BLOOD
OF MANY
NATIONS

A Simon Sol Dorsey Mystery

BLOOD
OF MANY
NATIONS

A Simon Sol Dorsey Mystery

Johnny Gunn

NEW PULP PRESS

Published by New Pulp Press, LLC, 926 Truman Avenue, Key West, Florida 33040, USA.

For information contact:
Publisher@NewPulpPress.com

ISBN-13: 978-0692717165 (New Pulp Press)
ISBN-10: 0692717161

Printed in the United States of America
Visit us on the web at www.newpulppress.com

BLOOD OF MANY NATIONS

A Simon Sol Dorsey Mystery

1

"Die, you son of a bitch, die," and the assailant, brows knit solid above angry eyes, slammed the cleaver down, again and again, parts and pieces splattered all over the kitchen. The strong, muscular man finally wore himself out, sat down at what was left of his kitchen table, an ironic smile spread across his broad face, and poured another cup of coffee. "I hate telephones," he croaked, reaching for a bottle of amber heaven to add to his coffee. His telephone was in a couple of hundred pieces, scattered all around him, but still ringing. His booze fogged brain slowly told him it was his cell phone ringing. "I'll kill it too, if I knew where it was." Sunday mornings are hard on the man whose card reads, "Simon Sol Dorsey, Private Detective."

Known to his enemies as Son of a Bitch, what few friends still around have referred to him as Sol. He was in his mid-thirties, a hulk of a man, and one who carried an attitude even when alone in his kitchen. He was standing in the middle of that filthy kitchen, holding the cleaver, buck naked, and didn't give a damn about anything. "I need a nap, or a fair to good woman, or maybe another drink. Damn that phone."

He knew the sun was up, he doesn't remember coming home, and it is now dawning on him that he has no clothes on. "Must have been a good night," he muttered to himself, feeling a bruise or two, an ache here, a scratch there. "Guess I didn't bring anybody home with me. Shame."

He glanced out the kitchen window at swirling gray fog, rivulets of water slip sliding down the dirty glass, and his mood grew proportionally to the grime. He stumbled to the fridge, found a beer, popped the cap, and took it down in slightly more than five seconds. That was followed by another cup of coffee, well laced. "Come on Dorsey, get your head together." Another session of one-sided conversation, something he was almost famous for, and then a short nap.

Some people sleep and work based on the clock, not Dorsey. He spent most of last night on the prowl, up and down the filthy streets that surround Franklyn Street in this fair city. Working for a client? Nay, good person, he was looking for as much fun as he could have, and with a lady of the night simply known as Simba, he had lots of fun. He was paying for it this morning, and a long nap, mid-morning would help his attitude, some.

His attitude toward crime, criminals, law enforcement, lawmen have derived from what he read as a young boy; swashbuckling lawmen, private dicks with the ethics of an angry water buffalo, and criminals beaten into submission. The first third of the twentieth century would have been a fine fit. He was a lost soul in the twenty first century. Modern technology and prevailing social mores were not his best friends. He destroyed his first two computers before he discovered their value in research. His laptop was capable of taking abuse, his telephone wasn't.

When he woke up, a couple of hours after the cleaver episode, he was back sitting at his kitchen table, his telephone was still spread around the room, his head hurt more than his knuckles, and that caught his attention. His knuckles were bloody and bruised. "Strange," he said out loud, "Usually when my knuckles look like this, my jaw hurts, my ribs hurt, and I have at least one black eye." He felt about, tenderly, and found no serious bruises or broken bones. A bang on the front door brought him around, somewhat, and again, that moment of truth; he wasn't wearing pants, or anything else, for that matter. "Must have been some night," he mused, and ripped off the tablecloth, spreading even more debris around the room. With the stained rag wrapped around his ample body, Sol Dorsey found his way to the door.

"Well, now I've seen it all. Simon Sol Dorsey in a wraparound skirt. May I have this dance, Miss?"

"Laugh it off, asshole. Laugh it off. What the hell are you doing here? Did you bring Bloody Marys?" Police Captain of Detectives Ulysses S. Elmo was laughing so hard he couldn't speak. He did a quick bow, maybe expecting a curtsy back from Dorsey, and stepped into the apartment, wound his way through piles of trash, ancient newspapers, dirty clothes, other unknown items, and made it to the kitchen, only to behold more trash, more newspapers, and one totally mangled telephone. He was carrying a briefcase, unusual for a Sunday morning.

"The next time you have a party like this, I better have an invitation." The laughter continued as he moved things around and found a chair to sit on. "You're an amazing man, Dorsey. Amazing."

"Go to hell. Again, what the hell are you doing here before sunrise?"

"The sun came up hours ago, Sol. I've been calling, but

3

I guess you were still passed out." He was looking around at telephone parts and pieces, "Or something." Serious Elmo squared around in the chair and became the "Serious" part of his name.

"I may have a job for you, if you can put yourself together." Captain Elmo's nickname was Serious, and the change in his attitude at that moment was how he got it. He was damn serious when he needed to be. Sol Dorsey on the other hand was generally angry, contemptuous of any and all, and ready for a knock-em-down, drag-em-out brawl on a moment's notice.

Simon Sol Dorsey was a private detective who would have been very comfortable in 1928 or 1942, but he was trapped in the twenty first century. "Crime is rampant today because of the Miranda ruling and judges rewriting the constitution. Give me ten minutes with a perp, and we'll have that confession, or we'll know he's clean." Dorsey was a mountain of a man. He stood well over six feet, weighed more than two hundred fifty pounds, and had less than five percent body fat. He wore his once blondish hair, with shards of gray interfering with the picture, in what was called a flat top or butch cut years ago. "Style? What the hell does that mean?"

Dorsey's idea of weight training was lifting pints of beer, booze, and broads. He' was a throwback and feels good about that. If he was pushed, he could probably press three hundred pounds, "but I prefer doing it one pint at a time, thank you very much for asking." He hadn't cooked anything other than coffee in the decade he's occupied his apartment, and for that matter, many believed he had not used a broom or mop during that same time period.

Interrogations were the "Dorsey Method", not correct police procedure.

Dorsey does have a wardrobe of fine clothing but was much more comfortable in jeans and a sleeveless tee shirt, always with western boots. "See how the toes are pointed? Fits nicely right up some fool's butt. Now, that's kicking ass," he told anyone who would listen.

Serious Elmo was chuckling over the big man wearing a tablecloth and filthy tee shirt, no shoes, and with a two or three day beard. "You're a mess, old friend. Get cleaned up. I'm buying."

Dorsey floundered his way through the chaos of his apartment, talking to himself the entire time, reached his bedroom after a quick detour to the boy's room, found a clean tee shirt, shirt, pants, even boots and sox, and did a ta-da entrance for Elmo's benefit. "Just shut up and go to hell, Serious. Just go to hell," and the two huge men left for a nearby saloon.

"Wait," Dorsey said, went back into the apartment and turned off the stove. "I'm gonna burn this place to the ground someday."

"Probably the best thing for it."

"Do we need the car?"

"No, let's hit Maglio's." Maglio's Tavern was about a block down the street, two blocks from the waterfront docks, and served fresh caught stuff right up from the sea. The place had an atmosphere that fit the pair; professional fishermen, hardworking dockworkers, truck drivers. They took a large banquet for six and filled it. "Bring a couple of pitchers of cold beer and keep the crab enchiladas coming until we say no, Maglio. Nice to see you too. You ever smile?"

Surrounded by the history of the area, faded photographs of fishermen in boats without motors, photos of miners, Chinese dock workers, ancient sailing ships just off the coast, and interspersed with all that, photos from Maglio's home country. Maglio when just a youngster, standing in the middle of Palermo, Maglio on board a sailing fishing boat off the Sicilian coast, and Maglio when he arrived in New York City.

There were ship's bells, frayed ropes, navigation lights, even a stray compass decorating areas of the bar and grill, and always, the place was full of people, people that called each other by name, very few tourists. Most called out a 'howdy' to Sol Dorsey when the two arrived, and Sol called each back by name. Comfort can be spelled many ways and that day, it was spelled Maglio.

Serious Elmo was settled in, Dorsey was moving the table a bit so he would fit, and Sunday almost-noon was underway. "You mentioned job, Serious. I don't much care for working for the police. You know that. The cops in uniform? They're OK, but the suits? Most of them can go to hell."

"I wear a suit, Sol. Don't forget that. Besides, this isn't a cop job. I got to say, though, it's probably gonna be damn dangerous." A comment like that would get Dorsey's attention right away. Danger was honey to that bear.

They drank two pitchers each of Bloody Marys, after their beer, and ate platters of crab enchiladas over the next couple of hours. "So a sixteen year old girl doesn't come home from school one day. Jeez, Serious, I bet that happens every day. What's the deal?"

"The deal is, shit head, her father is Hank Jacoby, the cop I fired when dope and guns from evidence lockers were disappearing. I'm still sure he was selling the stuff. Just haven't ever been able to put the pin in the ass. Her name is Melissa and I would bet her disappearance has something to do with narcs, guns, and her father."

"Has to be more to it than that or you wouldn't be banging on my door, Serious. What's the whole skinny, pal?" Dorsey and Elmo have had a long relationship that started when the captain of detectives was still a uniformed cop walking a beat. Together they would top a quarter of a ton of muscle and bone, and they have had more civil rights cases brought against them than any other two men in California. They also have solved more major crimes than any other two men in the Golden State. Elmo's bosses tolerate him because he produces. They don't speak to Dorsey.

Sol Dorsey's hands were too big for most baseball gloves, the fingers long, tapered, strong. He had a nasty habit of grabbing people by the throat and lifting them off the ground, holding them there until they decide to talk to him, and then giving them hell for being such weaklings. Dorsey was a category five in high overdrive when he smelled a liar or a tweaker. Serious Elmo knew this, and with drugs playing a large part of this job, he was about to get Dorsey on the job.

"There really should be an open season on those that sell that shit," Dorsey said. "Put a bounty on those heads and I'd be a rich son of a bitch, Serious. Rich, I say." Captain Elmo quit listening to those rants years ago.

"Jacoby is married to a woman from the Ukraine, and

when I was investigating the evidence locker thefts, I think I discovered that she has ties to Ukrainian organized crime. It's just a hunch, but I brought you my old files on this, and I'll let you put it all together. I think you will be moving into international criminal activity. You up to it?" He set the hook.

"Stupid question. Of course I'm up to it, but you said something about this being a job. That would mean me, Sol Dorsey, PI, making money off the investigation. I haven't heard the word dollar or client yet." This was always a sore point between the two men, because they worked well together, but Elmo was on the city books, and Dorsey was on credit collector's books. "I have heavy expenses, you know."

"Yeah, I know. Those wrap around skirts cost lots of bucks eh, big man?" Dorsey frowned, actually clenched one of his fists, Elmo laughed out loud, then settled down a bit. "When Melissa was born, her mother arranged for membership in the Free Children of the Ukraine, an American organization that was formed to help children of Ukrainian émigrés. It wasn't the Jacoby family that filed the missing person report, it was the FCU, and that's the part that brought me to you. Jacoby knows I will do what is necessary to nail his ass to any cross available, and I still believe his wife is involved in international criminal activity, so they enlisted this FCU group to come to the police.

"This group has money, Sol, and I told them you would be calling on them." He pulled a set of file folders from his briefcase and handed them across the table. "Here's everything I know, including the address and phone number of the FCU. I'm available to you at all times, Sol. Go get 'em big guy, and bring me in whenever you want." This time the smile was genuine, not a smart ass smirk or out and out guffaw.

"Anybody else in on this, Serious? The DA, the DEA, the FBI? Sometimes, you know, I have a hard time taking you at your word. Am I bumping heads with a bunch of other idiots?"

"I'm sure the DA got the report, but it's probably hidden under fifteen others, and as far as I know, no federal agencies are looking at the Jacobys. I'm being straight with you, Sol, and I'm looking forward to being able to help."

"OK, one more question then. Why aren't you on this case? Why bring me in?"

"Simple, pal. It's a missing person's case, not even criminal. Yet. Somehow, Sol, this is the kind of caper that just fits you. Even if you do wear skirts on Sunday mornings." The scowl on Dorsey's face prompted more loud laughter from Elmo, and another ugly stare from Maglio.

"You know, Serious, I don't think that man likes it when people are having fun. Come on, Maglio, give us one nice smile." All the two men got was a gruff harrumph from the Sicilian gentleman.

Dorsey played broke when they got up to leave and Serious Elmo popped for their Sunday morning breaking of the fast. Dorsey went back to his apartment, Elmo went somewhere else, and Maglio smiled closing the drawer of the cash register.

Dorsey's apartment had been a disaster for all of the ten years that Dorsey had lived there, and it generally took some athletic agility to just navigate from one room to another. The big man simply wiped the kitchen table clean with a swoop of one long arm, scattered even more stuff onto an already filled floor, turned the coffee pot on, and sat down with an open file, about an inch or so thick. His laptop, the only part of the twenty first century he acknowledged, was pulled from a shelf and booted up. "Serious and these people seem to know a lot about Melissa Jacoby, but not much about her folks."

Almost anyone who knew Dorsey would tell you, "that man spends more time talking to himself than he does talking to real people. We're talking full blown conversations here." Sol Dorsey would tell you it's how he was able to get a handle on whatever was going on in his so-called mind at the time. It was a noisy time in that kitchen as he worked his way through the files that Serious Elmo had given him. More than once he got up from the table, wandering around with a fresh cup of coffee, digesting what he was reading. Prosecutors and defense attorneys all agree that Sol Dorsey was one sharp investigator, even if his "Dorsey Method" wasn't always lawful.

Dorsey would not be able to tell you when or even if the fog had lifted, if sunshine was pouring through his filthy kitchen window. His head was buried in background, in police reports, in what was shaping up as a large drug dealing operation in which a little girl might have been sucked in. Beautiful spring days along the California coast would not get in Dorsey's way of something like this.

"This is an interesting family," he was saying. "Papa is a discredited cop with a mail order bride from the Ukraine that may or may not be an international drug and weapons dealer, and a daughter with very high grades and the personality of a dead frog." As he got deeper into the files he found one name that kept cropping up.

"This isn't making a lot of sense right now. Mavis Brownell is an investigator for the district attorney, and it looks like Elmo was trying to tie her into Illiana Jacoby's operations. After I meet with the people at the FCU, and make sure this is a paying case, I'm going to pay a visit to Brownell. She's a looker, that's for sure." Dorsey's girl of choice was usually one of the hookers from Franklyn Street, but he would always give the big eye to a beautiful woman. The street ladies idolized the big guy. The society types were frightened half to death.

2

Friday afternoon, spring time sun shone on hundreds of high school students streaming from ugly classrooms, only thinking of weekends, parties, fun and games. Among them was Melissa Jacoby, sixteen years old, beautiful in every way but one. While she carried a 3.9 GPA, she had the personality of a dead elephant. With long legs, a cute little bottom end that jiggled provocatively when she walked, most of the boys wanted nothing to do with her. She walked home alone with a blank stare and empty head.

She didn't have any really bad traits, didn't do drugs, wasn't interested in drinking, had no desire for a boyfriend, or any of the other things teenaged girls were supposed to be into. She played volleyball, on the hardwood courts at school, and on the beaches that surrounded this town of hers.

A block from the Jacoby home, a black Lincoln Navigator SUV with heavily tinted windows cut Melissa off, almost driving up on the sidewalk. Doors were flung open, Melissa was grabbed, her mouth clamped shut, and she was jammed into the big truck. The kidnapping was over in less than five seconds, done in broad daylight on a busy street in a nice neighborhood. Nobody remembered seeing it, nobody called the cops. All the Jacoby family knew was that Melissa did not come home from school, and Hank knew he couldn't go to the cops.

Jacoby hadn't carried a badge for several years, not since the investigation into missing drugs and guns from an evidence locker. Some of those involved in that investigation were still working to pin the thefts on him. "This is making me vulnerable again. That bastard Elmo won't let up. You know it, and Sheik knows it, and he has Melissa."

Hank Jacoby was a weasel of a man, never what might be considered a good cop, always looked for the easy way out, the cheap answer, regardless of the consequences. He was average in most ways, height, weight, and below average in others, intelligence, common sense. Jacoby found Illiana in an ad promising love and happiness with a lovely bride from the Ukraine. Illiana found her way to the U.S., and a different brand of happiness.

Illiana brought her drug contacts and organization with her and it didn't take much convincing to get Hank involved. Even stupid ex-cops understood the power and strength of the almighty dollar. When she outlined the amount of money that would be flowing through their lives, all thoughts of being an officer of the law went into the scrap pile. His lack of intelligence, and his slovenly ways brought problems to the business, often, and Illiana spent many hours cursing her choice of mates. More than one of the international dealers Illiana worked with would not work with Hank under any circumstances. He had ruined more than one big deal in the past, and recently caused an entire shipment from the Middle East to be lost to federal agents.

The newspapers called it the largest foiled drug deal on the west coast. They estimated the worth of opium, heroin, cocaine, and methamphetamine at more than two hundred million dollars. Incredibly, it was found in shipping containers that were simply left of the docks. Federal agents took full credit for the bust.

"Illiana, I told you it would come to this. They have Melissa, I know it. My poor little baby. Contact those friends of yours and we'll put the word out. This has to be the work of Omar Sheik. He still believes that we screwed him on that last deal. If we try to get the cops in on this, that prick Captain Elmo will zero in on me again. This is a mess, Illiana. Call your friends."

"I will, Hank." Illiana sighed lightly, took a deep breath, understanding fully that Hank was simply inadequate for her needs. "Let's talk for a minute, first." Illiana knew Hank wasn't the smart, capable man she thought she married so many years ago. More often than not, Hank Jacoby cut corners, took needless risks, and was going to get the two of them killed one day soon if she didn't do something about it. She thought that marrying an American cop would open many doors for her and her group. Her partner, Sheik Omar, were more than willing to let Hank Jacoby in, thinking a nice line of police protection would aid the business.

"You know that last caper was screwed up because of you," she said, "but can you be sure it is Omar Sheik behind Melissa being snatched? What if it isn't? What if we send out the wrong message? How can you be sure?" There he was again, she thought, coming up with an answer before knowing all the facts.

"That last deal we made with Omar Sheik went sideways, Illiana. It wasn't my fault, but he blamed us because he lost so much money. Do you remember what he said? He promised to get back at us. This has to be him and that bunch of Egyptian bastards that work for him. I know it. Now, call that group of yours and get some help. What's their name?"

"Hank, you know damn well that deal was screwed because of you. And, yes, Sheik lost a lot of money, but you idiot, so did we. You simply won't ever be a real man, will you? You screwed up that deal, cutting corners, costing us millions. Don't blame Omar."

Jacoby had never taken responsibility for anything, except of course, those things that ended up on the plus side of the ledger. Anytime something went wrong, it was always someone else's fault. When he worked patrol, those assigned to work with him found their jobs in jeopardy regularly.

"You fouled up that deal, Hank, and you know it. If Omar is behind this, it's because of you. That group is called the Free Children of Ukrainians or FCU. They have contacts, Hank. If she's been snatched, they will find her. If this is Omar Sheik's snatch, we may never see Melissa again. I've worked with that man for well over twenty years, Hank, and right now, I know he hates your ass."

Illiana, born in the Ukraine forty years ago. She had been married to Henry Jacoby for seventeen years, and up to her once gorgeous neck in international narcotics, weapons, and money laundering, knew how the Omar Sheiks of the world work. She had already written off Melissa. She glared at her mail order husband, walked to the desk and called Lori Baranek at the FCU.

"Lori, this is Illiana Jacoby, I think Melissa may have

been kidnapped." She spoke very fast, tried to get everything said in one breath. Baranek told her to slow down, and Illiana continued, a little more collected. "We can't go to the police. It would be too dangerous for Hank, but we have to do something. Please, can you help us? Please?"

Her body felt like it was tied up in chains and steel cable, knotted, her fists clenched tight, she tried to calm herself. Anger at Hank, worried about her daughter, and first and foremost, worried about her business interests, it was difficult to calm her anger. This was the first time she had contacted the FCU, and hoped they didn't have a dossier on either her or Omar Sheik.

The FCU was organized when the Soviet Union came apart, designed to help Ukrainians immigrating to this country, in particular the children. It was well funded and over the years had done a fine job helping get those from the Ukraine settled into the American way. They were known for helping the children cope with the many huge changes in their lives, and providing financial, medical, and educational help to the families. Illiana had registered Melissa with the group when she was born, even though Melissa had never spent one minute in the Ukraine. When Hank questioned the move, Illiana explained, as to a child.

"This is just another form of insurance, Hank. These people are not involved in any questionable dealings, but they know and understand the ways of the Soviet Union, of those that really make things happen, and will have ways of protecting Melissa if something happens to us." As the Soviet Union broke apart, the Russian Mafia formed, or reformed if you will, and held sway over politicians, many former KGB agents helped things along, bankers came forth with money for those that could help them, a system of oligarchs formed out of the vacuum of disintegration.

In the Ukraine, organized crime was rampant, but was different than the Soviet or Russian elements. Criminal organizations were alike in some respects. There were narcotics, financial and political crimes, and in the Ukraine, much of this was determined by regional influences. For instance, smuggling was popular in Odessa, financial crimes more prevalent in Kiev. Narcotics distribution was often handled through contacts in Israel and areas of the Middle East that were in turmoil more often than not. Illiana's background in narcotics, money laundering, and kidnapping for profit, indicated she probably began her criminal life somewhere near Kiev. Omar Sheik brought her in when she was very young, taught her well, and they had been business partners since. Their business had grown to include dealing in arms on an international scale.

Their business was primarily along the western third of the US, but they also had made deals with gangsters on the east coast and in Canada. The Asian gangs in western Canada were good customers, and brought Illiana's organization many millions of dollars. Omar Sheik made deals all over the world, Illiana worked the distribution end of the business, and they shared and shared alike.

Illiana could see all of that going up in flames if she continued her life with Hank. "He must go," she said often, and wondered how she could have been so stupid as to pick him. The background on Illiana that Jacoby was given was of course written to make her a gem, the ideal little romantic beauty that every lonely American man was searching for. He didn't give a damn about where she was born, what her real background was, he was lonely, bored, and this was a quick fix.

Illiana Jacoby, at the dining room table, sat back in the wooden chair, a slight woman with early wrinkles forming around her mouth and eyes. Her nose was straight and thin, her lips were straight and thin, her eyebrows were straight and thin. Her once flawless high forehead showed the strain of her life. At one time, Hank could remember, she was very attractive, but most of that had worn off. She never left the house without a Glock in her purse, and was proud of the fact she had used it more than once.

Often she had hired thugs follow as bodyguard and security, and some of the men and women that worked for her were known to every police agency in the world. They just didn't know where they were.

She was the commander, the boss, and Hank simply fell in line with what she wanted. She married a cop and turned him into an international drug dealer, and rued the day. "I had such big hopes for you, Hank. You knew the laws and rules and I was sure you would be able to work all of that in our favor. Melissa probably won't live through this, and I just hope that we will. Maybe the FCU will at least be able to find her.

"I knew that group would come in handy one day, Hank. I told you so, didn't I? We have to be very careful now. I have two shipments coming in from Afghanistan this week, and we have those AKs to get delivered. If you really believe that Omar Sheik is behind this, we will have to make some new arrangements. He has been good for me, it would be a shame to lose him now."

Omar Sheik bin Ali was Egyptian by birth, there are some who think he had ties to Saudi Arabian royalty as well, had spent many years in the Ukraine during the Soviet years, and was close to criminal elements in the Middle East, particularly Israel. Sheik and Illiana go back many years, many deals. At some point, probably during the Soviet occupation of Afghanistan, the two hooked up and had shared deals ever since.

Illiana was a teenager, seventeen or so, when they met. She was very pretty, very intelligent, wanted to learn the ways and Omar Sheik was willing to teach. They made a fine partnership, and Sheik wanted to make a move into the American market. That led to Illiana becoming a mail order bride. "Don't marry that fool, Illiana. He isn't the right man for you. He's stupid, weak, boorish. Get to America, but get rid of him."

Most called him Omar or Sheik, and he was known to have a vicious temper, doesn't follow any religious tenets, dressed in Europe's finest, drank only green tea, and used none of the drugs he distributed. While Hank believed it was an accident that caused the last deal to go sour, Sheik was certain that it was Hank that went sour.

"I will see to it that stupid son of a bitch dies, and soon. I bring two tons of opium to his front door and he forgets to open the door? He will suffer for that." It wasn't quite that simple, but almost. Hank was to meet the freighter at the deep water terminal with a stake side flatbed, pick up the crates, marked as pottery and ceramics, and take them to a warehouse south of the city. This wasn't his first pick up, and good old Hank pulled a stupid stunt, rented a truck from an old friend instead of the commercial rental agency.

It was a junker, and the thing quit on him half way across a bridge leading to the docks.

Illiana was furious. "You stupid son of bitch, a deal worth millions of dollars and you try to save fifty fucking dollars on a truck? If Sheik doesn't shoot you, I will," she screamed.

He was hours late, finally showed up with the miserable truck. The crates sat alone on the dock and caught the eyes of the customs boys. Hank almost walked into their trap. The headlines talked about tons of opium found on the docks "He is the most stupid man I've ever dealt with. He will die." Illiana had Sheik almost calmed down within a day or two, but Omar Sheik was fanatical about never working with Hank Jacoby again. "I don't care how you work it out, Illiana, but I will not work with that man again. You would be much better off to kill him yourself. He is a burden, a burden that will sink you some day."

~ ~ ~

"Hank, we need two things right away. We need money, cash money, much more than what we have, and we need a new set of contacts. If Sheik is burned, we have to make some big changes. Go to the man tomorrow, and don't screw things up. Don't try to cut corners, don't try to save money on stupid things." Illiana was as worried about their business as she was angry at Hank. On top of all that, someone had Melissa, but that was third on her list right now.

"I'll call Socrates in the morning. He will be able to make some contacts for us in case we lose Sheik. I know the man was angry, but I really didn't think he would be so pissed as to hurt our daughter. If it isn't Omar Sheik behind this, where else should we look, Illiana?

"We've been so careful to keep Melissa out of this, and now she is being held by who knows. God, I hope they contact us, not just do something terrible."

Illiana had those same thoughts, knew how Omar Sheik operated, how she had operated. "Hank, when that fool Paul Fordham turned over on us, you remember how I handled the situation? I had his pregnant wife killed in front of him, slit her throat inches from his face. Do you remember? That's what's in store for Melissa, and you better get it through your stupid head that you are responsible."

In his private jet, as it descended from 35,000 feet for landing in Paris, Andrzej sat fuming, slowly opening and closing both fists, flexing muscles more used to being gently massaged by silk and warm oils. From his first foray into the world of illicit drug smuggling, now more than twenty five years ago, Andrzej, known as The Man, had only used the single name, which in the world of Romanian Gypsies means, The Man. "Sheik Omar and Illiana have lost their last shipment, Henri. Two million American dollars lost because of one stupid man."

Andrzej was heavy set, deep black eyes capable of searing fear into one's soul, glared from under bushy black eyebrows. His jowls quivered some when he spoke, he's never been known to smile, much less laugh, unless it's watching an enemy drenched in blood, and that he enjoyed as much as his nightly hashish pipe. He had been known to enjoy the company of young boys as much as that of young girls, which often created problems on international flights when those on board should not be there.

His tastes were those of the very rich. His jet was always the most expensive, the fastest, and the best looking. His home in France was more than luxurious, his retreat in the Swiss Alps had the best skiing, his home just off Aruba was filled with the expensive and exotic. He had offices in

California, New York, and Paris, and a large mansion complex just a few miles from Serious Elmo's police headquarters. Andrzej lived as a prince might have a thousand or so years ago.

Henri Bargon, an international killer, kidnapper, man that made things disappear, was on Andrzej's private jet in order to slip into Paris unnoticed by Interpol or some French police agency. "Here's what I want you to do, Henri," The Man was saying. "Illiana has a daughter, probably as stupid as her father. I want you to fly directly back to California, put together a team, and get that girl. I will not allow a stupid person to cost me a million dollars."

Bargon started to say something and was cut off. With a quick wag of his finger, The Man said, "Money is not a problem." Andrzej motioned to his on board butler. "Tell the captain he is to return to California as soon as possible with Mr. Bargon, and Pepe, get Bargon some traveling money.

"Henri, there will be a payment to you and your team of $250,000 when this is done. Use the big house, and there is a fine big American SUV available. It's a Lincoln, black, and with deeply tinted windows. Now, here's what I want you to do with the girl."

Only three people involved and with a payout of $250,000, Bargon was more than ready to take the job. "I had plans while in Paris, Andrzej, but this is far more to my liking. I'll keep you advised. Will you be coming back to California?"

"Maybe later, Henri. Maybe in time to watch Jacoby and Sheik do a little dance for me," and the scowl softened, just a bit.

~ ~ ~

She tried to scream, but a foul tasting rag of some kind had been shoved in her mouth, her sweater had been pulled up over her head, which kept her from seeing anything, and gave at least two of the three men eye's full of lovely teen aged breasts. Her hands and arms had been wrenched behind her and tied. One of the two men in the back of the large SUV slapped her across the side of the head, snarling in a heavy accent to "shut the fuck up." Melissa could feel that the car was moving very fast, weaving through traffic and taking turns so fast the tires screamed. After about fifteen minutes, maybe more, maybe less, the car came to a sudden stop. The terror driven bile in her throat almost caused her to vomit.

She was a protected, selfish, American teen-ager who had never been physically abused by anyone. The word terror screamed through her system, she desperately fought off the urge to throw-up, her body was wracked with cramps. She couldn't see, felt hands in inappropriate places, was slapped, and even hit with hard objects. They were big guns, but she couldn't know that.

Melissa was jerked out of the vehicle by a man with strong hands that held one arm and shoved her down a pathway. She tripped and stumbled up some stairs, and into a building. She was sobbing, trying to get free, when something big and hard slammed into her head, knocking her out cold. The tallest of the three men stepped forward, "Easy now, Armand, he said he wanted her alive. Put her on that divan over there, and no funny stuff."

"Henri, she is so pretty."

"If you touch her again, you will die. No funny stuff."

25

Henri was a large man, one would think Algerian with his heavy French accent and dark complexion. His black curly hair was cut short and he sported a pencil thin moustache. In Europe, the ladies were always friendly, and in Algeria, they flocked to his side. His eyes were narrowed in anger at Armand, darkened from deep gray to almost black. "I have not slit a man's throat in a long time, Armand. You touch that girl and I will have my chance.

"I'm going to go see the money man now. When I get back we will know what to do with her. That girl is worth a lot of money to all of us, and to Andrzej, she is worth even more. He has lost face, a large amount of money, and he wants revenge. Do you understand what I'm saying?" The two men, indicated agreement and Henri walked out of the building. Henri Bargon was an international snatch expert, was often called on to take from those that have taken from the wrong source, and was feared by many.

Armand spit at the girl, and his accomplice had to laugh at the gesture. "You will get us killed someday, Armand, always thinking with your dick. We are looking to make a lot of money here, and all you can think of is a quickie. Wake up, fool." Sean Sorenson, short and heavy, black as the darkest night, far more intelligent than Armand, got right in the other man's face. He spent about half an hour every morning shaving his head, and as the late afternoon sun streamed through a window, it made that magnificent head shine and sparkle like a large black Panamint Ball.

Sorenson found a blanket in one of the rooms and covered the girl. Armand had hit her pretty hard, but she should be coming around soon. He kept her sweater pulled up so she would not be able to see. "When she comes to, we have to be quiet. The old man said she was very smart, so we don't want her to be able to ID us by our voices. And you stay away from her. I have a sharp knife too." He had to smile to himself when he said that, knowing what a pleasure it would be to get rid of the fool.

Sorenson had done jobs for Henri before, and he knew there would be good money in this one. *If this fool screws this up for a quick piece of ass, I will cut him into so many pieces they'll never put them all together. We have a classic place to live while we're here, we eat and drink only the best, and we're in line to make a lot of cash money. What a fool, and I'm stuck with him.* He walked into the kitchen of the large house perched on a cliff overlooking the Pacific Ocean and opened a beer.

"Armand, get the hell out of that room. Your hours are numbered, fool. Get away from that girl."

~ ~ ~

The Man had hired Henri to set up the pick, and Henri went to his friend Sorenson right away. "This should be a pretty easy snatch, Sean, probably even easier than when we grabbed that old man in Bahrain. And, that my friend, was pretty easy. The Man says he will pay a quarter of a million, and he wants her alive. He's going to dangle her in front of the parents, and if he's paying us that much, how much do you think he's going to get from them? I think we need a third man, Sean. Got any ideas?"

"That job we pulled in Morocco went well. Armand did his job, and he has very cold blood in his system. He did well taking out the man's wife."

"Yeah, he did, but he also raped the broad while she was dying. I don't know, Sean, this is a teenage girl we're taking.

27

Can we keep Armand in check?"

"He is a fool when it comes to women, but he's got a good handle on situations as they develop. Let's talk to him." They found Armand, got promises of behavior, and made the deal. Both men had their doubts, but knew they needed a third in the caper and wouldn't find anyone better suited to the project.

As Sean Sorenson looked back on that conversation, he couldn't help but question his own thinking. "I may have been wrong about you, Armand. If you even look at that girl, I'm taking you out."

Armand gave a sly smile, shook his head as if to say, fuck you, spit on the floor, and walked over to an armchair. "I don't want anything from a white American girl." He wanted everything, and the ache between his legs was growing stronger.

Armand was a polyglot of mixed races and nationalities that would stymie the most grizzled census taker, had no idea himself who and what he was. He had passports from several countries, had identification from many more, and answered to Armand among those he worked with and for. International police agencies knew him by many different names, many different crimes, most not knowing it was all one person.

In American slang, Armand would be called horn dog, and Sean Sorenson feared that this job could go to hell in half a second. Armand woke up horny, spent his days thinking sex, and went to bed horny. No woman, young, old, lovely, or ugly was safe if left alone with the man.

"Enough. Damn, all I've done is read these stupid files. Enough," and Sol Dorsey slammed the lid on the last one. "What is that taste? No, it isn't a taste, it's a lack of a taste." He stood up, stretched so high his fingertips raked the ceiling over the kitchen table. "I want a beer. I want a six pack of beer," he roared, trying to intimidate his kitchen, the place that still held pieces of a destroyed telephone. He had the shoulder holster strapped on in quick time, slipped the .45 caliber revolver into its shell, put on a clean blazer, and was ready for a night on the town. The 9mm was in his right boot, and a mean looking ultra-sharp knife sat comfortably on his belt at about his hip line, if he had one. "Serious did a good job on this case. There are some people mentioned that I need to know more about. It looks like another horrible night in the saloons of this fine burg."

Springtime along the coast of California meant evening and late night fog, so thick vision was impaired. Tonight, the fog was heavy and wet, it was cold, the kind of wet cold that would cut through overcoats and sweaters, make the bones ache. Vision was distorted too, and the neon lights along Franklyn Street were almost gauzy. "It's a good night to spend hours in a warm saloon, pints flowing, warm and friendly ladies of the night to cavort with," he murmured when he left the apartment.

The large man's friends had more ties to the underworld than the society page, and Franklyn Street was more like home than slum. Besides feeling fatherly toward working girls, Simon Sol Dorsey's other love in life was his 1956 Cadillac convertible. When parked in certain neighborhoods, that car sent messages. "Watch out, Simon Sol Dorsey is on the town."

He had made some big changes from when the car first appeared in high scale show rooms more than half a century ago. There were no door handles on the outside or inside, for instance. "They're electric," he would point out to anyone that showed the least interest, "and the buttons are on my side of the dash. If you tell me what I want to hear, I might let you out in one piece. If you don't, those doors don't open." The original engine had been replaced by a four-fifty-four with massive carbs and headers. "She'll do one sixty without much trouble. Yeah, I have a copy of the ticket to prove it." He had dreamed of this ride since his entry into puberty.

The kids at school learned not to tease Dorsey about the time he was twelve. Before that, he was a normal sized boy, but then things changed. His shoulders broadened, his legs lengthened, his hands grew enormous, and he developed the Simon Sol Dorsey attitude. He couldn't remember ever having a father, his mother drank herself stupid most days, and it was pulp magazines and novels that became best friends, mentors.

He told Serious Elmo one time, "I never got in a fight until I was thirteen, and that was with a kid in high school. I didn't even know how to throw a punch, and damn near killed that little jerk. One of the teachers that helped pull me off of him suggested I take some boxing and judo training, and possibly some anger management classes. Probably the best piece of education I ever got."

He loved the old gangster movies, knew most of the dialog by heart, yearned to pack some heat and make the bad guys cry for help. If there were bullies at the schools Dorsey went to, he never met one. Girls went out of their way to be near him, particularly the ones with slightly clouded backgrounds. Dorsey never participated in sports of any kind, except for the boxing and karate classes off campus. Football and wrestling coaches spent many hours learning that when the big guy says no, that's what he meant.

"All those guys in the books and movies had big powerful cars, and I wanted mine. They slept with beautiful women, chased and caught the bad guys, and drove powerful cars. Now, I've got the biggest, strongest, meanest ride in town."

Dorsey wheeled the shark-finned monster onto Franklyn Street and looked for one of the saloons that didn't have two dealers lounging around on the sidewalk. He had a passion for druggies, those that take the stuff, those that sell the stuff. His passion, he explained, "is simple. Eliminate the bastards any way I can." The tweakers had just as much of a passion for Dorsey: Stay out of his sights.

"Hi, Sol. That was some party last night. I've never met anyone as strong as you are. Is your hand OK?" Sometimes the answers come late and from a strange quarter. This answer came from a charming young lady, probably early twenties, no more than five feet tall, and no more than eighty-five pounds. She sold pleasure down by the seashore, and Dorsey was more friend than client. Her long auburn hair hung in curls splashed across shoulders, back, and breasts, and Dorsey actually had a smile on his square face as he thought about the possibilities.

"How many of these lovely young ladies have I known in the last ten years or so? How many are dead because of drugs, booze, and the bastards they pretend to love? Each one is special. These girls are my friends, and too many have died so young." Those thoughts came in a flash, and he was back on the job immediately.

"Nice to see you Star. I take it we had some fun, eh? If you can lead me close to where ever Chago Navarro is we can have a cocktail or twenty." Navarro was a small time hood with too many answers, most of which were correct. He sold small amounts of drugs, sold merchandise provided by those unwilling to give it up, and was the kind of slime ball Dorsey loved to punch.

"He's at Smiley's. Sol, don't make me sit with that freak. Come on, you're supposed to be a friend."

"It'll be worth a hit if you'll be my girl for an hour or so. Your rate is one hundred? That'll work for me."

"The hundred rate is for a quickie, Mr. Dorsey," and she pounded on the word mister, "not an hour or more. Come on, Sol, don't do this." He slipped a couple of hundred dollar bills into her hand, and smiled the Sol Dorsey smile that made these girls love him so.

They walked into the saloon called Bar and found Smiley working the early shift himself. "Mr. Dorsey, nice to see you." The Bar, like hundreds of others, reeked of stale whiskey, fouled tobacco, and warm beer. The air was musty, warm, and with Dorsey in the building, filled with danger.

Smiley was smiling when he said, "...nice to see you," but he was also aware of just how dangerous Simon Sol Dorsey was.

"Yeah, I'm sure," Dorsey snarled. "Where's that tweaker Navarro?" Some of the saloons along Franklyn Street welcomed Simon Sol Dorsey, others tolerated him, all made money because of him. Smiley pointed at a table in the back near the card room. "Give Star here anything she wants and I'll take a couple of shots of Early Times. Oh, yeah, back 'em up with a pint of ale, old friend." The smile was almost genuine and Smiley knew not to get heavy with a wisecrack or he'd have some loose teeth.

Dorsey looked toward the back, saw that he had been seen, and drummed his fingers. "Come on. Smiley. Today would be a good time. You wait for me here, Star. Yell if something starts."

"Thank you, Sol," was all she needed to say, he gave her a nice peck on the cheek, pinched her butt, grabbed his drinks, and walked toward the back. Navarro was sitting with two other low life losers who split as soon as Dorsey got close.

"Santiago Navarro, we need to have a nice little chat." Navarro let his fingers gently caress his neck, remembered the last time he had a 'chat' with Dorsey. "I'm going to mention a name or two and you're going to fill in the blanks. That's rather simple, even for a fool. How's your neck?" He chuckled, finished off his first double shot, and spread his hands on the tabletop. They were massive, threatening, and brought painful memories back to the scumbag.

"I'm clean Dorsey. I don't do junk no more. Honest."

"Honest, my ass. Tell me about Illiana Jacoby. Don't

screw with me Chago, it won't be pretty."

"I don't know nobody by that name." The hand flashed, it was a backhand across the chops and the little pig bounced off the wall behind him, blood oozed from an ear and his nose.

"Like I said, prick, it won't be pretty. Hank Jacoby? Remember him?"

"Oh, yeah, the bad cop. He stole things, right?"

"You want to take a little ride with me, Chago?"

"No, no man, no. I remember now, Illiana, the Russian. Sure, I remember."

An invitation to take a little ride was an invitation to serious pain. Dorsey liked to take those he needed information from out to the dunes on the north end of the bay. One tweaker remembered the trip in full multiplex color. "He slapped me so hard I almost passed out, then picked me up by my neck and held me there until I did pass out. There was blood everywhere. Then the bastard left me there and I had to walk back." Dorsey had one spot he called special. Santiago Navarro had never been there, but he was well aware of the stories that have been told.

"You come clean with me, Chago, and we won't take that drive out to the sand dunes. You remember them, don't you? Wasn't that where we were heading when you told me about the guy that killed little Red? Sure, you remember, I was gonna hold you a couple of feet in the air by your neck, and you remembered everything." Dorsey was smiling like he was talking to a little boy and offering a candy bar. He owned Santiago Navarro.

There was a spot north of town, right along the coast where sand dunes were high and silent. Rolling dunes meant there were little valleys where one could hold conversations without being seen. Boys and girls frequent the dunes late at night to watch the submarine races. One such little valley belonged to Dorsey, and buried in the sands were great splotches of blood, probably some teeth, possibly some evidence that a Dorsey client didn't want discovered, and no one around to discuss what went on or when.

Back at the bar, Star was about to make a deal with some guy in a business suit and Dorsey walked up and shoved the guy aside. "This is my action, pal. Beat it." Star wanted to complain but knew better. "I just picked up a name I don't know. Does the name Timothy Socrates mean anything to you?

Before she could answer, Smiley did. "He works at a bank, Mr. Dorsey. One of the big banks downtown. They had a story about him in the paper the other day. Something about him being gay. I just remembered the name is all. Like, you know, I'm a Greek too, so the name stands out."

"Thanks, Smiley. That's a big help. Now, go listen to somebody else's conversation, eh?" He nudged the pretty girl, pinched her butt one more time and motioned her to follow him. "Let's take a little walk, kiddo."

Every other doorway on both sides of Franklyn Street opened into a saloon, many with raucous music, and many with raucous idiots who had drunk past their capacity. Often, young men would stand nearby selling drugs and attractive young ladies would stand nearby selling other merchandise. "Let's try the Black Out, Star, and see who's doing what to whom, shall we?"

~ ~ ~

"Wake up, Star. Come on, it's late and I have work to do. Come on you little cutie, it's Monday morning. Get up. And I hope your head hurts." Mornings were tough on the big guy, and he had a long day ahead of him. "I really appreciated your help last night. I learned a lot about these people I'll be dealing with." He tucked three one hundred dollar bills into her purse while she was in the bathroom, and headed out for the kitchen, still filled with broken telephone parts. "Damn," he cursed, trying to miss the sharp plastic pieces of telephone with his bare feet. Coffee, toast, Star out the door, and it was time for the day to begin.

His to-do list was simple and to the point: Lori Baranek, FCU; Mavis Brownell, DA's office; Timothy Socrates, Bank of wherever. Dorsey's only recognition of the 21st Century was his computer, and with a few strokes pounded onto the keyboard as if it was an old Royal mechanical, he found out that FCU was pretty legitimate. "There's a surprise. I would have bet I would find ties to the Ukrainian mafia or money laundering goons somewhere."

He still wasn't sure he would be doing some paid work by way of the FCU, but it appeared as though their checks wouldn't bounce. "Lots of money there, and only to protect kids from the old country? I don't see any ties to criminal activity, but with that much money, I'm willing to bet there will be." He vowed to tread lightly when he made contact later in the morning.

"Groups like this have high sounding ideals for others to appreciate, and usually, if we look deep enough, we find out the true purpose of the thing. Feed the kids, protect the poor, save the whales, it's all the same thing. Get more money coming in than you spend on your projects, and take nice full salaries every month." It was not a fine, handsome face he was wearing during those thoughts.

"A guy could make a good living exposing most of these kinds of operations. I wonder how many also have ties to the criminal world? Narcotics and weapons bring big bucks, money laundering, now there's where an operation like this could really be swimming in lots of dollars. I got to look into this someday," and he let his thoughts drift off in other directions. His mind never slowed down.

He had to rummage through most of the house before he could find his cell phone since the landline was destroyed. "Lori Baranek? Yes, this is Sol Dorsey, Police Captain Elmo asked me to call you. It's about Melissa Jacoby. May I come over?" He was out the door and in the old Caddy inside of five minutes. "Damn it," he muttered, going back in and shutting off the stove. "Someday."

The FCU offices were in an old building in the financial district, which made sense to Dorsey. "Damn immigrants have more resources than we do. Oh, well, at least these people seem straight. Not out to gouge the system. I wonder if they do background checks, and if they do, what do they know about Illiana Jacoby? Easy, Sol. Let's go one step at a time." It's an old trait with Dorsey; No investigation without promise of a paycheck.

"My mother drank every dime that was made, I never remember new clothes, only hand me downs from some agency. Never again. Never. I will never do a job without getting paid, ever."

Lori Baranek was a tall thin woman, classic is how Dorsey put it in his mind, with deep golden hair streaming down her back. She was in a cashmere business suit, light green, with a soft yellow blouse showing ample cleavage. "This is how I like to start the week," he muttered to himself before the introductions. Evil thoughts of Star were replaced by evil thoughts of Lori. Baranek had a very slight accent that seemed more Spanish or French than Ukrainian.

"We're not in the habit of hiring private investigators, Mr. Dorsey, but you come with high recommendations and we are fearful for Melissa's safety. Captain Elmo said you normally charge one thousand dollars per day, is that correct?" Her smile seemed to be an old fashioned invitation to happy and warm places, and Sol Dorsey was concentrating on soft, pink, delicious lips, not business.

"Um, yes. A grand a day, plus expenses. What exactly do you know about this? Is this missing girl a runaway, or does it seem more criminal in nature?" First Star spent the night and then Lori Baranek all but invited him somewhere. It was almost more than Dorsey could take. "Sixteen year old girls can be a bit flighty, you know. I would hate to spend a lot of time and your money on something that could be cleared up by a cop on the beat. Tell me what you know."

That delightful smile was crowned by lively blue eyes, almost as bright as the emerald greens Dorsey wore. "Melissa has never given any indication that she would want to run away or do something equally stupid. Her mother and father are sure she has been kidnapped."

"Two questions, Lori. Has there been any contact with the kidnappers, if that's what this is? And, what do you know about her parents?" They were sitting across from each other in a conference room, shared coffee, even sweet rolls. The dark wood panels on the lower halves of the walls were reminders of history, of glory days when gold and the open sea paid for things in this area. *That question*, he thought, *will open the door to finding out what she knows about Illiana.*

"I've known Melissa since she was born, Mr. Dorsey."

"Please, call me Sol," he smiled, offering his own invitation.

"Alright, Sol it is." The smile was generous, and Dorsey was hooked.

I think I'm going to invite this lady to have supper with me one day soon, he thought, and offered a full Sol Dorsey smile back.

Baranek continued, "Anyway, when Melissa was born, Mrs. Jacoby, that is, Illiana had her registered with us. Illiana came to this country as what some call a mail order bride. She and Henry Jacoby met through an agency and he traveled to Ukraine to marry her and bring her to the U.S.

"She had trouble as a young girl," she said, as she lowered her eyes, slightly. "Her parents were very poor, and she got in trouble trying to help the family. I'm not sure exactly what she was accused of. And then, her husband, a police officer, was accused of stealing items from the police. He was set up, he says, by some officers that didn't like him. That's why they came to me for help. Mr. Jacoby is afraid the police will continue to harass him if he tried to get help from them."

Dorsey's notebook filled up fast with this conversation. He didn't dare let his thoughts *drift off into bedrooms and lingerie and heaven and all that crap.* Out loud, he said, "Was Melissa involved in drugs or any of the other teenage problems?"

"No, she wasn't. Her mother assured me of that, but said she liked a boy, Sammy Ochoa who did drugs a lot. She had forbidden Melissa from seeing Ochoa, but she was sure they did see each other."

"How about the Jacobys? Are they involved in drugs or illicit activities?" He knew they were, deeply involved, but he wanted to see what this woman had to say about it. He was looking directly into those azure eyes, tried desperately to remember he was on an important investigation. His thoughts were explicit in his mind, bedroom after bedroom after bedroom. *Damn, this is one good-looking lady, and I would love to spend some quality time alongside her.* He brought himself back to reality by thinking that he could never invite her to his apartment.

"There have been whispers that Mrs. Jacoby was involved in drug dealing while in her home country," he said, and hoped to get some kind of response. His eyes were devouring the lady, and his thoughts had traveled long distances back and forth, bedroom to conference room, to bedroom.

"I haven't heard anything about that since they came to this country. Here is a current picture of Melissa, and all the information I have." She got up to escort Dorsey out of the FCU building. "Please call me if you find out anything. Anything," and that smile again lit up the fantasy world of Sol Dorsey.

"Thank you, Lori. I'll call you soon." Very soon, he meant to say, and headed out the door, down the street, and found the old Caddy. A large black SUV with heavily tinted windows drove by slowly, and Dorsey squinted trying to get a look at the driver. The windows were too dark, but he did get the license number.

His next stop was going to be the DA's office, but that car caught his attention. "Somebody wanted to know what I look like and what I drive. Interesting. Interesting. Did that little drive by come from last night's visits or the one this morning?" He felt to make sure the .45 was tucked under his shoulder and the 9 mm was in his boot. "Man, was I a target."

He needed to go somewhere to sort out his conversation with the Baranek woman, to give more thought to that big black SUV, and to what appeared to be a narcotics driven kidnapping. "The FCU doesn't know about Illiana Jacoby's past other than she got into some trouble when younger? I'm not buying into that fantasy. A roll in the hay with lovely Lori Baranek might loosen things up somewhat there." He realized then that he had driven down to the docks and was parked in a "compacts only" space, which was something he loved to do, and was thinking clam chowder and cold beer. "I must have pinched somebody's ass last night, asking about Jacoby and finding out about some dude named Socrates. That would sure as hell answer the big eyes from the black car." He sat at an open-air table, ordered, and took out his cell phone.

While he waited for Serious Elmo to come to the phone, his mind was alive with FCU probabilities. "They have to be connected to something illicit. It isn't logical for them to not know about Illiana, to have that much money available, and not be connected. I'm looking to have some real fun, I think, getting info and other things from Lovely Lori.

"What is it about the drug business that brings so many people in, spits so many wretches out? Attorneys representing punks snorting cocaine go home after court and snort cocaine. Aspiring prosecutors get thrown out of law school for going on methamphetamine binges. Judges get picked up buying pot from a corner dealer, and then they all go on TV to proclaim a war on drugs. You want a war? Hire my ass," and he let his mind go back to what he really wanted. "Yeah, Lori B."

~ ~ ~

"I can't help you on this one, Sol. Those plates were either stolen or you wrote the numbers down wrong. The numbers you gave me are for a Honda Civic, and have not been reported stolen. What did you find out at the FCU?"

"Not a hell of a lot that I don't already know. This has to come from a drug deal that got screwed up some way. Somebody will get their two cents back by way of darling daughter.

"Last night I kept hearing the name Timothy Socrates. Ring a bell?"

"Only from I what I read in the paper a while back. Seems his job at some bank was in jeopardy because of an indiscretion. I guess he's gay and did something stupid. How does he fit in this?"

"I don't know yet. What you just told me I heard three times last night. There is some connection between Socrates and the Jacobys, but I don't know what." His mind was still putting Socrates, a banker, in some kind of money laundering situation. He had those thoughts last night, and they were still with him. "OK, pal, I'll do my best to keep you informed. You screwed up giving me this case. That Lori is a charmer, and I'm going to do some charming of my own. Ta, ta."

His late spring morning was filled with great thoughts, the aroma of the docks, and a large sour dough roll filled with fresh clam chowder. "You know," he said to the couple sitting at the table next to his, "this is a beautiful day." They looked at him like he was some street nut, he smiled a charming smile, stood up, and strolled slowly back to his Caddy.

"I love mornings like this," he said out loud. "No fog, warm sun, fishing boats all lined up, their innards being cleaned for display on ice trays at markets all over town. And, I just met a beautiful woman, got hired at a fair price, and drive a dream car. Damn me, but this is a good day."

5

enri swung the large SUV up the driveway and into the garage, hitting the garage closer button even before getting all the way in. "Sean, get Armand to change those license plates again. And, I want you to bundle up our little prize. We have to move, and fast." All of this was said as he was getting out of the car. Then he saw the look on Sean's face and the blood spattered all over the black man.

"What the hell happened?"

"The simple answer is 'Armand' happened. I was in the back yard, by the pool when I heard the girl scream. Armand raped her while she was asleep. When she screamed, he slit her throat. She's dead, Henri, and of course, so is Armand." He looked like a defeated little boy that had just lost a football game, large shoulders just hanging, his head and face downcast. "All I did was walk out into the yard for a little sun and that fucker went to work on the girl. Son of a bitch."

"Doesn't that put a topping on everything else? We have to clean up this mess fast and get the hell out of here, Sean. The family hired a private detective to find the girl, and from what I heard, he is about the best, about the meanest, and is already on the job. I made him at the FCU offices, and he made the car.

"Our damn prints are all over this house, Sean, and now

we have two bodies to get rid of. Plan, old friend?"

"Let me think. Let me think." He was pacing around the big black car, clenching and unclenching his fists, kicking the tires, scowling, seeing thousands of dollars float away, and then a slight smile spread across his black face.

"We need to soak the house and Armand in gasoline and torch the place. We can take the girl's body out to one of the beaches somewhere and dump her in the surf later tonight. OK, let's get those license plates changed, get the girl wrapped in a blanket and in the back, and then, when it gets dark, torch this place."

"That will get part of this problem taken care of. A very small part. The Man will have our heads when he finds out. And that damn detective will be coming down on us as well."

"What did the Man tell you when you went downtown?"

"He wanted us to take a picture of her, then cut off a finger and take another picture. He is planning to send those, one day apart, to the family. I've never seen him more angry, and he will explode when he hears about this." Henri had been on the phone with Andrzej for more than an hour. Andrzei was now in Jerusalem arranging for a shipment of arms.

"Alright, we'll torch this place, dump the body, and then, my friend, we need to split up and get the hell out of this country. We are now on a big hit list, on several big hit lists. I wish you hadn't killed Armand. I wanted that pleasure.

"Besides raping the girl, what else did he do?" Henri was thinking that the fool might have cut her or marked her in some way. It would be Armand's way.

"He damned near cut her head off, Henri. Blood was still pumping when I ran back into the house. I was so mad I wanted to cut him into little pieces. How can a simple snatch go this bad this fast?" He walked over to a work bench, grabbed a couple of license plates, made sure they matched, and began the exchange, muttering, cursing, making sure the whole damn garage knew how angry he was. Henri walked into the house to see the damage for himself.

"I wonder if we will live through this?" he asked, as he walked around the carnage. He wrapped the girl's body in the blanket Sean had brought out, even though it was pretty much soaked in blood. Sean came in and the two moved her into the back of the SUV.

"Let's wrap Armand in a blanket or two as well, and make sure he is drenched in petrol. Then we will have to change clothes and pile all ours on as well. We need to soak the entire house. This house has to burn to the ground Sean. To the ground." They lifted Armand onto the sofa where the girl had been, covered him in a blanket from the bedroom and peeled off their clothing to add to the pile. There was blood on everything and they didn't want to carry any of it with them. "It really doesn't matter if they know this is arson, what matters is that Armand not be identified right away and our prints are burned away."

Sean was thinking timing as well as burning. "By the time we shower and dress it will be getting dark and we can start soaking this place. We have about ten gallons or more in the garage, and that should give the place a good start."

"Why don't you drain another ten or so from the car? I filled it up before coming back, Sean. We have to get rid of as much evidence as we can. Our prints are on everything." A wry grin spread across his face, as he commented, "After all, this is a safe house, you know."

They showered, dressed and spread more than twenty gallons of gas throughout the complex, drove the car out of the garage, and Sean went back into the garage, lit a pile of newspapers they had spread on the floor, opened the door to the house, hit the garage door closer and ducked under it as it closed. They were two full blocks away when the house exploded.

"Let's hope the fire department is slow in getting there, Henri. Oh, that man is going to be pissed when he finds out. I've never been to South Africa but it's looking mighty nice right now. How about you?"

"Being French Algerian, they will look for me in France or North Africa somewhere. I'm thinking Russia or one of the little countries around there. Lithuania maybe," and he had kind of a rueful smile on his rugged face. "A quarter of a million dollar piece of ass is what Armand got and cost us." The expletives that followed were probably Algerian, or maybe Lithuanian.

~ ~ ~

The bank sat on a busy corner in the middle of the city's financial district, but was overshadowed by the big boys in the game. "First Reserve Bank? What kind of name is that?" Dorsey said to himself. He parked the Caddy in a parking lot about a block away and snarled "don't screw with this car while I'm gone," at the kid handing him his ticket. Cadillac's of that vintage, 1956 convertible, with their massive shark fin tails, long and heavy bodies, and big balloon white wall tires had an emotional impact, even on the young and dumb.

"I'm looking for Timothy Socrates."

"I'm sorry, Mr. Socrates is no longer with us. Can someone else help you?"

"Uh, no, it's rather personal. Do you know where I might reach him?" Dorsey was sure he was lied to about not knowing where Socrates might be, but you can't wrap long fingers around someone's neck in the marble flanked lobby of a bank. He took his time walking back to his car, wondering why a banker's name would come up following questions about an ex-cop and a possible drug dealer.

Back at his apartment he rescued his phone book from a threatening pile of old newspapers, and found Socrates, Timothy listed. The address was in an old industrial building converted to lofts and such and rented out for more dollars than most people have ever imagined. "I wonder what kind of banker old Timmy boy is? Having the laundress in a bank makes it easy to clean up the money." His musing was cut off by a phone call.

"Simon, this is Mavis Brownell in the district attorney's office returning your call. How are you? It's been a long time."

To himself he said, "Long time my ass, we've never met." To Brownell he said, "I'm fine Mavis, just fine. Can we meet somewhere? I'm working on something I would rather not discuss on the phone."

"Sure. Ever been to Buchko's on Third? Nice little place with good wine."

"Sounds like a plan. Three O'clock OK?"

"I'll see you then."

"I know the body goes with that voice, but I wonder why

she thinks we've met. And, now that I think about it, why is she so willing to meet with me? Didn't ask one single question, or even hint at one." He picked the phone book back up, paged to Buchko's on Third. "Here we go. Ukrainian food and spirits, dinner served from five to eleven, bar from two to midnight. Well, well, well.

"Illiana from the Ukraine, Melissa missing and a Ukrainian children's group has hired me to find her, and the D.A. wants to meet with me at a Ukrainian restaurant. I might just enjoy this little meeting." He knew Brownell was striking, and mingled his thoughts about Lori Baranek with those of Mavis Brownell. "Sometimes it's nice to think of a lovely woman that isn't a prostitute." And then the thoughts about Serious Elmo putting Mavis Brownell into the Illiana Jacoby situation, and he was back on the case immediately.

"Once again, talk narcotics and the strangest mix of people get in the conversation. Right now, we have a dirty cop, that fits, a mail order bride with drug connections in the old country, a lady running a non-profit that makes lots of money, and a prosecutor. Strange bedfellows, two of which could jump in my bed any time they wished."

~ ~ ~

The drive out to the coast took about an hour, and it was very dark when Henri parked the black SUV. The two men carried Melissa's body out to the water line and threw her into the surf. Sean Sorenson turned toward his comrade, pulled a Glock nine millimeter automatic and put three rounds through Henri. "Remember, old friend, a secret isn't a secret if more than one knows it." He drove back to the city, parked the car near the docks and dropped the weapon over the side, into about thirty feet of water.

Jamal King spent the night at an obscure little hotel, and in the morning, Marion Smith bought some clothes and shoes at a cut-rate store. Jamal King then took public transportation to the airport where Sean Sorenson bought a one-way ticket to Mumbai, India. On the following day, Sorenson bought a one-way ticket to Cape Town, South Africa.

"I've never been on a safari, and it might be a good way to get lost for a while. How could such a simple thing as grabbing a teenage girl go so wrong so fast?" Sorenson was far more afraid of The Man than he was of cops finding him. "I have to disappear and fast."

She was long and graceful, a wool suit, pastel for spring, skirt not too short, cleavage just right, in a simple muted flower pattern, working to highlight a deep auburn mane and bright gray eyes. She walked directly to Sol Dorsey, seated at a cocktail table toward the back of Butchko's. Mandolin music played in the background, and some that were there were not speaking English. He thought he saw her nod to the bartender, but the smile was for him alone.

"Hello, Sol. You're even bigger than I remember." Dorsey was standing to greet Brownell and towered over her. "I saw Captain Elmo earlier today. Then got your call, so I was expecting it. You and Elmo have been friends for a long time?"

"We go back a few years. I went straight, he became a cop." A gentle chuckle followed and Mavis Brownell joined the joke. "You have me at a disadvantage, Mavis. I don't remember us meeting." It was a question and a challenge.

Her smile appeared genuine and warm, and she met Dorsey's brilliant greens head on. "You rousted a drug dealer a few years ago, I had just started at the DA's, and saw you testify during the trial. I don't think we actually met, but I have seen you."

"I was afraid old timer's was starting to settle in." His smile was genuine and warm as well, and Dorsey was fully aware of just how attractive Mavis Brownell was. "I have been doing some work on a drug case and a name keeps popping up that I simply can't put into its proper place."

"Captain Elmo said something about international drugs. What is the name? Maybe I know it."

"I heard the name three times last night while I was moving up and down Franklyn Street. Timothy Socrates. Supposedly a banker, but the bank he is supposed to be associated with says he is no longer with them. I don't remember running into that name in other cases. You know how the same names keep cropping up." She was leaning forward, listening to every word, he believed, and he could almost taste her lips. *I spend too much time with the working girls,* he was thinking. *I gotta get out with a little class once in a while.*

She was giving Dorsey as much time as he wanted to enjoy the view, and said, "Good old Franklyn Street. If it's ugly or illegal, it happens on Franklyn Street. I hope you only go down there on business?" He mumbled something back, and she continued.

"Socrates got into some kind of a jam recently, lost his job at the bank, and the papers tried to make it a federal case. I don't know anything about drugs, though. Just another gay man being a bit too public for his employers." Dorsey rocked back in his chair, recognizing a flat out lie.

She just dismissed the fool, and lied about what she knows, he was thinking. *I need to find out more about what's in this lady's mind. For that man's name to come up as often as it did last night and she doesn't know anything? I better keep my distance here, I think.* He was also working on keeping a semblance of a relationship even though he

54

had a great distaste for liars. "How about a little dinner, Mavis? This has been a long day for me."

"I'd love to Sol, but I have a meeting at six. But, understand, big guy, this isn't a flat out no. You have my number." She got up from her chair as she spoke, and he took her hand, squeezed it gently, and they said goodbye. The little wool skirt did a delightful dance as she left Butchko's Grill on Third.

The waiter asked if Dorsey wanted another cocktail, which of course, he did. "Have you known Ms. Brownell long, sir?"

The question caught Dorsey short. "Um, yeah, for a while. Why do you ask?" That was strange, he thought, for a waiter to come out of the blue with a question like that.

"When her grandfather owned Butchko's, Mavis was just a little girl, and almost grew up in here. I just wondered. We all love her."

"Her maiden name was Butchko?"

"No, no, sir. While Butchko is an old Ukrainian name, the family name is Dziuba. She married Mr. Brownell, and then he was tragically killed. She didn't go back to her family name. She is so lovely."

"Indeed she is. When did the family emigrate, or am I getting too personal?" He was trying his best not to get excited by this turn of events, but it was hard to do. *I'm in the middle of little Ukraine,* he mused, and the atmosphere proved him right. Drapes, lighting, the music, most of the staff wearing what might be considered traditional dress, and everyone speaking with a distinct accent spelled Ukraine.

"It was during the revolution that some of the family

came to this country, and many followed later. I'm not sure when old Mr. Dziuba got here. I'll get your cocktail right away, sir, but if I might suggest, our vodkas all come from the old country. Have you ever tasted real vodka? It's sacred sir." The smile was that of a true salesman and Dorsey enjoyed the situation.

"No, but I think I'll stick with good old Kentucky Bourbon, straight, no ice."

It was several cocktails and a large roast lamb dinner later that Sol Dorsey arrived back at his apartment. "If I don't get all this written down, I'll never remember. Damn, I'm investigating what might be a Ukrainian drug organization, a Ukrainian's kidnapping, and find out an assistant DA is Ukrainian and a liar. I wonder how old man Brownell met his end?" The chatter was Tommy gun fast as Dorsey got the stove going, got his laptop opened, and never shut up.

"The waiter said 'tragically killed.' I'm sure glad I didn't go into any detail about that with Mavis. I could have blown my case into smithereens. I don't like it when people lie to me, even if I do want to get the little darling in bed." It was many hours, a six-pack of pale ale, and a pot of coffee before Dorsey wrapped up his day. His to-do list was growing longer by the minute.

As he was putting things together in his mind, he kept returning to the condition of his apartment. "The little working girls have no trouble putting up with this mess, but how could I invite Baranek or Brownell up here? Maybe I can hire someone to clean this place up. Bullshit," he exploded, laughing as he headed to his bedroom.

"I'm going to connect Brownell to all this, to Jacoby, to

Baranek, and in the process, might even find a little sixteen year old girl. A member of the district attorney's office lying to an investigator. That just about tops it." He had maneuvered his way through a hallway and was almost into the bedroom. "That roast lamb dinner and cocktails will look good on my expense report. A Ukrainian dinner at a Ukrainian restaurant, paid for by a Ukrainian organization that protects children. Yeah, right." And he wandered off through a maze of "stuff" to his bedroom.

~ ~ ~

He found the morning paper after relighting the coffee, and was startled to read about a couple of bodies washed up on the beach near the bridge. "A young girl knifed to death and a middle aged man shot to death," he read, and started the search for his telephone. "Damn it, now where the hell did I leave my cell phone?" He spent almost five minutes searching, only to discover it was sitting under the newspaper. "I hate telephones," he mumbled while dialing Serious Elmo's home number. Luckily for the cell phone the meat cleaver wasn't handy.

"You see the paper yet this morning Serious? Is that Melissa's body? Have they ID'd either of them? It looks like a snatch gone bad to me. Did you know Mavis Brownell is Ukrainian? And a liar?" The questions were flung out faster than Elmo could respond.

"Slow down, Sol. Jeez, old man, at least take a breath. They found the bodies late last night or early this morning, and I put a lid on releasing identification. It is Melissa Jacoby and she was raped, apparently after or during her murder."

"That's about as low as you can get."

"Well, there's more, old friend. The man is Algerian, a known smuggler, kidnapper, and killer. He goes by the single name Henri, and he probably had a lot to do with this. Don't interrupt yet, damn it." Sol Dorsey was ready to jump down the telephone line, but held up.

"There was a big fire in one of the north-bay mansions, and the fire department is sure it was arson. Inside, they found the remains of another Algerian named Armand. I've got a forensics crew scouring the place right now. Fires don't always burn away fingerprints, and blood samples can still be taken. It's my guess that this is all connected. I'll see you in my office in half an hour." Dorsey agreed and started the great hunt through the garbage pit he calls home, looking for his pants. He did remember to turn the coffee off when he left.

Dorsey parked the big Caddy in a 'compacts only' spot reserved for official vehicles. They quit writing him parking tickets years ago. "If Henri is dead and Armand is dead, we need to be looking for number three. Somebody got rid of witnesses, Serious. I left a note at the FCU that I would be checking the identity of the girl whose body was found on the beach. That will hold them off for a couple of hours.

"How sure are you that this originates with Illiana Jacoby and drug smuggling? The assistant DA lied through her pretty whites last night about knowing anything about Tim Socrates, and I would bet he's connected here somehow. Up and down Franklyn Street, when I mentioned Ukrainian drugs, Socrates' name popped up immediately, and Mavis Brownell said she didn't know anything about that. Did I tell you she's Ukrainian? I wonder how well she knows Illiana Jacoby?"

He finally slowed down enough to take a breath and Serious Elmo, settled back in his big office chair, smiling slightly, got a chance to say something. "You're like a freight train, did you know that? Start slow, build a head of steam, and can't be stopped. Your man Socrates has been in the shadows for some time, never fully investigated, but looked at by the district attorney and the feds. More than likely he's in the money laundering business, and probably on an international scale.

"If Brownell told you she doesn't know anything about him, it's time for you to start being very careful. Here are the preliminary autopsy reports, and I'll send you whatever the forensic boys pick up. What's on your schedule?"

"I want to talk to Socrates, but I don't want to scare the hell out of him. I also need to go by FCU and let them know that Melissa is dead. I guess that ends my employment there. I really don't have a handle on this yet, Serious. Too many questions, not enough answers.

"Something else. Dead Algerians and possible drug connections everywhere kind of tells me we should expect visits from the feds pretty soon. The DEA has screwed up so many of my investigations that I really don't want to have to deal with them again.

"Well," Dorsey finished, "I'm heading over to the FCU. Anything you want me to pass along to them? Hell, I'm probably out of a job. One day on the job and the girl turns up dead." His mind was playing tricks on him as he left to find his car. "I'm out of a job," he was thinking, "and I'm still working on the case." A passerby looked at him, almost in fear when he stormed, "I don't work for free, damn it."

He also knew that he couldn't give this one up. "There

are hundreds of questions that simply have to be answered. Boy, my next client is going to pay through the nose to make up for this."

He was chuckling as he got into the big Caddy. "I don't work for free, my ass. With Ukrainians coming out of the walls, selling drugs and guns, laundering millions, and protecting the hell out of each other, there is no way I can give this one up. Sure as hell I'll find myself working for the damn cops. That would top this morning off."

He never noticed the morning fog was lifting, spring time sun was warming the air around him, or that he could actually put the top down on his beautiful Caddy if he felt like it. "I really do have my nose deep into this case," he thought, "and there is no way I can shake loose of it. I hate druggies and all those connected to them."

~ ~ ~

"Hank, you get some kind of an answer from the money man. I'm going to go by FCU and then try to make contact with Sheik. If he's behind this, I'll know right away. If he's not, it could be that we are being rousted by Israelis or maybe even Russians, although the stupid Russians don't do well in the smuggling business. We need to get some money back in our control right away." There was more anger in her tone than worry.

"If Omar Sheik is behind this, Illiana, I will kill the bastard. I will."

"Yeah, yeah. Get tough when nobody's around," she chided. "Get your ass down to Socrates' place. Melissa will only live if we have some hard cash, and only if she was snatched for money, not for intimidation. And don't try any cheap ass tricks." She slammed the door and stalked to her car.

On the way to FCU, she turned the radio on and heard about the two bodies found on the beach. Instinctively, she knew Melissa was dead. She just drove around aimlessly for about an hour, and finally, went to the Ukrainian children's center.

"Hello, Lori. It was Melissa, wasn't it?" It was just a cold, hard statement, no emotion, no indication that Melissa was her daughter. "Have the police contacted you? No one has called us."

"Come in, Illiana. I'm so sorry. It's just horrible. The private detective we hired to find Melissa just left and confirmed that she was killed. Her body was found on the beach near the bridge. Can I get you something?"

Illiana didn't cry or scream or tear her hair. She was taught from early on not to show emotion, to save outbursts for when you are alone. Don't give away personal feelings to anyone, and so, all she did was give Lori Baranek a hug, and go back to her car. *If Omar Sheik is behind this, Hank will never get a chance to kill that man.* She couldn't get it out of her mind that the Israeli mafia might be behind this horrible crime. She called a number in a town about one hundred miles inland and waited for an answer before driving off. "I'll be there in a couple of hours, Sheik. This is very important. No, Hank is not with me."

Simon Sol Dorsey parked the big Caddy two streets over from where he believed Timothy Socrates lived. "I don't know who this jerk is, but he is involved up to the top of his Greek neck. Interesting neighborhood, anyway." The walk on a spring time day was delightful, lovely ladies were out in their springtime frocks, cute little bottoms dancing with each click of high heels, and the world felt good. When one lived near a coast, left or right, the sound of the ocean and bay, the current weather, and the current season played a large part in emotional outlook.

The aroma of a lively ocean, fishy to some, fresh to others, coupled with warm, bright, springtime weather allowed for bright thoughts of iced cracked crab, of mussels on a grill, of steamed clams, of beautiful women. The women were always beautiful, and willing to meet new people. Always. In Simon Sol Dorsey's case, all of this was filtered through thoughts of murder, drugs, and evil people.

"Mavis Brownell and Illiana Jacoby are Ukrainian, Tim Socrates is probably Greek, I have two dead Algerian smugglers and a dead Ukrainian teenager, and many indications of international narcotics smuggling. I'm mighty deep, and I got here mighty fast." As he muttered to himself, he found he was walking just a bit too fast.

"I'm really hyped," he said. "Slow down big boy, let's see

where this Socrates fool lives." The building was one of several industrial complexes turned into condos for those that made too much money. "Even the rent on these is sky high, more or less the purchase price. Damn me, but I don't think I could live in one." Considering the condition of his apartment, it's a safe bet.

"Bankers don't make this kind of money. People that own banks might, but people that work in banks don't. Those that make lots of money from drugs need a way to clean up that money, and those that do the laundering make lots of money. If Socrates is the man to go to, he would be making this kind of money. How will he be able to continue if he doesn't work at the bank? This is really starting to be fun."

He was still half a block away when he saw Hank Jacoby drive up and park in front of the complex. "Here we go. Ex-cop Jacoby coming to visit ex-banker Socrates on the day his daughter is murdered." Dorsey couldn't remember ever meeting Jacoby but knew who he was by way of Serious Elmo. "I hope he doesn't know who I am or what I look like." Dorsey slowly continued his jaunt, walking right up to the door as Jacoby got a ring back from Socrates and the front door unlocked. He let his humor take hold for a minute and even held the door open for the man. "Go right ahead, sir," he said, smiling.

Dorsey got on the elevator with Jacoby and let the ex-cop push his floor first. Dorsey pushed the button for the floor below. "The fifth floor is the top floor, so that might be a private entrance. I wonder if there are stairways that aren't protected?" The hallway on the fourth floor was broad and well lit unlike many apartment buildings. "These condo people live well," he mused, as he strode down the main hallway. He found the cleaning and storage room, and then the staircase. He went back to the storage room, found a couple of towels and draped them over his arm and was ready to go upstairs.

"If Socrates has the entire floor, I could be walking into a problem." He slipped the .45 out of its holster and tucked it under a towel. "Just in case," he thought. "I don't think anyone uses these stairs, ever." There was dust and dirt on the steps and the banister, but no scraps of paper or junk. He reached the door to the fifth floor and found the stairs going up one more level. He went to the top, and the door opened onto the roof. Dorsey noticed that the building next door shared a common wall with this building, and he took the staircase of that building down to ground level.

"Isn't this convenient. A way in and out without having to worry about getting that front door open." He made sure the building next to Socrates' building didn't lock up at night and made plans for a late night visit. "I better make sure I have a job first," he said as he pulled the big Caddy away from the curb. He mulled over the question that had been in the back of his mind for the last half hour. "Why would Hank Jacoby be visiting an unemployed banker on the day his daughter's mutilated body washes ashore? Why did that banker's name keep cropping up the other night? What the hell kind of a mess have I got myself into?"

There were no answers, of course, but the questions wouldn't go away. It took the vision of Lori Baranek to clear them. "Hello, Lori. I'm very sorry."

"Thank you, Sol. It's horrible."

"I won't take any more of your time, then. I do think you

need to know that the death of Melissa Jacoby is probably associated in some way with major international criminal activity. How deep that conspiracy is, who is involved, how many other people may be in danger, I don't know. I'm telling you this so you can protect yourself and whatever other children might be at risk. There is a definite Ukrainian influence in the conspiracy." He was coming close to disclosing too much information, but felt this lovely lady needed to know.

"Thank you, Sol. This is something I've been afraid of for some time. The organization I work for is dedicated to protecting the children of those that have come to this country, and you are telling me that some may be in danger?" It was a question and a statement, and Dorsey had the same question in his head.

"I wish I could tell you. I'm seeing kidnapping, drug smuggling, possibly money laundering from some with Ukrainian backgrounds. I'm afraid that the Jacobys are right in the middle of it. I just want you to be able to protect yourself."

"I have been aware of some of the problems that Mr. Jacoby has been involved in, you know, with the police, and I'm aware that he isn't the smartest man I've ever met, but do you believe that there is danger to children other than Melissa?"

"I can't answer that. I just feel you need to be aware that it is possible." He smiled, took her hand, felt it tremble, and squeezed it gently. For such a huge man, Sol Dorsey had a soft spot that was even bigger, and he was holding the hand of a beautiful woman that he wanted to know better. They had moved from the reception area to Baranek's office, and they settled onto a small sofa along a wall opposite the doorway.

Springtime sunshine streamed through high windows, and Dorsey couldn't keep his eyes off Lori. Her hair actually sparkled, and he knew he was being flirted with, was willing to just about do anything the lady asked. "I'm not trying to create a fear factor here, Lori, but you must understand that those that deal in narcotics, weapons, kidnapping are very dangerous criminals. Melissa had her throat slashed and was raped following the kidnapping. It's potentially very dangerous right now." Once again, he had her hand in his, and once again thoughts of bedrooms and evil actions flooded his mind. The smile was specifically for Lori.

"I don't want these children to be in danger, Sol. We have too much of a drug influence in this country now, and too much danger from criminal activity. Can you help?"

"If you mean follow this out, find Melissa's killers, yes, I can, but you must understand that it will be expensive. It could entail travel abroad, it could mean paying for some help, it could get very dangerous. And, it could embarrass some of the Ukrainian émigrés."

"I understand. There's someone you need to meet. Can we have dinner tonight? I can fund most of what you're talking about, but I have an acquaintance that can help with some of the background you will need." She wrote a quick note on a piece of paper and handed it to him. "I'll see you at seven?"

"I'll be there. Thank you." They touched hands again, and Sol Dorsey was aware that their relationship just changed, dramatically. If he knew how, he would have tap danced down the stairs and out to his car. "Son of a bitch," he said, smiling. He drove back to his apartment, spun a U-turn half way down the hallway, and headed down the street to Maglio's for crab enchiladas.

Half way through his first platter of enchiladas, Serious Elmo called. "That third man you talked about has about forty different names and addresses. He's mostly known as Sean Sorenson, a dedicated kidnapper and smuggler who has worked with Henri many times in the past. Henri's last name is probably Bargon.

"How was your visit with FCU? Are you still employed? This is turning into a very big case, and because of the murders, my department is now fully involved. You have full access to anything you need, old friend."

"I'm meeting someone tonight who might have some background on the Ukrainian criminal organizations in this country, and yes, I'm still employed. For some reason, the FCU is funded well. The Baranek woman didn't blink when I outlined how much this might cost. I'll call you in the morning."

He washed the second platter of enchiladas down with a couple of mugs of cold ale and headed back to his apartment. As he left Maglio's, he saw two men giving his big Caddy a good look-see. When they spotted him, they took off running and Dorsey knew he would never be able to catch them. "So, first that big black SUV, now two bogey men giving me the once over. My visit down Franklyn Street must be paying off."

~ ~ ~

"Come on Dorsey, get your head on straight. This is one good-looking lady you're about to have dinner with. Come on, clean slacks, nice sport coat, don't forget to shave, stupid. Come on, you're running out of time." The patter continued for half an hour, and he made it to Lori Baranek's apartment on time.

"Hello Sol, please, come in." She was wearing a delightful gown that proved just what a good looking woman she was, her eyes dancing with friendliness, her perfume spreading evil thoughts through Dorsey's head. He took her outstretched hand, kissed it lightly.

"This is very nice, Lori. Thank you for inviting me." He spent hours trying his best to remember his manners. *I spend too much time with rough people with no manners,* he kept telling himself. A large man was seated on a sofa as they entered the living room, and he stood up, towering over Dorsey.

"Sol, this is Charles Dolinski. Charley, meet Sol Dorsey." The two men were sizing each other up, Sol knowing Dolinski was probably the biggest man he had ever met. Two saloon brawlers eyed each other, hoping to find where the first telling punch, kick, or bite would go. The moment passed quickly, the two shook hands, smiled and said hello to each other. Dolinski had a heavy accent, thick with the Baltic regions of earth.

"Charley was in the police department in Kiev before coming to this country. I'm sure he will be able to help you sort out some of the things we talked about today. He has some of the same misgivings as you concerning a conspiracy from Ukrainian sources."

The dinner was splendid, with too much lamb, too many vegetables, and a cake to wrap things up that was simply too sweet and too rich. "I will have to buy new pants and shirts tomorrow, I'm afraid," Sol laughed. Dolinski had eaten even more, and simply sat back in an easy chair, groaning like a ten-year-old boy.

They said their thank you's, their goodbyes, Charley Dolinski left in a cab, Dorsey lingered for just a couple of minutes, knowing he hadn't given anything away but had learned far more than he expected. He held her hand, felt the vibrations of anticipation running through his body, and did not want to go home. "I'll keep you fully posted on what I find out. Would it be better to call you here, or at your office?" That might get the right answer, he thought.

"You can call me here, any evening, Sol." He drew her close, they kissed as softly as it is possible, and he knew he had to leave right then, or do something very stupid.

"I'll call you in the morning." The drive to Socrates' neighborhood was long and slow, and Dorsey allowed his mind to play as many games as it wished. He finally broke his reverie and got himself back to business.

"I wonder if Mr. Dolinski is still a cop?" he was thinking. "For the second time, I've had a Ukrainian tell me they don't know the name Socrates. First Brownell, now Dolinski, and I'm positive that Brownell is lying. For Dolinski to tell me about Illiana Jacoby's background and not know the name Socrates has me baffled. I wanted to say I saw Hank Jacoby at Socrates' home. I should have.

"I think I should have brought Brownell's name up in the conversations, too. He did pass on some good information on drug pipelines and sources. I need to find out more about this Omar Sheik character. He sounds like one bad ass son of a bitch." He parked the Caddy a block from Socrates' building and walked over. As he came around the corner, he spotted two men near the entrance to the building. Dorsey ducked back quickly, then slowly moved so he could see the front of Socrates' building. Then a third came to meet the two. "I'll be damned. So, Mr. Dolinski isn't a cop, he's a friggin' member of the Ukrainian Mafia. Well, well, well."

Dorsey watched for a few minutes as the three talked. "I'd love to hear that conversation," he said to himself. Dolinski went back inside the building and one of the other two left in a cab. "The third fool must be the lookout. OK, no home invasion on my plate tonight. I wonder if those two were the ones I saw near the Caddy earlier. That makes sense." He headed home with more questions than answers and could feel a long night coming on. He was right. He woke up every hour on the hour with hundreds of unanswered questions.

She drove along the river, looking for East Bank Blvd., spotting the sign too late and had to drive another half mile before she could turn around. The trees along the street were dressed in their spring finest, great blossoms and overbearing limbs of green blotting out street signs, none of which brought the slightest bit of brightness to Illiana's soul. She parked immediately in front of the large Victorian style home, and was about to ring the bell when the door opened.

Illiana remembered how impressed she had been the first time Sheik Omar brought her to this house. Immense compared to what she knew in the Ukraine, filled with expensive antiques, expensive carpeting, expensive foods. This, she also knew, was what she wanted out of life. Instead, while she had access to massive amounts of money, she had no life, only Hank.

In some way she knew that before she could have any of the imagined good things in life, she would have to dispose of Hank. The first thing he would do, she knew, would be to exaggerate his position, spend too much money foolishly, broadcast to the world that he had money, and most would know that he didn't have a job nor did he marry into money.

"At some point," she often told herself, "After Hank is

long gone, I will get an inheritance from long lost family in the Ukraine, and then, it will be OK to spend a little bit here and there, and just on me." That always brought a smile to her face, something that few ever saw.

Her mind was filled with these thoughts of a good life, with antiques on antique tables, with lamps and shades hundreds of years old, with sofas and chairs from Persia along with the carpeting underneath. She always had thoughts of fine food and wine, of evenings spent at theaters and parties. She dreaded having to go home later today and face Hank. "I hate that man," were the thoughts in her head as Sheik Omar greeted her.

"You made good time, my dear. Come in and tell me why you're so upset. You sounded terrible on the phone." Omar Sheik bin Ali, neared the six foot mark, dark and obviously Egyptian in every handsome way, was a gentleman of honor, a throwback to better times when courtesy and manners meant something important. Others say he was a born killer with no soul. Dressed in an open neck silk shirt, slacks, and Arabian style slippers, he ushered his Ukrainian partner into his home, his robe flowed in the breeze.

Omar Sheik wasn't really a collector, he just had 'stuff' as he calls it. Victorian lamps, once lit with coal oil, now electric, period furnishings from around the world, the envy of many a visitor, and carpets from every village in Persia. A bit cluttered, but warm and friendly. It would not be far off the mark to see Sheik Omar in a tent in the hot sands of Egypt or Saudi Arabia.

"You don't know why I'm here, Sheik? You don't know about Melissa?" She settled into a large wing back chair, and challenged her partner. He seemed confused as he sat across from her.

"I don't know what you're talking about, Illiana. What's wrong with Melissa?" Was this genuine concern or simply evasion? Illiana got right to the point, again in a threatening manner.

"She's dead, Sheik, her throat cut from ear to ear and her body thrown to the fish, that's what's wrong. Are you behind this?" There was tremendous anger as she spat out these words, and Omar Sheik was stunned. He was also aware that a Glock semi-automatic weapon was always in her possession, and probably within easy reach.

"No, Illiana. No." They sat in silence for a couple of long minutes before he spoke again. "Tell me what happened, exactly, and why you would think I had something to do with it.

"Let me get us some tea" he said, but Illiana shook him off.

"Hank's stupidity cost all of us a lot of money, Sheik, and you vowed to kill him at the first opportunity. I know your temper, I know what you're capable of. She was kidnapped, raped, her throat slashed open, and her body dumped in the ocean. This has Omar Sheik written all over it.

"We have been together for a long time, we've made lots of money, and I am very aware of just how stupid Hank can be. I'm already making plans to end that problem, but if you are attempting to punish me or Hank by way of killing our daughter, I'm going to kill you now."

He sat very still, knew she could do that, would do that. He stood slowly, opened the silk dressing jacket to show

75

Illiana that he was not armed, and sat down next to her. "I am not involved in this." He put his arm around her shoulder, which brought memories of when they first started working together, when Illiana was a very young girl. "Melissa is sixteen? I believe you were fifteen or so when we made our first hit, eh? We have done many things, you and I, and there is no question I want to kill your husband, but only your husband. Melissa is like a granddaughter."

"Then who, Sheik? Who?" She wanted to scream, cry, hammer the walls with her fists, but would never do that in front of anyone. "Is someone moving in on us? Is this a message from someone wanting our territory? Who, Sheik?" On the hour and a half drive up, she had given this much thought. Sheik Omar and Illiana Jacoby had been in business for well over twenty years, had territory that they had defended from many angles, and had succeeded in keeping it because both were ruthless.

"Over the years, Sheik, we have fought off many who wanted in on our territory, on our buyers. We have defended our business well. There have been attempts by Israelis, by Russians, by Italians, by so many, and we have always worked together. We're a team, Sheik, we work well together, and we have made lots of money. In the process, I'm sure we have made many enemies, but who is this that kills my daughter instead of me or you?

"We buy our merchandise from people we have done business with for years, people we trust, and they have been paid well for dealing with us. Have we made enemies we don't know about?"

"I have heard rumors of another group that wants in on

our area, but I didn't believe them. A cop from the old days in Kiev. Give me a day or two, Illiana. Go home, kill Hank, grieve for Melissa, and be prepared. We have a large shipment moving our way, guns, opium, and cocaine in several boats and airplanes. The Israelis are prepared to ship more ecstasy and opium and the Afghans are sending tons of opium and heroin. There are large crates of AKs arriving as well.

"If someone is moving in, we need to be on our toes, my lady. Have you ever run into a large Ukrainian named Dolinski? I think it's Charles Dolinski. Biggest man I've ever seen, and there are whispers that he's trying to set himself up in the business. I'm sure he has Ukrainian contacts, probably some from the old KGB, but I doubt he has the kind of contacts that would challenge us."

"I remember a huge cop in Kiev, but I don't think I ever heard a name. I don't know anyone named Charles Dolinski."

"Keep your eyes and ears open, Illiana, and I'll get back to you in a day or two. Believe me, I had nothing to do with Melissa's death. Nothing." He walked her to the door and she gave him a hug goodbye. "Be prepared for anything and get rid of Hank."

Going back into his living room, he knew who killed Melissa. "The Man is still pissed about Hank screwing up that last shipment. I was sure I had him calmed down by making this new order." He would have to kill Hank himself, he feared, and ship his head to Andrzej to pay him off.

Neither one noticed the large black SUV that moved out of a parking space half a block away as Illiana drove away.

~ ~ ~

"Hi, Mavis, Sol Dorsey here, how about a crazy mixed up lunch?"

"Whatcha got in mind, big boy? For lunch that is." They both laughed over that, and Dorsey invited her to meet him at Maglio's for crab enchiladas, cold beer, and just a touch of business talk.

"I'm not much of a beer drinker, Sol," she said as he held her chair for her. "But I do love fresh crab with some nice wine. I don't think I've been here before. There's a lot of character to this place. You fit nicely." A warm smile woke up all the thoughts and ideas in Dorsey's head, and he knew he had to get the business part of the meeting out of the way quick.

"I was hired to find a missing girl, a teenager named Melissa Jacoby, and it was her body they found on the beach. I don't know if you remember Jacoby, he was a cop allegedly stealing dope and guns from evidence lockers. Anyway, it was his daughter."

"Who hired you, Jacoby?"

"No. It wasn't the family, and that's what's just a bit strange. I was hired by a group known as Free Children of Ukrainians. Apparently Jacoby married a Ukrainian girl, a mail order bride type thing and this group supposedly protects or helps the children of Ukrainian immigrants. Is Jacoby in the drug business? It's a strange murder that has drugs written all over it."

Sol Dorsey wanted to let Mavis Brownell hang herself, but in his mind he created pictures of the two of them wrapped in warm sheets and blankets, smothering each other with passion and heat. He created pictures of her making him proud to be a man, and then remembered she boldly lied to him about Socrates. Would she do the same here?

"I read the reports, Sol, and I see it a little differently. A young girl, mixed up with an older man, he won't take no for an answer, rapes her, then kills her. I don't think Jacoby is smart enough to get into the drug business." Dorsey wanted to reach across the table and slap the beautiful prosecutor across the chops. He had to let it go, but all thoughts of spending a delightful couple of hours in the sack went out the door with her big time lie. And, he remembered later that she didn't even mention that the older man had been shot to death.

His thought centered on what he knew, and what he knew she knew. "She has to know that Henri Bargon is an internationally wanted criminal, found shot to death with a missing American teenager who was raped and murdered. She has to know about Illiana Jacoby and Omar Sheik. She is one hell of a liar." His thoughts continued in those directions, as he tried to keep up some kind of conversation.

Small talk, a large platter of cracked crab, a platter of crab enchiladas, a pitcher of cold beer and a couple of glasses of white wine, and the afternoon drifted lazily into evening. He let the conversations go where they would, and finally cut the meeting short.

"We will have to do this again, very soon, Mavis. Maybe we'll find a couple other little bistros to enjoy." She didn't want the day to end, but he knew that he would never enjoy a romp in the hay with her. "There's a couple of people looking to pay me some money, so I have to cut this off." He watched her long legs and cute bottom walk out of Maglio's, so did half a dozen other men in the joint, and headed to his apartment and more muttering to help his investigation along.

"There's one thing I wish I had right now, and that's at least one contact in the Ukraine. These people are imbedded and apparently take care of each other. What the hell is the connection between FCU, Dolinski, Brownell, and Jacoby? When I get that figured out, I will be able close the case, I guess," he muttered.

"And, let's not forget good old Timmy boy Socrates. Brownell, though. She's the big answer, I think." Dorsey was pacing through the apartment, talking, growling, muttering, even found time to make a pot of coffee, giving the pot a full measure of conversation.

"That lying little bitch. Somehow, Mavis, the Jacobys, Socrates, and those Algerian goons are all tied together. And, now, an ex-cop from Kiev. If the FCU is tied up with Dolinski, I wonder if they are tied up with Illiana's drug and gun business, and if that's the case, why have they hired me? My ass is hanging out the window here." He spent several hours on the computer before heading for the sack. "Damn. Why can't I remember to turn the friggin' stove off?"

Back in the bedroom, about to jump in bed, and the phone sounded off. "Dorsey," he bawled after a short search for the cell.

"Sol, this is Star. I need some help." She told him where she was, he dressed and was out in less than two minutes, cussing the fog, feeling its cold and wet tendrils already reaching inside his black leather jacket. He scrunched that beat up fedora down on his head and nursed himself into the big Caddy.

Dorsey was mean, according to most criminal types he dealt with, surely and angry to those he needed information from, but to the working girls of the city, he was the biggest, cuddly teddy bear of an insurance policy any had ever known. Star had no question that he wouldn't answer her call for help.

Down to Franklyn Street, one more time, he snarled. "This filthy street needs to be burned out. Star, baby, what have you done now?" He parked the Caddy where it was very visible, headed to the saloon called "Bar" and made his presence known the way he liked. "Fling the doors open and go in like a cannon ball. That's the way to let everyone know you're there. Don't screw with me, is the answer."

Big men like Dorsey walked with a built in swagger, an all but visible chip that hung off broad shoulders, and a look that cracked glass. Dorsey fit the bill in every way, as if he practiced often. He was more than just assured of himself, he was proud of the fact that he could and would get in someone's face, could and did intimidate. He was more than at home in what most would call a slum neighborhood saloon, lights too bright, stale tobacco aroma permeating everything, warm whiskey served in dirty glasses, and beer by the glass, cheap, not always cold, and often splashed when served.

Burt was tending the long plank and Sol put it to him gently. "Star called, said she would meet me here. I don't see her Burt."

"I think she's in the card room, Mr. Dorsey. In the back." High stakes poker, table limit, was the draw at the "Bar," and Dorsey pretty much knew who he would find back there.

"Anybody with her?"

"Not that I could tell. Might be trolling or looking to meet someone."

Dorsey was pissed, worried about the little prostitute, and angry at Burt for his lack of respect. "I'm going to have to pop that little prick soon." He walked to the back of the saloon, noticed two guys who sat near the pool tables. They had eyes on him the whole way as he went into the card room. Star was standing off to the side of one of the three tables, intent on a five-card stud game underway. A big smile spread across her pretty face when she spotted the big man.

One of the tables was empty, the other two filled. Dorsey recognized everyone at the tables except one, a small man, probably mid-forties, slicked back hair, hadn't shaved in a couple of days. He wore a pastel pink shirt, no tie, and a black ill-fitting, suit. "He has a little bulge under his left shoulder, probably an automatic. This is a set up, and I'll bet Star knows it. Those two out front are back up, and this guy is going to take out these two tables."

Dorsey walked around both tables, looked at the pots, checked the cards, pinched Star on the butt, and settled in slightly behind and to the right of the dude. Star sidled up to him, and he gave her the nod to keep quiet, which she did. The dude knew where Dorsey stood, and tried to squirm around to keep an eye on him while still playing his cards.

"Sit still, you skinny little prick. You trying to look at my cards?" It was the man to his right that snarled.

"No, man, just sittin' too long."

"Then get up and walk around, but don't be trying to look at my cards. I'll put your skinny ass through the wall. Hey, Sol, how you doin'?"

"Just fine, Guy. Nice to see you." The dude got up, and in a quick move pulled a nine-millimeter automatic from his shoulder holster, but not fast enough. Dorsey's forty-five barked twice and the dude was dead. His two friends came through the door, and the forty-five howled a couple more times.

An acrid blue smoke filled the room, along with blood and dead bodies. It was very quiet in the card room in the back of the saloon named "Bar". That was, until the sound of men as they broke away from the tables, overturned chairs, broke glasses, did their best to not be involved, but were, found they couldn't get out.

The chaos settled down within moments, replaced by sirens and screaming tires slip sliding on wet pavement, and the cops, milled among those in the place, seemed as confused as the poker players and winos at the bar.

Once again, gunfire, sirens, death splashed across Franklyn Street. Once again, Simon Sol Dorsey in the middle of it. "I make most of my money from what happens on this street, but I think it really is time to close it down, take out the gangsters, hipsters, druggies, and prosties. If anyone asked, I don't think I would ever say that in public." An ironic smile slipped across his craggy face, and probably no one noticed.

Murder, narcotics, money laundering, kidnapping, it all happened on Franklyn Street, where every other doorway opened into a saloon, the rest split between pawnshops and tattoo parlors. Upstairs in every building, the ladies of the night offered their wares to men, boys, women, and girls. If it was criminal in nature, it could be found on Franklyn Street. Tonight, with a cold and dangerous fog, the criminal nature was rampant.

It was hours of police procedural before Dorsey even had a chance to say hello to Serious Elmo. "Serious, I really don't know any of the background on this. Star gave me the impression she was in deep doo-doo one more time and I came down here. I spotted the two guns in the lounge, and when I came back here, the third was at the table. I pick it as a straight up robbery, but there could be more to it. Star might have some of the answers."

"Talk to her, Sol, and I'll keep good old Lt. "by the book" Simpson away from you." Orel Simpson, was natty in his dress, precise in his speech, and always by the book, had been the first on the scene and was ready to put the cuffs on Dorsey. Serious continued, "Is this connected to anything you have going? Any connection to the Ukrainian mess?"

"I don't think so. I don't think I've seen any of these three before tonight. We do need a long talk on the Ukrainian case, though. I'll see you after I have a chat with Star," and he walked over to the hooker, patted her bottom, kissed her cheek, and walked out the door, with Lt. Simpson held in check by Serious Elmo.

~ ~ ~

He had a pair looking at him, swimming in a puddle of grease, and four limp strips of half cooked bacon sloughed onto the chipped blue platter added to the cholesterol heavy breakfast. Star munched on a stale sweet roll. "How can you eat that stuff? Have you even heard the word heart attack? Geez, Sol, that looks horrible."

"It would taste better with a double shot of cheap whiskey, but the coffee is old enough that it's working. Tell me about tonight. What brought all that on? Who were those idiots? Why did you call?"

"The guy at the table, the one you shot first, hired me for the night, but said he had to make his mark first. He and his two friends said after the card game that I should find a couple of my friends and we would party for a day or two. When I saw all those guns I got scared and called you."

"I didn't recognize any of them. Any names?"

"The two big guys called the one that hired me Coon Dog, but that's the only name I heard. I don't think I've ever seen them before either. Wait. Yes I have." Her eyes lit up and she sat straight up, a sweet roll half way to her mouth. "When we were out the other night, Coon Dog was in two or three of the saloons that we went into. I remember him, Sol. Do you think he was following us?"

Sol Dorsey stuffed that bunch of info into his Ukrainian file. He thought these might be part of the new drug organization moving in on the Jacoby operation. "When Coon Dog or either of the other bums spoke, did they have any kind of accent? This is important, Star."

"Yeah, Sol, one of them did. Kind of guttural, you know what I mean?"

"Thanks, baby. You able to get home OK?" He handed her a couple of hundred dollar bills, paid for breakfast, and headed for that beautiful Caddy, parked right around the corner.

"You even look like you're gonna touch that car and you die." He snarled the words out, went into a fast lope, and pulled the reloaded forty-five, all in one motion. Two men, one he recognized from Socrates' apartment, were standing next to the Caddy. "Move away from that car now."

The two were pretty casual as they moved back, and one started to reach inside his sport coat. Dorsey aimed the big revolver at the guy's nose and both men froze.

"That's better, boys. Much better. Now, one at a time, you first," and he indicated the man reaching in his coat, "put your guns on the hood of the Caddy. Very slow, gentlemen, I've already killed three people tonight, so two more won't hurt a thing." Three handguns found their way to the hood of the car and Dorsey then demanded wallets.

"You boys been on my ass for several days now. Want to tell me why?" There was no response at all. He took the drivers licenses from each wallet and gave the wallets back. "You, in the blue shirt, get the fuck out of here now. Don't look back, just get away from here as fast as you can." The man took off like a jackrabbit, and his friend was about to run also.

"One little move, asshole, and you're dead." Dorsey pulled a key ring out, punched a button, and the passenger door opened. "Get in." He slammed the door, pushed another button and the trunk opened. He put the armament in the trunk, pushed yet another button and got in the car. The hit man was trying to get the door open. "Electric, stupid," and he slammed the guy across his nose with his revolver. Blood splashed generously across the guy's face, and a whimper followed by words that Dorsey couldn't understand.

"We're going for a little ride, now, so behave and enjoy the scenery." It was a beautiful morning, with a grand sunrise as they neared the dunes. The surf was crashing on shore, birds of many colors and species were singing and dancing their way into the new day.

It was spring, the air was fresh, no fog, no wind, not even a chill. Dorsey tried to remember whether there had been fog when he went to Star's rescue. He forgot the chill that fog can bring, particularly when danger existed.

"It doesn't matter," he thought. "Yes," he muttered, "no chill except for the blood running through this man's veins." He snickered as he looked over at the whimpering man. He wasn't very big, didn't have large hands or broad shoulders. "Just another puke who needs a lesson in courtesy, compliments of me."

The man had been tailing Dorsey for several days, had heard some of the stories about the big man, wasn't really willing to believe most of them. And now, he was in the front seat of this huge American car, going somewhere, and didn't know if he would be coming back. To Dorsey, the fear was palpable, and that was how intimidation worked. "I own you," he snickered, backhanding the fool.

What does it take to kill another human being? For Sol Dorsey, the answer, while complicated, as it should be, was easy. "It takes that person to be involved in a criminal activity that hurts or kills other people. I feel that killing people that kill other people is fully justified. There is no other way sometimes." He was thinking about earlier in the evening when the three men died. "That situation could have ended with many people in that room dead or wounded, people that weren't involved in anything other than a card game. I did what I had to do, and I have no regrets." The man in the passenger seat listened to this jabber, not understanding a word.

A young cop asked Dorsey one time what it felt like to kill another human being. "The first one is very difficult," the big man said, giving the rookie a serious answer, not his trademark smart ass remark. "Many thoughts ram their way through your mind, and even if everything is fully justified, it's hard. After the first one, when you understand that what you did was the right thing, it ain't quite so hard. Always make sure you're justified. Sleazy attorneys abound," he said, allowing the smartass to return.

It was a quiet half hour ride out to the sand dunes on the north side of the bay, and Dorsey used the time to put answers to "about ten thousand questions." He parked the car, got the big man out, and walked him into a ravine between high hills of sand and salt brush. He never said a word, just slammed the guy in the back of the head with his revolver.

"Get up, big boy. I need some answers," and he picked the guy up by his neck, almost squeezed off the guy's breath. "First, whose money is it that has you on my tail?" The man was hanging five or six inches above the sand, kicking and squirming, not being able to breath.

The man didn't say a word, and that brought an open handed slap that put the dude back in the sand. Dorsey helped him up, again by the neck, and put the revolver right under his chin. "Whose money?"

"Dolinski," was all he said and Dorsey slammed him across the side of the head with the heavy pistol.

"Thanks. Have a nice walk back." Dorsey headed back to the saloon named "Bar", hoping that Serious Elmo was still there. He was. So was By the Book Simpson.

"**G**et out of my way Simpson. Serious, we have to have a long talk. There's a war about to break out around here." The Bar was closed, there were twenty or more cops, uniformed and otherwise, all over the place, some even stringing more crime scene tape. Dorsey and Elmo walked over to one of the cocktail tables, each with a cold beer, and settled in. It was almost mid-morning now, and Dorsey was willing to add a couple of shots of bad whiskey to his table fare. Orel Simpson fumed, and knew that he would be turned away from that table.

"Heavy guns have been following me since I took the Jacoby case, these three dead ones are part of a major Ukrainian drug organization moving into the city, maybe the whole damn state. Because of what you started, I now know that Illiana Jacoby is a partner with a man called Sheik Omar, and between them they own the heavy narcotics distribution in most of the western states. They also deal heavily in importing arms, particularly the big assault weapons."

Dorsey stopped long enough to take a deep breath, which brought a smile to Serious Elmo's face, and continued. "I have no idea if the feds have a clue to the size of this operation, Serious. This is your call now, and you know that I'm going to have to quit the case shortly. I'm almost sure FCU is involved, somehow, some way.

"Now, this new group is either looking to take out Jacoby or to join forces. I don't know which, but I do know they are on the hunt. A big son of a bitch named Charles Dolinski, you remember? He was a cop in Kiev, seems to be heading up the group, but Tim Socrates and Mavis Brownell are in this also. I think Lori Baranek and the FCU have a lot to do with it too.

"I can't go any further with my part of the investigation. I'm being paid by FCU, and that would implicate me. Damn me if I'm going to let that happen. I'm going to give you everything I have, Serious, and bow out. A grand a day and I'm quitting. Shoot me, Captain Elmo, just shoot my ass."

The case was building fast, getting interesting in so many respects, and now, Simon Sol Dorsey, PI, is turning it over to the cops. 'This just isn't right, Serious. It just isn't right. Go ahead, damn it, shoot me. You know as well as I the DEA will screw it up and all the bad guys will get off scot-free."

He got contemplative for a moment, then continued, "You know, Serious, private investigators don't have the best reps in the world, including me, but I do have my limits, and there is no way I can continue taking money from an organization that I know is involved in what I'm investigating. Call me a jerk if you want, but I simply can't take their money.

"Yeah, it is best if you just go ahead and shoot me."

"There are times I'd relish that choice, Sol, but not today. I guess you probably don't want to tell me how you know all this, eh?" He got that twisted little boy look back from Dorsey, shook his head, motioned for another round of beers, and continued.

"There's someone I want you to meet." He motioned to an attractive lady in a blue business suit to come join the two big men. Dorsey had spotted her the minute he got back to the Bar, but thought she was either with forensics or maybe the DA's office. He didn't make her for a cop.

"I was hoping I'd get to meet this lovely lady."

"Sol, meet Felicia Bogdanovich, assistant commissioner of the Ukrainian State Police. Felicia, this is the man I told you about earlier, Simon Sol Dorsey. You two are on the same case, but from different angles."

Dorsey was giving her the big eye, from her thin ankles to her blazing blue eyes, with several stops along the way. He stuck a big paw out and shook a small hand with a strong grip that was returned, also very strong. "Nice to meet you," he said and they all sat back down. "Ukrainian State Police, eh? You must know this Dolinski ape."

"I know him very well, Mr. Dorsey, very well." There was just a hint of an accent, but Dorsey recognized that the lady was very comfortable in English.

"Call me Sol. Are you investigating his narcotics operation?"

"That and many other aspects of his life," she said, giving Dorsey a nice full smile. Bright teeth, full damp lips, tongue wetting them slowly, and eyes, oh those eyes. They were designed to be seen on soft pillows for hours on end was how Dorsey was describing her to himself. "Captain Elmo has briefed me on what you have been doing. I understand you are on the FCU payroll?"

"I was. I'm sure they are connected to Dolinski, so I will terminate that deal."

"Good because I need an American investigator to work with me. The government of the Ukraine will pay you what the FCU has been paying, and we will work together. Because I am a foreigner, I need an American as a partner. I think we'll work well together, don't you?"

All the large investigator could say was, "Yeah." Serious Elmo was guffawing, By the Book Simpson was ready to shoot Dorsey, and Felicia had a grand smile brightening the scene. The sun was high in the sky when they left the Bar.

"My car is right around the corner. Can I give you a lift?"

"I have a motel room down by the waterfront, Sol. I'd love a lift." He took her hand and gently steered her toward the Caddy. Her eyes got even brighter when she realized the big car was Dorsey's. "Cars this big are rarely seen at home. I like this, Sol. Take me for a drive and tell me what you have learned." The little key ring with all the buttons was out in a flash, as well as a broad smile across Sol Dorsey's mug.

The top was down in quick time, the sunshine offering a bright spring day, and he pulled the boat out onto the street. *This is why I have this car,* he was thinking to himself, not talking out loud for a change. *Look at me, escorting a high-level police agent from a foreign country that is with me because she wants to be.* He could have lit the city with his smile and bright green eyes if it had been a dark day.

"I've learned that it's very nice being with a Ukrainian government agent," and the conversation began, continued, and ended a few hours later at the motel by the waterfront. "Yes, ma'am, I've learned a lot today."

He wanted to take her home, but that might be a big problem. He was mumbling and it was probably a good thing she couldn't hear him. "How can I bring this beautiful woman to that garbage pit I live in? Maybe it's time to do what Serious has suggested several times. Hire some down and outer to clean the place once a week or so." He was through talking to himself, had plans to walk the lady to her motel room door, and go home and cry in his beer when all plans ended.

"We can continue going over the case inside, Sol. And maybe have some dinner a little later. I'm still all messed up on time. Kiev is on the other side of the world from here, so I don't know when to eat or when to go to bed. We'll work on that, eh?"

Oh yes we will, Dorsey said to himself, and to her said, "Yes Ma'am, anything you say Ma'am." There were broad smiles from two excellent investigators off on a spree.

Inside the motel room, the conversation started out in a less than business-like manner. "Captain Elmo said that we would be able to do most of our work from your apartment. Is that right?"

"Probably not. There probably would not be enough room, and it's not a nice place to be. I'll bring my files and computer here. This is very comfortable." He cringed when she brought up going to his apartment, and at the same time vowed to ram a fist down Serious Elmo's throat.

"My files are pretty compact, and I have most of the background stuff on my lap top, so we can set up shop right here. I have all the stuff that lets me do background work. They have names for that stuff, but I don't know what they are or what they mean." *What the hell does app mean, anyway?* He gave her a big smile. "This will be fine." He slipped an arm around Felicia, and she melded right into

93

him. "Yes, this will be fine," he said again.

"Don't stop doing that, Sol." She was pressed up tight against him, their lips bare inches from touching, each able to feel every inch of the other. "We're partners on an international crime investigation, but I think we're also going to be good friends. Let's start with the investigation part and work toward the relationship part," she said, giving the big guy a hug and slipping away from him.

He knew she was right, hated the thought that she was right, but did as instructed, went back to his apartment and gathered up files, laptop and printer, and came back, breaking every speed law on the books. They made themselves comfortable at the little motel room desk.

"You certainly are thorough, Sol. I knew about lots of what we discussed today, but not to the depth that you have. Tim Socrates is the money man, he launders for organizations all over the world, Near East, Israeli, Asian, South American, and obviously Ukrainian. Dolinski, Omar Sheik, and Jacoby cannot operate as freely as they do without his ability to keep the money line clean."

"Are you putting Dolinski and Jacoby in the same organization?" Dorsey asked, moving some files around. "For some reason, I'm putting Dolinski and FCU together working to take out Jacoby. Which way do you see it?"

"What I see is at least one, maybe two groups working to take out Jacoby and Omar Sheik. What I meant was, without the benefit of Socrates and his ability to launder money, none of the groups would be able to exist." She sat back in her chair, frowning slightly. "There are some people in Europe and the Near East that are as good, maybe even better than Socrates, but he's right here where they need him. He's a big pivot point in many syndicates and gangs."

Dorsey wanted the meeting to go in another direction, one much more personal between them, but that investigator's mind of his followed along. "It's strange to me that Socrates would be laundering money for opposing organizations. I'm thinking that Dolinski is working to take over the Sheik Jacoby operation."

"Yes, I'm pretty sure that is what's happening," she said. "Socrates works as a middle man for many different criminal organizations, some involved in narcotics, some in guns, some in financial crimes.

"There's another person involved that I was hoping you had a handle on. Omar Sheik and Illiana Jacoby have someone higher up that they deal with, and I believe that is the person Dolinski is trying to find as well. Have you heard another name, Sol?"

"I've had that in the back of my mind right from the start. When I found out about Omar Sheik, I figured he was the one, but he and Jacoby have been tight for years. Would Socrates have enough push to be the big guy?" Dorsey got very contemplative, and as usual, reverted to thinking out loud.

"You said that this Omar Sheik guy teams up with Illiana Jacoby, and moves large amounts of weaponry and narcotics all around the world, including our port here. Are you suggesting that they are doing this for someone higher up the ladder? The Israeli mafia, the Ukrainian cartels, the American mobsters all come to mind, but the only name I've heard that might fit the description is Tim Socrates, the money man."

"I'll put all my notes together, and then we can get a lot

deeper into this," she said. "Let's make our two sets of files into one, and we'll have a better picture. These operations bring in hundreds of millions of dollars a year, and the people we're dealing with kill anytime they are threatened. We need all our notes in the same place."

"I agree," he said. "I think I left one file on the kitchen table. Let me run back and get that. Anything I can get you while I'm out?"

"In the Ukraine, late in the day, you know, before cocktail hour, I like a cold beer once in a while. Think you could find something like that?"

"You are my kind of woman," he said, gave her a quick kiss, stole a little pinch on her butt, and headed out the door. Felicia Bogdanovich sat back down at the little desk.

~ ~ ~

I've worked with men like Sol Dorsey before, and I always learn something from them. I've never been close to an American, though. As she thought about that, she was thumbing through her past. There were, of course, Ukrainian men, Russian men, but it was always the foreign, the different, and probably a taste of intrigue that led her to arrangements with men outside the USSR realm of influence. As she remembered specifics, she stopped the process quickly.

"I think the men from France are the most difficult. They feel they have a reputation to uphold, and lucky for them no one has ever done a real survey on the issue. Top of the list right now, Italians followed very closely by Japanese. Oh, my," and while she was aware that she was completely alone, she found she was mumbling to herself, and also just embarrassed herself. "It was Takeo Oka. Oh,

96

my," she said again and sat down at the desk immediately. "Actually, it may be Japanese, essentially Takeo Ota, who are first, and the Italians, led by that northern border area god, Umberto Fazio, second." Her cheeks were brilliant red, her hands were shaking, and she had very evil, but wonderful thoughts swirling in her head about what might happen with one Simon Sol Dorsey.

She had her notebook out, shuffled some papers around, and pulled one sheet out, and put it next to the telephone. "No, I better not use this phone," and she got her cell phone out of her purse, punched some numbers in, and began a long conversation with her immediate supervisor, the head man at Ukrainian Police Headquarters.

"Thank you, Commissioner Babyak. Yes, I'll keep you fully informed on how this moves. Mr. Dorsey has some vital information, and I'll pass that to you as soon as I have it. I think we'll work well together, and no, sir, I won't be bringing him home with me." She giggled like a little girl saying that, and continued, "It seems as though our friend Dolinski may be here in America. It looks like he may be setting up a network, and possibly using other Ukrainians to work for or with him."

She listened for a minute then brought up the possibility of the Dziuba Family Gang getting into international narcotics and weapons. "I heard rumors when I was in Israel, Babyak, and I'd like you to do some background on this for me." She said goodbye, and went back to her notes.

"This is very much like the investigation that led me to the assistant commissioner's position, and may pump me up again when it's over. Babyak and I brought down some

Russians that were bent on spreading narcotics and weapons all over the Ukraine, but also into some of the old Soviet republics. Chechnya came about because of that gang. What a damn mess that is turning out to be. It's a Russian mess, though, and that's fine with me.

"Babyak and I were a good team then, but he's become just a fat old man sitting in a swivel chair and depending on all of us to do the dirty work." She put her thoughts aside as she heard Dorsey come up to the motel door.

~ ~ ~

She looked deep into Dorsey's bright green eyes, took his hand in hers, and let it go where it wanted. For Sol Dorsey, the hands went to some warm and wonderful places. "We've picked up a lot from each other," she said. Her smile warmed the room, and her words warmed the big investigator when she said, "Let's sleep on this for a few hours, and then get back to it." He hadn't even had time to close the door and didn't give a damn either.

"Yes, Ma'am, right away Ma'am. This is the proper way to conduct an investigation," and he helped her out of her things, she helping him out of his. "It is important to keep up proper international relations." As the sun was setting, Dorsey said, "What a long and wonderful day this has been. And it is going to continue," he smiled. It was several hours later that two exhausted investigators finally fell into a deep sleep, her legs and arms wrapped tightly around him and his.

~ ~ ~

"Come on, Dorsey, pick up the damn phone." Captain Elmo was more than impatient at the moment. "Son of a bitch, pick up," and he did.

"Dorsey," he bawled, after spending a minute trying to find his pants. He was standing in the middle of the motel room, stark ass naked, still with a little boy's grin on his mug.

"Dorsey, this is Elmo. We have another body, and I guess I can quit harassing Hank Jacoby. He washed ashore sometime this morning. Where are you?"

"None of your damn business, Serious. So, the war has started, eh?"

"Looks like it. Can you find the Bogdanovich woman and come down to the station? You two are the leads on this right now. Mavis Brownell is working to butt in, and you will have to fend her off."

"Be there shortly," he said, and slipped back into the warm world of Felicia Bogdanovich.

"Who was that?"

"Captain Elmo. Hank Jacoby's been killed and he wants to see us. Mavis Brownell is the name we've missed, I do believe.

"Once more, pretty lady, and then we have to go to work."

"Yes, sir, boss."

~ ~ ~

"It wasn't me, Sheik. The cops say he was shot once in the back of the head, taken out in the bay and dumped. I had the same plan, but it wasn't me. He left to see Socrates, set up the money for this next shipment, and move enough into our own accounts to keep things moving.

"Is Socrates screwing us, Sheik? Is that bitch Brownell getting more involved than she should? What's going on?" The world was collapsing on Illiana Jacoby. Melissa was dead, Hank dead, her moneyman appeared to be involved, and now, Omar Sheik still questionable in her mind. "I need some answers, Sheik."

"Socrates may have jumped in with Dolinski, but I have access to all our money. Socrates lost his bank position and I stepped in before he was able to set up new accounts. Don't worry, your assets are safe, Illiana. I have put out the word to take the fool out. We'll have to find another banker, but we won't have to deal with that little butterfly anymore. He won't be mincing through our lives much longer."

"I never did really trust the little queer," she said. "Who can we trust with these shipments that are already on their way?"

"I'm working with an Israeli banker, Illiana. He's damn good. Much better than Socrates. I'll be coming into the city tomorrow to put the finishing touches to the deal. I think it would be a good idea for you to be with me. It's just us again, Illiana, and let's keep it that way." It was Omar Sheik's idea for Illiana to get to the U.S., but when she married Hank and brought him into their business, it put a big wrench in their relationship. He had no romantic ideas about Illiana, but he also didn't want her to come up with another husband that he would be forced to deal with.

His conversation with The Man did not go well, he knew that Melissa died because the last shipment had been fouled up by Hank, and he was worried that Andrzej might be looking for other major dealers to work with. Dolinski maybe? Brownell? An unknown? Omar Sheik had to make sure that he didn't screw up his relationship with Illiana. She ran the outside business, made the right contacts, picked up the goods, had delivery people and big guns at the ready all the time. He ran the inside, and he needed her.

Illiana had the west coast filled with men and women that answered to her, that distributed the narcotics she provided, that found buyers for the guns, and that would come to her bidding, and rescue, at a moment's notice.

He gave her the time and place to meet, they said goodbye, and Illiana gently put the phone back on its cradle, took a step back from the table, and for the first time in twenty years, let her emotions run wild. Screaming, beating of breasts, tearing of hair, and stomping of feet finally took its toll and she collapsed on the bed, crying herself to sleep.

It was hours later that she stumbled into the kitchen, made some strong tea, and tried to put her mind back to the job. "You're right, Sheik, it's just us again." She spent the next several hours on her throwaway cell phone planning how to get the next load picked up, who it had to be delivered to, and how many guns she might need to protect the entire operation. "No more screwed up pickups with borrowed trucks that don't work. No more dealing with a screwed up husband that never did work right." She made one more phone call and half an hour later a delightful young Chinese boy brought her dinner.

~ ~ ~

"What exactly does that mean, 'you can't get at the funds right now'? I have made lots of money available to you so I can make a move on Omar Sheik and Illiana Jacoby, and you tell me I can't get at it?" Dolinski pulled a little automatic from his jacket pocket and shoved it up Socrates' nose. "You are a dead man, Socrates."

"No. No, Mr. Dolinski, it just means there will be a slight delay. It's not easy keeping these large amounts of money from being traced. I can't just cough up a million bucks. The money is there, all of it, just give me a day or two to make sure no government agencies know where it is or who gets it."

"Tomorrow, little man. Tomorrow morning or you die." Just being in the same room created the effect of Dolinski domination, the man was so large, and his temper equaled his size. "Jacoby is crab food, Socrates. Have my money or you will join him. I will be here tomorrow morning," and he walked out the door, over to the elevator, and left the building.

Socrates slumped into a large chair, found his phone and made one quick call. "Mavis, please come over as soon as you can. Something has gone horribly wrong and I can't fix it."

~ ~ ~

"Do you always park like this?"

"Why should people that drive little toys have special places set aside for them?" That was the Simon Sol Dorsey philosophy and attitude on more than just parking spaces. If anyone should get special treatment, he believed, it should be him. "I don't believe in parking meters, either." And they went into the police station, upstairs to Elmo's office, and both felt warm and sated, thank you.

"Where have you two been?"

"None of your damn business. What's with Jacoby?" He held a chair for Felicia, found one for himself, and sat down to face Serious Elmo with a broad smile that explained everything to the older cop. Elmo had a cup of coffee half way to his mouth, and gave Dorsey a bit of a smile back. Dorsey couldn't scowl back, no matter how hard he tried.

"You are right about a war. Jacoby was shot one time in the back of the head with a small caliber pistol, probably a .32. A couple of fishermen found him floating in the bay. He was naked, Sol, but easily identified. One of the cops knew immediately who he was."

Felicia said, "That would be the way Dolinski would handle an execution, and we're pretty sure that he is moving in on the Jacoby/Omar Sheik organization." She wanted to say more, Serious and Dorsey were thinking, but stopped there.

"What else are you thinking, Felicia?" Dorsey asked.

"Captain Elmo, can we talk safely in here? No bugs or recordings?" That would be the way in Kiev, she knew, and wasn't going to be comfortable giving away state secrets in Elmo's office.

"I could eat a ton of crab enchiladas," Dorsey said. "Let's go to Maglio's. I don't think we ate last night." He knew she had something to say and wouldn't say it unless she felt safe. Even though she was a Ukrainian police commissioner she didn't feel safe in Elmo's office. Dorsey had to laugh, as he thought, *Cops never trust other cops, all around the world.*

~ ~ ~

They had been more than two hours at Maglio's, and Dorsey and Elmo opened up with everything they knew. Felicia asked important questions, and it narrowed the playing field down quickly. "I'm sure that Dolinski gets his money from the FCU, Sol. The only way a group like FCU could operate would be with large amounts of cash. Those coming to this country from Ukraine don't have large amounts of money. They are fleeing, and they are broke."

Dorsey sat back a little as she continued. "But, you know, they do have their old contacts, and it wouldn't be hard to use those from this end.

"Drugs and guns bring in lots of cash. Illiana Jacoby and Omar Sheik have been running their operation for years without giving back, so to speak. The FCU knows about that, and brings Dolinski in to take over." Felicia Bogdanovich was a very good investigator, but Dorsey had more questions.

"OK, I'm with you to that point, but there are missing parts. Where does Mavis Brownell fit, where does Socrates come in? Sure, he launders their money, but he appears to be in a stronger position than that. I think that either Brownell works for Socrates or the other way around."

Captain of Detectives Serious Elmo hadn't said a word for the entire time. "You two are pretty damn good at what you do. If we were in a position to move on someone right now, who would that be?"

Dorsey immediately said, "FCU then Dolinski."

Felicia piped up with, "I think Dolinski and have him implicate FCU."

"Interesting," Elmo said. "I would have thought Jacoby or Sheik. Well, there we are, many wonderful suspects, several murders, narcotics flowing like the Volga, and knee deep in AK 47s."

Dorsey said, "Don't you just love it?"

The conversation lasted for several hours, and they continued to spar about Brownell and Socrates. "If there's a third, they are damn well hidden. No other names have come up. Let's let this go 'till tomorrow," Elmo said, which should have ended the session, but didn't. "Listen, Felicia,

Sol's apartment is just up the street a bit from here. Want to see it?"

Dorsey's face turned black, eyes glowered, mouth set for a growl to be heard blocks away. "I'd like that, but Sol says he doesn't want me to see it. He thinks I wouldn't like it. I bet he's wrong."

"He's not wrong, lady. You would gag."

"All right, that's enough nonsense. My apartment is off limits to everyone except me, and that's final. No more crap, Serious. Let's get back to the problem at hand. Damn." The scowl would be in place for many more minutes, and Serious knew better than to push any further. Felicia did not understand, but did recognize how serious Dorsey was about the situation.

"That was very good, Sol. Thank you," she said, changing the direction of the conversation. "I think Mavis Brownell is probably more like a director than the big boss. I think you were right, that Socrates is the man. He has access to everyone's money, and gets paid very well to boot."

"Let's leave it at that," Elmo said. "We've got a good handle on this case right now, and you two still have a lot more work to do. International drug cartels are really none of my business. I'm a homicide man, so I'm investigating Melissa's murder, and you guys are working for an International agency.

"Hopefully, we can do all this without being overwhelmed by DEA or the firearms and tobacco cowboys."

They got up from the table, Dorsey and Elmo shaking hands, and Elmo sneaking out before Dorsey could stop him. Maglio was on his way to the table with the bill, a big smile spread across his face. "For you," is all he said, handing it to Dorsey.

Felicia saved those in the deli from hearing howls of pain

when she asked, "How about a little tour around the city? I've never been here before, actually never even been in America before. Maybe you could show me Texas?"

Dorsey almost spit his ale clear across the restaurant on that one. "I have something almost as interesting and fun in mind." Her smile gave him the head's up he needed, and the meeting came to a halt. It was almost three in the afternoon, and Maglio's bill was a big one.

"Have you got some clothes you don't mind getting dirty? I have found a way into Tim Socrates' apartment, but we may have to do some roof walking. OK with you?" They had spent several hours going over the investigation at Maglio's, it was getting late on an overcast spring day, and Sol Dorsey needed some action. A home invasion would do fine. "I love figuring these things out, but I hate sitting around."

"Yes, of course. Swing by the motel, I'll change, and we can go. Socrates is one of the answers that we need. When you brought up the name Mavis Brownell, it didn't register, but when you added the Dziuba, everything clicked into place. The Dziuba family has had underworld businesses for generations. Strange that she would be a prosecutor in the district attorney's office.

"I talked with the Ukrainian Police Commissioner about the Dziuba family, and he's putting together a file for us. It will have many names that we haven't run into, at least not yet."

She caught herself, almost in mid-sentence. "Sure. What a nice way to keep tabs on everything that could destroy the organization. Come on Sol, what better way to know your enemy than to work for him." She laughed gently at that, and Dorsey got a snort or two out as well, and then got serious.

"According to a life-long friend of Mavis's, Mr. Brownell died of a tragic accident and Mavis didn't take her maiden name back. Maybe too many international investigators would have been interested." He was driving slower than what would be the Sol Dorsey standard, letting it get later and darker. Felicia got her tour of the city, but not quite the way she expected.

"Mr. Jacoby, then Dolinski have both been visitors at Socrates', and within hours of each other. Brownell claims not to have any information on the jerk, but those that she might be working with or for have intimate relationships. This guy has a lot of answers for us." When he didn't get any reaction to his comment, he looked over at Felicia. "Are you with me?"

"I'm sorry, Sol. I'm trying to do what you're doing, and not getting anywhere. The Dziuba family is on every watch list there is in the Ukraine, as is Sheik Omar's name. To find them here, not back home, has me confused. My people sent me here to follow up on a series of crimes that related back to our narcotics operatives, in particular Sheik Omar, Illiana Jacoby, and Charles Dolinski. Now, because of you, I'm about to help break up a major international war amongst those gangs.

"I've been lucky in my career, Sol. Very lucky to have worked for some of the finest investigators in the Soviet Union, and now, it seems my luck is holding, being able to work with you and Captain Elmo.

"I just thought of something. In Kiev we have a large set of files on Omar Sheik, but just a sentence or two on Illiana Jacoby. I need to find out what her name was before she married the cop. Would Captain Elmo have that?"

"He would indeed. Wouldn't that be something if she traced back to one of the family names we already know about? Good thinking, old girl. I like your style." If he could have managed to keep the Caddy on the road, he would have reached over and pinched the lovely lady's cute little bottom right then and there.

They arrived at the Socrates' apartment and parked two blocks away, walked hand in hand back toward the building. Along the coast of California, springtime evenings are often accompanied by layers of fog, sometimes cold and wet, filled with anger and danger, sometimes light, barely moist. This night, it is the latter of the two that the investigators are walking through. There was a storm on its way, but not tonight.

"He lives on the top floor of the building on the right, but the front door is locked and a buzzer system is used to keep people like me out," he said as they turned the corner.

"What kind of license plate is that, Sol?" Felicia asked as they approached.

"That, dear lady, is an official car belonging to the District Attorney's office. What do you know? This might be our lucky night. Wouldn't that be just about perfect if we find that Mavis Brownell is visiting our gay little banker?" Unlike on his previous two visits to the area, there weren't any bodyguards lurking in the doorway. They quickened their pace and entered the building next door, took the stairs to the roof and slipped into the stair well of the Socrates' building.

"That was almost too easy, Sol," she whispered. "I hope this isn't a set up." They hadn't made a sound nor had they heard anything out of the ordinary. "Let's start getting really slow in our approach. If someone from the district attorney's office is around, maybe it isn't Brownell, maybe it's another investigator doing what we're doing.

Sol Dorsey was about to open the door onto the fifth floor when he heard voices in the hallway. "It's Socrates and Brownell," he whispered. He cracked the door and the two could see them. She appeared to be saying goodnight, and it also appeared as though she was angry.

"If you screw this over with Dolinski, he will kill us both, Tim. Make it right with him, I'll deal with Omar Sheik and Illiana Jacoby, and then we'll have to fight our way out from under Sol Dorsey's big damn investigation. I think I can make him look like a fool by way of the FCU. Don't screw this up, Tim," and she walked toward the elevator.

Socrates stood in the hallway, watching her leave. When the elevator door closed, Sol Dorsey leaped out of the stairwell door and grabbed the little man before he could get back in his apartment, Felicia Bogdanovich a half step behind. "Are you up for a little conversation, Mr. Socrates? I hope so, because this lovely lady and I have some questions for you." He pushed the man back into the apartment. "Strange, where are the big guns that usually hang around, Tim?"

"Who are you? What do you want? Get out. Get out before I call the police."

"We'll talk about the police in a few minutes, Socrates. Right now, let's talk about the assistant district attorney, shall we? Why was Mavis Brownell here? That's a good question to start with, don't you think, Felicia?" His big hand, fingers splayed open, reached out and took Tim

Socrates by the neck, lifted him about a foot off the floor, held him there for a minute or so, his legs, feet, arms, and hands flailing about, and dumped him on the sofa. His other hand, fingers splayed as well, reached out and slapped the little man across the side of his head knocking him to the floor.

"Well now, you do live a rich life for an unemployed bank employee. These furnishings must be worth hundreds of thousands of dollars, don't you think, Felicia? Persian carpets, lamps from the Tiffany line, original art, museum quality. My, my, Mr. unemployed banker, we have much to talk about."

Socrates was a thin man with a dark complexion, dark eyes, and dark hair. He had a hawk's nose, now bleeding, and a pointed little chin. Physically he would have been no match for almost any man in half way decent shape. "Your name is Socrates," Felicia said to him, "but you aren't Greek, are you? You're from the other side of the straits, you're Turkish.

"That's why Mavis Brownell and Dolinski are working with this piece of shit, Sol. He is the middle moneyman for most of the Ukraine, Turkish, Israeli narcotics operations in this sector of the world. It never entered my mind because of the name Socrates."

"Like I said, you are good lady."

In a three-piece suit, Mr. Timothy Socrates would even look like a banker. Few would associate him with international crime and conspiracies. At this moment, as he slid onto the floor, his eyes were open to saucer size, his nose was bleeding, and he was whimpering and crying, begging not to be hurt. It was a pitiful sight with Dorsey's huge frame menacing the little man and Felicia scorning him.

"We have a few questions that need to be answered, Mr. Socrates, and I believe that we have all night to get the answers."

"Don't hurt the little man, Sol." She was smiling when she said it, and Sol stood back, bowed slightly, picked Socrates up and gently placed him back on the sofa. "That's better. Now, why was Mavis Brownell here?"

It took about an hour to get all the information they needed from Socrates and they decided to stay until Dolinski showed up for his money. They bound and gagged Socrates and spent the next several hours taking his apartment apart.

"I thought we couldn't do this," Felicia said. "In Ukraine, sure, but in America? I thought we had to have a court order or something to make our search legal."

Dorsey just sniffled something, as he opened drawers in a file cabinet. "The cops have to have a search warrant from a court, but, my little shamrock, we're not cops. At least I'm not. Actually, you aren't either, so just keep looking." They worked for hours and had a fair sized mound of file folders and documents spread out on a large table.

"Most criminals don't keep extensive records like this, Sol. We have large amounts of money in bank accounts across the country. There is money in offshore accounts, in Swiss accounts, in safe deposit boxes, and in open accounts.

"This little fool is very thorough, and equally stupid for keeping records in his own home. Makes it a little easier, though. Isn't this the right time to bring Captain Elmo in on this? Before Dolinski gets here?"

"You're right, I'll call him. You are aware that he is going to be highly pissed about this. Of course, since I'm not a cop, all I've done is break and enter, not foul up police procedures. You wait," he smiled to her, "he'll accuse me of that right up front."

She returned his smile, kissed him in such a way that he was ready to put aside the investigation for a few hours, if she wanted to. And, he knew they couldn't do that.

"I'm only a man, Felicia."

"And, a damn good one. Our next adventure is going to be you giving me a tour of your apartment."

"Not going to happen," is all Dorsey said in reply. The comment about the apartment changed the atmosphere, Dorsey scowling, clouds as thick as library ivy settling into the apartment. "Let's not bring that up again."

Felicia, eyes downcast, seemed to understand that she may have overstepped, just a bit, and started working over the accounting as Dorsey finished the call to Elmo. "We may have our answers right here, Sol. Socrates may not be the big man, and I'm sure that Brownell isn't either. There is a third person, someone that is able to put tremendous pressure on everyone involved." She spread the pages of one of the accounting ledgers across the coffee table. "These are print outs from his computer.

"Each transaction has two debits attached. The smaller of the two is Socrates' commission, and the larger, much larger, is for the boss. And, there's no name attached to that account."

While they waited for Serious Elmo they went line by line over each of four ledgers, and found back up for each on the computer in Socrates' bedroom. "That name just doesn't show up anywhere, but that person is swimming in big bucks. I think this section is probably Dolinski, this is probably Brownell, and this account might be Omar Sheik. Sheik and Jacoby have the largest operation in the western U.S. That's probably why Dolinski and Brownell want in. Sol, these are huge amounts of money. And each of these accounts, besides paying small tribute to Socrates, are also paying vast amounts to that unknown person. He's the one that pulls the strings."

Dorsey was quick, Felicia was too, and they could not figure who that missing person is. "Dolinski will be here later this morning to get money for his next deal. Did you notice that a large amount of money has already been paid out to Sheik and Illiana? They have a deal in the works, too."

"Either that or they are ending their relationship with Socrates." Felicia smiled when she said that, and Dorsey was smiling as well. "If Melissa and Hank are killed because of a bad deal, does it lead directly back to Socrates?" The buzzer from downstairs ended their conversation.

~ ~ ~

"I hope you didn't screw up this case, Sol. Did you read him his rights?" As soon as the words were spoken, Dorsey and Felicia traded looks and smiles, Elmo caught them, and was scowling almost as hard as Dorsey was smiling. "All right, can it. Did you?"

"I'm not a cop, Serious. He has no rights when he is dealing with me. And Felicia is a visitor to this country, not a cop. If you think he has some kind of rights, you go ahead and tell him," and the smirk continued to be splashed all over his big mug. "Hell, man, all we did was ask a couple of questions. Necks bruise real easy, he isn't hurt. Are you hurt, Tim? Doesn't look hurt, and I think he'd tell you."

"Alright, can the BS, Sol. What time should we expect Dolinski?"

"Probably not too long after the banks open. He'll give old Tim boy here time to get the money and get back to the condo. I'm sure he'll have a couple of guns with him, they have sure been keeping track of me the last week or so."

Serious Elmo made some quick phone calls, which would bring several cops, out of uniform to the area. "For Pete's sake, don't get Orel Simpson in on this. Geez, we'll never get a bust. Can you put a tail on Mavis Brownell? And, we need to keep track of Illiana Jacoby too."

"Anything else the city's cop shop can do for you, Dorsey?"

"Sometimes, Serious, you are just too serious." That eased the tension a bit and Felicia helped out the cause by coming up with a pot of hot coffee. "Socrates and Brownell seem to have been working to take out Omar Sheik and Illiana Jacoby when Dolinski started making his move. It's hard to say which one came up with the idea, but it appears they are working with Dolinski just long enough to dump Sheik and Jacoby, and then they'll take him out.

"I haven't got the FCU connection figured out yet, but Brownell knows what that is. If Socrates knows, he ain't talkin', Captain, Sir." He sat down with his cup of coffee. "Actually, Brownell even mentioned FCU when she left here earlier. When we leave, Felicia, let's pay Lori Baranek a visit. Too many of our questions are aimed right at her and that organization.

"Did you ask your boss in Kiev about them?"

"I did, and he will send that in the file also. It's strange that the name doesn't ring a bell on my desk. It must be an American front and go by another name on the international scene."

"I'm amazed, Serious, that DEA hasn't shoved big noses into this. Have you had any kind of whisper from those jerks? They will foul it up if they show up."

"Not a squeak, Sol. You're right though, they must know something about a conspiracy this big. Damn, how many countries have we got involved so far?"

The three drank a full pot of coffee, talked about what each was thinking, and the morning wore on toward bank opening time. "With these ledgers and what's in that computer, this little puke will be in prison for the rest of his life. I just hope we can tie these numbers to names like Brownell, Dolinski, Sheik, Jacoby, and FCU. I'm amazed, really, to find this kind of crap. Good work, you two." Serious Elmo was living his nickname, and was more than aware that, while they may have some answers, the questions were still open.

"We should have visitors at any minute, now. Are your people in place on the street?"

"All accounted for. They'll give us a heads up when the Dolinski crowd shows up."

"The last time I saw him, he had two guns with him. One stayed downstairs near the front door of the complex and the other came in with him. Interestingly, when Brownell was here last night, she was alone. Is it too late to get a man or two in the stairwell?"

"They are already there, Sol. Take it easy, it's my name that's Serious." Felicia's tinkle of laughter brought a scowl to Dorsey's face, and then, he too, had to chuckle.

"He's here, Captain." That's all the guy on the radio said, and in less than thirty seconds the buzzer sounded. Elmo rang back to unlock the door, and the three of them got into position to take out Dolinski when he walked in.

"My boys will neutralize the hired gun, and we'll have two coming in that door shortly. Put Socrates on the couch, all trussed up nice, so Dolinski will see him right away. All right, now. Nobody gets shot except the bad guys." They could hear the elevator doors open, and had big guns out and cocked when the door opened.

~ ~ ~

"I don't think I've ever seen anybody that big, Dorsey. You could have given me a heads up, you know." Serious Elmo had just put cuffs on Dolinski, was nursing a badly bruised jaw and black eye, and Dorsey was sitting on the protection guy, already cuffed.

"You looked good, Serious. He knocked that gun of yours thirty feet and punched you pretty hard. Good thing Felicia was there to calm things down. Your feet were actually off the ground when he nailed your ass." Dorsey was laughing hard, but also knew he would take a ribbing soon as well.

Felicia Bogdanovich sealed her partnership with Dorsey when she swung a small sap across the back of Dolinski's head, just above his neck, spewing blood over everyone and put the giant to sleep. "Yeah, sweetheart, you can work with me anytime. That was nicely done." She gave him one of those smiles that said he could collect his thank you later, when no one else was around.

"Well, Mr. Charles Dolinski, we need to have a little chat. Do you remember me? I can see it in your eyes that you do. I'm Felicia Bogdanovich, Ukrainian State Police Commissioner. Ah, yes, now you remember. After the Americans get through with you, I'll see you back in Kiev. I think you know what that will mean, eh?"

The big man had been interrogated before, probably many times, and gave Felicia no response at all. They picked him off the floor and slammed him onto the couch where Socrates was sprawled, and the two jostled around to get separated. Before Dolinski could get fully connected, Dorsey threw a set of leg cuffs on the big man. Even with hands cuffed behind his back, he was a threat simply because of his size.

Serious Elmo took command of the situation, invited two officers from downstairs to bring the other hired gun up, and do all the legal things that bug Dorsey. "OK, you've given him his right's speech, let's get on with this." He scowled at the big man, gave the impression that he was going to punch his lights out. "Who set you up on this little caper to take out Sheik and Jacoby, Dolinski? Who opened the door for you?" There was, of course, no response.

"Dorsey, once in a while, you need just a touch of concern when you question these fools." Serious took out a note pad from an inside jacket pocket, used a touch of the theater as he got his pen out, and prepared to question the ape. "Now, Mr. Dolinski, in order for me to keep this gentleman next to me from ripping your head off, I need a couple of answers." Elmo's right fist came out of nowhere, blasting Dolinski's nose all over his face.

"Dorsey, I've told you before, I don't believe in this type of interrogation," and Serious Elmo slammed the big man one more time. "Dorsey, you must not hit this man again, do you hear me? You must not use violence on criminals during questioning." Dorsey was roaring his approval and Felicia blasted Dolinski across the back of his head again with her little sap. The three cops in the room who work for Serious Elmo, were doing what they could to not see, hear, or touch anything.

"Now, sir," Elmo said, in all seriousness, "we need some answers. You are here to collect some laundered money from our little banker here, and we need to know where that money came from. Care to enlighten us?"

Sometimes, big men can't take being blasted the way Elmo and Bogdanovich blasted Dolinski. For most big men, they have been in command all their lives, and for someone smaller to knock them around, is a tremendous loss of face. For anyone, an open handed slap is also a personal affront. Elmo reached out and slapped Dolinski with his open palm, measuring well more than the traditionally accepted eight inches, and rocked him back a foot or more.

"Now, sir, about that question." The drug dealer was bleeding from his nose and the back of his head, one eye was swelling shut, and the sting from that slap had him infuriated, incensed to the point of rage. "Sir? I won't wait much longer."

The radio crackled. "You've got company coming, Captain. I don't recognize the woman, but she is heading upstairs now. We had the door propped open, so she didn't use the buzzer. The elevator is coming to the fifth floor now."

Dorsey, Elmo, and Felicia all had guns in hand when they heard a key in the lock and the front door of the condo was opened. Elmo grabbed the woman and was about to smack her when Dorsey bellowed to stop. "Well, I guess we have our answer about where you got your marching orders, eh Mr. Dolinski? Welcome to interrogation room number one, Lori. Captain Elmo, sir, this is Lori Baranek from the FCU, one of the better-funded organizations working for the welfare of children through the distribution of narcotics and weapons.

"Sit your cute ass down, Lori, and give us a nice explanation so your face doesn't end up looking like Charles's." Dorsey thought for some time that Lori Baranek was somehow connected, but it was still a surprise when she showed up. He motioned Felicia to join him away from the crowd.

"She showed up at the precise time Dolinski was to pick up the money. There's something very strange here. She introduced me to Dolinski, to help me in my investigation. I'm thinking out loud here, Felicia, but I'm wondering if Dolinski was supposed to take me out, and the two hired guns didn't do it. We need some background on the lady. Whoever she works for is the big man we've known about without having a name. Can your people in Kiev get something going? And I'll do the same thing here."

It was a quick conversation with Sol Dorsey doing just about all the talking, but Bogdanovich was in agreement. They rejoined the group in time to hear Lori Baranek demand to have her attorney present. "Guess it's a good thing I didn't pop her, eh, Captain, Sir?" He turned to face her. "You are going to need an army of attorneys, Lori. We have enough on Socrates, Dolinski, and you to put you all away for the rest of your lives. And that's just on our end. Wait till some of the other countries start checking in.

"Oh, damn, I've completely forgotten my manners. Lori Baranek, I want you to meet the Assistant Police Commissioner from the Ukraine. Yes, that's right, straight here from Kiev. Lori, say hello to Felicia Bogdanovich."

It was just a flash, and Baranek was taken aback. Dorsey stored that away, and knew that there was recognition. He didn't know if it went both ways.

~ ~ ~

"Illiana, meet me at Spiro's on the wharf. We'll have lunch and I'll bring you up to date on what is going on. Most interesting."

"Let's meet at Buchko's Grill instead. I'm more comfortable there."

"No, and when we meet, I'll tell you why. No. Meet me at Spiro's."

She had been waiting for some kind of message for a couple of days, and this was the one she wanted to hear. She tucked the Glock in her purse, checked her makeup and headed down to the docks. It was early in the tourist season, but when you lived near a seaport, and there was open air dining right alongside the same boats that brought your lunch or dinner, even the locals swarmed to the area.

Often, the restaurants and cafes would own their own boats, even full size fleets, which added to the gayety and flavor of the area. Along the north coast of California, halibut, snapper, cod, and crab were the highlights, and always, clams and mussels. The weather was fair, lots of sun, little wind, and there were throngs of people out and about.

"Sheik, I was starting to worry. Why didn't you want to meet at Buchko's? I like that food."

"That place is still owned by the Dziuba family, Illiana. I don't trust any of them."

Illiana frowned, but got back on the main subject right away. "We have some merchandise due in tomorrow, so is everything set?"

"Ah, my little songbird, we are set. We have eliminated anything that could get in the way. Sit, order, and we'll talk." Omar Sheik bin Ali was full of himself today, and even found he was capable of a generous smile as he helped Illiana at the table. She ordered a small shrimp salad and cup of tea, he ordered a crab Louie and tea, and began to talk immediately.

"I have said many times that I didn't trust Socrates, and now I know why. He has been working with Charles Dolinski, that's the name of the former cop from Kiev I told you about. I managed to get all of our money out of the various accounts Socrates used, and it's safe in the Bahamas, right now. I am looking for another moneyman, because we don't have the time or the resources to do it all.

"Socrates and Dolinski are in custody right now on many charges, including federal money laundering. We won't see them for years. I understand the Ukrainian government has a hold on Dolinski as well."

"You've been busy, Sheik. Who killed Hank?"

"It was Dolinski. It would be the way, thinking the man would be more in charge than the woman. You are unique, Illiana. There's something else, and it is worrisome. A private detective, Sol Dorsey, is working with Felicia Bogdanovich of the Ukraine state police, and they are the ones that had Dolinski and Socrates jailed. This could get messy for us."

Illiana sat bolt upright in her chair. "Dorsey was the investigator that Lori Baranek hired to find Melissa. The FCU is where I went for help when Melissa disappeared." She had a frightened look and Sheik was also caught off guard.

"That's awkward, Illiana. Awkward. There have been reports that seem to indicate that the FCU is somehow involved in the Dolinski move to take us out. How much does this Baranek woman know about us?"

"I've never discussed anything with her, but she is aware that Hank had been a cop and had been fired for stealing guns and dope. What is the status of our next load? How is all this going to affect our moves, Sheik? Damn." She muttered something in her native language, and Omar Sheik had to chuckle a bit.

"Not to worry, little one. The weapons are coming in on a special cargo ship from Nagasaki. They originated in China, of course, but bringing them in through Japan lowers all the flags as far as customs is concerned. Opium and cocaine will come as usual, through the port on a freighter that also carries passengers."

"You said something about the Dziuba family earlier, Sheik. What would they have to do with us?"

"Sometimes, my dear, you don't always pick up on things. Mavis Brownell is a Dziuba, and she too is working with Socrates. This is turning out to be one big octopus with many more than eight legs, and all of them are reaching out to strangle us and our operation. Illiana, my little shark, quit being a tough guy and start thinking, like you have always done."

They discussed how best to pick up all the cargo, get it

distributed to the right sources, and collect the necessary money, finished their lunch, and parted. Neither one noticed the black SUV that had been parked near the restaurant.

"Did you get that, Francisco?"

"Every word, Chago. Every word," and he turned off the tape recorder, folded the little antennae, and tucked the works into his brief case. "I'll meet you on the boat in half an hour. You were right, and I didn't believe you."

"Dorsey is still in this, Francisco, so we have to be very careful. My friends in Tijuana want this operation for themselves, and we are fighting people from all over the world. Dorsey can still fuck this up for us."

For the hundreds of locals and tourists that flocked about the fish markets, restaurants and dock areas, it was just a lovely spring day, oblivious to the fact that major international intrigue was taking place right in front of them. As philosophers like to point out, things weren't always as they seem.

11

"How long can we keep Baranek under cover? That was pretty quick thinking to not book her or hand her over to the feds like you did Socrates and Dolinski. We've lost them, but we still have Baranek and the FCU."

The feds showed up, but it wasn't the DEA or ATF. The FBI brought their money people in and took Socrates and Dolinski because of the purported money laundering. No questions dealing with narcotics, murder, gunrunning were even broached. "I don't think DEA is even aware that this international war is about to explode on my streets," Captain Elmo muttered.

"If DEA shows up," Dorsey said, "they will screw up the investigation, somehow. You can bet on it." Dorsey looked over at Felicia. "Have we heard anything back from Kiev?"

They had taken over a large banquet at Maglio's, not wanting to go into lots of details of the case inside Elmo's office. Maglio, scowling as always, but knowing that lots of food, beer, and booze would be paid for, let them have their way. Felicia's background, having to deal with KGB and other Soviet era privacy issues, came forward and she gave the place a good eyeball before settling in.

"You Americans," she said, getting settled into the banquet they chose, "are too willing to believe the good things of life. I would never discuss a case like this in a government office or in a business open to the public. You should worry more about your security than you do." She looked around the large open sitting area, up and down the long bar, and back at Dorsey and Serious Elmo. "How do you know that one or more of these people don't have a listening device or something? You are just too trusting."

"I suppose you are right, but I would rather trust and keep an eye out, than treat everything as conspiracy." Dorsey gave her one of his generous and seductive smiles, and closed the subject. "Now, back to Baranek and Brownell."

Felicia answered the original question about Kiev. "No, I haven't heard from Kiev yet, but I also put out questions on Mavis Brownell and her ties to the Dziuba family. I should have answers in the next couple of hours. If Brownell was working to rip off everyone by way of Socrates, and if Baranek was working to rip off everyone by way of Dolinski, I can't imagine that Omar Sheik and Jacoby don't know any of this?

"And, like you said, Sol, apparently there is a large shipment due in soon. It seems there are a lot of people gunning to be top dog here." Dorsey chuckled over her little Americanism.

"Somehow," Dorsey said, taking down half a pint of pale ale, "many of these people have stayed under the radar, in the Ukraine, here, and in other places around the world. We've only gotten a good handle on Sheik Omar and Illiana Jacoby in the last few days; Socrates has been an unknown as has Dolinski. Why doesn't anyone seem to know that Brownell hails from a well-known international drug smuggling gang?

"I hope I don't find out that DEA and other police agencies around the world have been holding out on letting local agencies in on their knowledge. This is getting damn serious, people are dying by the truck load, and we don't have background on anyone." Dorsey was in a full rant, and that type of behavior usually meant that someone was going to get hurt, or give up answers.

Sol Dorsey was one of those people that seemed to know things without benefit of being told as in his comment about federal agencies not sharing knowledge. He believed that too many people were involved in this caper and those people weren't known by those that investigated such behavior. "These people are up to their neck bones in international crime and if you do a criminal search, their names don't come up. You can't be this successful in a criminal activity without someone knowing it. Serious, I tell you, there is some agency withholding information, and that is a big problem."

Serious Elmo rocked back in his chair, rubbing his still sore jaw. The black eye was now a gaudy purple, and the swelling hadn't stopped its forward progress. There had been some strange looks thrown his way when they entered the little restaurant. Elmo was uncomfortable, and that made him just a little dangerous as well.

"Listen, Serious," Dorsey continued, "is it possible that the FCU or Baranek is the missing third party? Someone above Brownell and Socrates is pulling the strings. It's starting to fall into place, but I haven't heard any rumblings to that effect. We've already got several different countries involved here." He looked around the table, didn't get any response, looked around again, and angrily said, "Well, say something."

"You still piss me off, Dorsey. Damn that guy was big." His beer mug was empty and he was about to refill it from the pitcher on the table when his cell phone fired off. He barked, "Elmo," and even Dorsey was impressed not to mention the fright factor to some of the patrons around the joint. Here was a massive man sporting a magnificent black eye and ruptured nose growling at a tablemate then all but yelling into his cell phone.

Felicia didn't understand the two men at all, knew Dorsey was enjoying making fun of Elmo, knew Elmo was large and strong, and was frightened. She leaned in close to Dorsey. "I'm heading back to the motel to wait for my calls from Kiev. I'm also going to get some answers on the FCU and Lori Baranek, hopefully without opening doors for a Kiev investigation. Come back to the motel as soon as you can, because, big shot, I'm not through interrogating you." Dorsey tried to pinch her cute little butt, but she was quick and side stepped the attempt. She blew him a kiss, which he acknowledged with a little jerk of his head. Elmo caught the act and grimaced while Maglio just chuckled.

Dorsey was muttering to himself, poured another mug of ale, motioned Maglio to bring another pitcher, and gave sidelong glances at Elmo. "OK, now let's get this show on the road. Get off the damn phone." Elmo never even heard the running commentary.

Serious Elmo was still on the phone as Bogdanovich made her way out the door. He listened for a moment or two, said thank you, and had a pained look on his face as he put the phone away. "We are about to be visited by an upstanding representative of the Drug Enforcement

Administration. Try to behave yourself, Dorsey." He looked around, almost bewildered. "I'm glad Felicia left, I would rather she not be here right now. I haven't told the feds about her work on any of this. And, as paranoid as she is, she would surely believe the feds were following us."

"She headed back to the motel. She'll be busy working the computer and trying to get more names." He looked up in time to see someone come through the front door of Maglio's. "This has to be our fed. Jesus, nobody dresses like that around here. Ask him if he's undercover, Serious."

He got a blistering stare from Elmo and had to laugh just as the federal agent arrived at the table. The agent was wearing a crisp white shirt, red striped tie, and very black suit on a wonderful spring day. His shoes were shined to a military sheen, his hair cut in a military brush, and on top of all that, he wore black horn rimmed glasses. "Captain Elmo? Good, I'm special agent Gerald Fleming, DEA. We need to talk."

Elmo stood up, towering over the man, the agent was engrossed, staring at a massive black eye and very crooked nose. "How do you do. Sit down. This is Simon Sol Dorsey."

The agent sized up the two large men and said, "I think we need to be alone on this, Captain Elmo."

"If we're talking about Socrates and Dolinski, then Dorsey needs to be in on the conversation. It is his investigating that put them in custody. Please, sit down."

"I don't deal with PIs, Captain. Dorsey, please excuse us."

Before Elmo could say anything, Dorsey did. "No, I think I'll stay. You see, Jerry, It's OK to call you Jerry? I probably know more about this case than you do, maybe even more than Serious does. Yes, I think I'll stay. Join us in a pint of ale, Jerry?"

He was smiling when he said it, Serious Elmo had a nasty grin on his face, and the second large standoff of the day was underway. Serious was more than aware that when Dorsey started talking that way, a big fist could fly up from nowhere and take heads off. He was hoping the DEA agent had sense enough to back off.

"Captain, I had a talk with Lt. Simpson and he pretty much filled me in." Elmo almost choked on a swallow of good ale.

"Simpson hasn't spent one minute on this case, Agent Fleming, he is not a part of the investigation, and if you wish any cooperation from my department, you will limit yourself to discussing the case with either me or Dorsey." His one good eye had narrowed, his breath was long, slow, and very controlled, and Dorsey expected the Captain of Detectives to deck the DEA agent. These two men were long time partners.

"Jerry, old boy, relax, eh? This is a big bad case, we already have at least four dead people, we have drugs and guns and money laundering, and two suspects in custody. Relax, old boy." Dorsey had used this same approach on some of Elmo's officers, and he knew how much it grated. Get this agent really pissed and he might say something important. "Tell me about Illiana Jacoby or Omar Sheik, if you've gotten this far along in the investigation. If not, then tell me a little bit about Sean Sorenson. Oh, I see. You aren't familiar with that name either. Hmmm." Elmo was having a hard time holding himself in check and was about to blow beer all over the table.

"Captain, Elmo, Sir," Dorsey continued, "It appears our fine comrade in arms here doesn't have a clue as to what this case is all about. Maybe he should be attached to the squad that is led by Lt. Simpson." That was the clincher. Fleming was boiling, his fists doubled, his breathing angry as hell, and his eyes, if they could, would gladly murder Simon Sol Dorsey at this point.

"All right, have your fun. This is now a federal case. Your interference will not be tolerated, and I want all the files in my office in the federal building by five this afternoon. Good day." The agent stormed out the door and Dorsey signaled, once again for another pitcher of ale.

"Better bring a platter of enchiladas, Maglio. We'll be here for a while." He had the look of the hunter that bagged the biggest deer because he was that good. His smile had egotism and arrogance written across His face, and he was already marking the 'I win' box on the DEA page of his scorecard.

"Serious, how is it that a guy who arrived from Palermo less than six months ago makes better enchiladas than most of the Mexican joints in this town? Now, I have a real investigation to get on. Right away, before the feds take over."

Maglio heard him and yelled out, "I been here twenty years, bucko, and don't a forget that." He pouted for just a second, then continued. "Yeah, though, you right. Best crab enchiladas in town."

"All right, smart ass, can it," Elmo snarled at Dorsey. "That SOB Simpson put the clamps on this. 'By the Book' my ass." He pulled out his cell phone and called Orel Simpson.

"Here's what I want, Lt. There's a file on my desk labeled Socrates. I want you to take that to DEA agent Fleming at the federal building. Here's what I want from you, and don't screw this up. You're one of the finest investigators we have, and I want you to work hand in hand with Fleming. Got that? Good. Clear your moves with me, but work hard with Fleming. Thank you."

"And you call me a smart ass." Dorsey was all but cackling, his eyes sparkling as he stood and saluted Serious Elmo. "That was the finest bit of flim flam I've ever seen from you." Fishermen, dockworkers, the idle, those that spent hours a week in Maglio's were fully entertained by Dorsey's antics.

"Well, we won't be bothered by that ass now for some time. I think he and Fleming will get along just fine." They raised their pints, toasted each other, and attacked a platter of crab enchiladas, baited each other, bantered back and forth, and got all but roaring plastered over the next couple of hours. Maglio just shook his head and continued ringing up the register.

~ ~ ~

"Socrates and Dolinski are in federal custody, Illiana. I was able to move our money and other stuff out of the country, but Socrates worries me. One good knee in his groin and he will tell them everything he knows. Do you have any contacts at all in the local police? If we know where he's being held, we might be able to eliminate the problem."

They sat on benches along the waterfront and spoke Ukrainian. The radio was calling for a big storm to come in, but the air had spring written strong. There were fresh breezes off the bay, boats moved through gentle water, the aroma of the catch of the day was strong, lingered in a warm spring. They did not notice.

"No one in that department would even say hello to Hank, so I doubt that I could get any info from them. I read that Socrates was in federal custody, and that a hearing was scheduled for some time tomorrow. I can find out the exact time."

"A broad daylight hit? I don't know." Sheik knew that time was short, that Socrates had to be killed, "but really, Illiana, hit him at the courthouse?"

"Do you remember Ivan Brodsky? He's available. He'd kill his mother in front of God if the money was right."

"Dangerous man. See if you can set it up, and if he pulls it off and lives through it, we'll have to eliminate him as well. If Socrates is questioned hard, he'll blab everything, Illiana. Everything."

"I'll go home and close up the house and disappear. Hank was the go-to person with Socrates, so I'm not sure how much he might know about us. I have never brought up your name in anything, so it is probably I who is in the most jeopardy. Hank was so stupid, it's hard to say what he might have blabbed." She wasn't worried. The feds had been trying to track their operation for years. "Sheik, we need to work fast on this. I'll contact Brodsky as soon as I get home.

"You take care of yourself, Sheik. I've already made the arrangements for pickup of these next loads of merchandise, so we'll have large amounts of cash soon. I'll let you know where I'm located, probably tomorrow." They said goodbye, grim faced as ever, and left the waterfront.

Illiana found the news article, got the dates and times,

and called Ivan Brodsky to arrange for the hit. "No less than ten thousand, Illiana. Because of vests and guards, a hit like this is very difficult. Put ten thousand in my account, when I know it's there, I'll make my plans."

~ ~ ~

Santiago Navarro was on his fishing boat, an eighty-five foot trawler, when Francisco arrived. "There's a large shipment coming in, according to street talk. I have heard that tons of narcotics are on board. I'm sure it's the stuff that Omar Sheik is looking for. That Jacoby woman set up a pick up for it when the boat arrives. We could ace them, Chago. We could tell the DEA about this and get them busted and out of business."

"Too many people, Francisco. Too many. Dolinski is in jail, Socrates is in jail, we don't know who else is in their gang, and Omar Sheik has a load coming in. No, let's let it come in and then take it from them, just like we planned. We have the people, and we know something that they don't. We know Dorsey, and he's the most dangerous of all of them.

"No, we'll do it like we planned."

Francisco wasn't happy with the plan, but Navarro had the contacts in Tijuana, had the guns available, and Francisco wasn't going to give up his nice comfortable second position just to make a point. "OK, Chago, we'll do it like we planned. I have two trucks and five good men ready to move. The boat should be docking tomorrow."

"Good. We'll put the stuff on my trawler, and we can move up and down the coast for distribution. Everyone is used to seeing this boat, so we won't raise any red flags moving in and out of ports. The guys from TJ will also help, and this will give us even more opportunity down the line. My deal with the Tijuana Cartel is going to make both of us rich, Francisco. Very rich. Good work, good work."

There hadn't been a fish in the hold of Navarro's boat in at least ten years, but any drug sniffing dog that walked by the docks would have a fit, would foam at the mouth over what the ventilation shafts were putting out.

"After the hit, move that stuff down here as quickly as possible. What kind of trucks do you have, Frankie?"

"They're the ones I got last year. Flat beds with stake sides, and I repainted the names. Now, they are from the All Pacific Fish Company. They'll fit right in along the docks, and we can then take them back to the warehouse and repaint them again."

"Good work. Sheik and Jacoby will be out of business, Dolinski and Socrates are going to prison, and the only one that could screw this up is that ape Dorsey. Damn, I hate that man."

~ ~~

Fleming and Simpson fronted a squad of uniformed and well-armed federal officers at the city jail, ready to transport Timothy Socrates to the federal courthouse for his preliminary hearing. There were holds on Charles Dolinski from the Ukraine and from Israel, so federal charges would wait for action on the holds. "We can expect something, Lt. Simpson, but I don't know what. Let's make sure that Socrates is wearing a flak vest and is surrounded when we leave here and when we arrive at the courthouse."

"Yes, Sir, Agent Fleming. I ordered the vests last night, and your agents have all been briefed on our moves this morning. I put special leg irons on Socrates myself, and his hands will be cuffed behind his back."

"Good. Bring him out and put him in the van. We don't want to be late, now do we, Lt. Simpson."

"No, Sir, we don't. I've never been late for a shift or for a court hearing. Never." The smug little smile, a trademark of Simpson's was well received by the agent who was known to wear one of his own regularly. Dorsey would be bent over laughing had he been lucky enough to be there.

There was a decided change in the weather, a breeze kicked up, a slight chill was in the air, even clouds were seen instead of the normal fog. Socrates was doing the world famous leg iron two-step, head down, staring at the ground as they moved him from the jail to the federal prison van. The feds had banned the press from attending the move, but even so, Socrates was trying to keep his head down. As he made the move from the last step to the ground, his head exploded, and about one second later, the rifle blast was heard. Socrates would not be testifying, ever, and the chaos that took place in the next several minutes would have brought another smile to Sol Dorsey's mug.

Federal agents and city cops dashed about, took cover, pulled guns, pointed them in half a dozen different directions, and lots of commands were howled into the wind. It was a known fact that one shot was always the best. It was the second shot that most people needed to identify the direction from which it came. It would take forensics to replay the event, and probably determine that the shot came from about two blocks away, high in a flophouse hotel room. There of course would be no prints or indication that anyone had ever been there except for a lack of dust on one windowsill.

Brodsky dismantled his weapon later that morning and packaged it in four different boxes and called UPS for delivery to four different commercial mail drops he had in several area cities. He then had money transferred to an account in Europe, boarded a plane for Miami and transferred to a flight to Madrid. He used three different passports from three different countries on his jaunt. He was out of the country before Lt. Simpson had finished writing his preliminary report on Socrates' death.

"It's done, Sheik, and well done for sure. Shipment is on time and should be moving before the day is over. I have three trucks scheduled at the dock, and only one will actually have the stuff, the other two, decoys."

"That's a good move, Illiana. Socrates may have spilled a lot of stuff, and too many people may know too much now. Did you arrange for two men in each truck?"

"All three trucks are painted alike, there are three people in each, two well-armed and a driver. We won't lose this load, Sheik." She settled back in an easy chair, looking around her new apartment. "By the way, here's my new phone number. It's from one of those quickie cell companies, so it won't be easily traced." She gave the number, they said goodbye, and she took a long, deep breath.

"Thank God Hank isn't involved in this. He would have it so screwed up we would never find our stuff. Dirty bastard is responsible for Melissa being gone, too." Illiana Jacoby would not be able to tell you whether she mourned Melissa more than the money that Hank had lost on the screwed up shipment. "I won't mourn that son of a bitch, ever. Just you and me, Sheik, just you and me once again." She smiled for

137

the first time in many weeks.

Her apartment was closer to the waterfront than the old place, and more comfortable. There was security of a fashion at the front, but Illiana was not one to put much trust in those things. "My Glock will handle whatever security I need," she thought to herself when being shown the place. Illiana was not one to have many personal things, the move was just a couple of loads in her car, and she was settled in.

All she could do now was wait for the call to tell her the new shipment had arrived and was safely ready for distribution. "That will put some cash back in the pocket," she said to herself as she idly turned the television on. "Well, look at that. Cops all over the place and one dead bastard sprawled in his own blood. Well done, Ivan, well done."

Illiana never was involved in picking up or moving whatever material they were importing, whether it was guns, narcotics, or slaves, and that was starting to be a nice commodity as well. She and Sheik had discussed the matter often. "If one of us was to be picked up, it would be the end of our operations," she told him. "If we lose a soldier or a shipment, we're still in business. No," she emphasized, "that's why we hire these people."

Another call was being made by Sheik. "Hello, Andrzej. We'll have everything fixed for you by this time tomorrow. As you are probably aware, the organizations that were setting up to take Illiana and me out of business have been eliminated. I'm aware of just how angry you have been, but the problems have been taken care of. They no longer exist."

"If something goes wrong, ever again, Sheik, I will

personally rip you limb from limb. I'm not in the habit of watching several million dollars go away and not do anything. The Jacoby girl was not supposed to die, she was supposed to get my money back for me. I still don't have it, Sheik. I still don't have it." The connection was broken at The Man's end.

12

The two burley men were loading crates of Persian rugs onto the flatbed trucks, using long woven fabric straps to secure them. When the three trucks were loaded, papers signed, they moved off the docks, going in three different directions. Truck number one headed north, the second truck was moving toward the central valley, and the third truck was going to a warehouse in the city's industrial section. It was that third truck that seemed to draw most of the attention. Two large black SUVs and a stake side flatbed followed number three. It wasn't exactly a parade, but even to the casual observer it would have been noticed.

"It's only logical, Simpson, that the drugs would be put in a warehouse in the city. Were you able to discern any differences in the way the crates were packaged or marked? I couldn't." Gerald Fleming had gotten just enough information from Socrates to set up this operation. He and Simpson, along with two other agents, were going to stop the flat bed at some busy intersection and make a very public bust.

"Persian rugs should be very heavy, Agent Fleming. This truck was loaded with the lightest crates. They all seemed to be marked the same, though. Crates filled with heroin, cocaine, and marijuana would not be as heavy as crates filled with Persian rugs."

"Very good, Lt. Simpson. That's why Captain Elmo depends so much on your ability. OK, then, let's get ready. I'll hit the lights and siren at this intersection coming up." As he started to move in for the stop, the second black SUV cut him off, then cut off the number three flat bed, ran it up on the sidewalk, and four men with AK47s jumped out and blew away the three men in the flat bed. Two of the four then got in the truck and got it off the sidewalk and back on the street, speeding off with the other two men following in the SUV. Neither Simpson nor Fleming saw the fish company truck that turned onto a side street as all the commotion took place.

Fleming, it seemed, had demanded that he be the driver of the DEA vehicle, and he wasn't up to a high-speed chase through busy city streets. He didn't live in this city of hills and turns and wasn't able to keep up with a large truck driven by one who was from this city.

He got close once, and the government car was shot up bad by some good shooters with automatic weapons. "This is Fleming. Code red. Code red. We've been disabled by gunfire, the shipment was hijacked, and I have one wounded agent. There are wounded and dead near the intersection of Third Street and High. Respond ambulances and agents. Also, notify Captain Elmo at police headquarters." The radio crackled for several minutes while Orel Simpson tended to the wounded agent and Fleming paced.

"Damn it, who was in that other car? Was it at the docks, Simpson? I don't remember seeing it."

"It was there. I thought you had arranged for back up, so I didn't say anything. I'm sorry, I should have said something."

~ ~ ~

The hijacked truck and black SUV were able to make it to the industrial section of the city and into a large warehouse. "Good work, men. Anyone hurt? Good, then let's get this stuff separated and moved out of here fast. There will be cops and feds everywhere, and soon. Get started on that and I'll call our man." Conner Figueroa had planned this hit for weeks, convinced the man that it would work, and believed he had pulled it off. He went into a back office area and the men in the truck and SUV started unloading the crates.

"Bull, this is Conner. We have the stuff." He listened for a minute, said he would, and went back to the main floor. "The man wants us to open at least one of those crates and make sure we have the stuff. Get a crow bar, Mr. Chop-Chop, and let's see what millions of dollars' worth of stuff looks like."

Chop-Chop got his name from a convincing way he had of getting information from someone. Chop goes one finger, then, chop goes another until the right answer comes forth. "I got it, Conner. This has to be the right one, though. These crates were much lighter than the others." He snipped the metal straps and pried open one of the crates. "Oh, shit. Conner, look at this." The crate contained ten or so Persian rugs and a few pounds of what they call popcorn, the filler used for shipping. "We're screwed, Conner. We got the wrong truck."

It was a very meek Conner Figueroa that made the second phone call. The voice that everyone heard screaming threatened all with death. "Clean your prints from everything and burn that warehouse to the ground. I want to see that fire on the news tonight. And find the right truck. This is the second load I've lost this year. Find it or die."

~ ~ ~

"Santiago, we got cut off by another bunch of guys with big fucking guns. They killed the men in the truck, then took the truck. We got nothing, Chago. Nothing." He listened for a minute and hung up the phone.

"I'm not sure he believed me, Jose. I have to get down to the docks right away. Get rid of these trucks. Get them back to our warehouse and repaint them." He got in his own car and drove down to Santiago Navarro's boat. "He's one pissed off Mexican right now, Jose, so make sure you do a good job on those trucks."

Captain Serious Elmo was a hair shy of guffawing when the news came up stairs of the DEA foul up. "Hey, Dorsey, Fleming and Simpson lost the load. It was hijacked right in front of them and they didn't even get a shot off." The two men talked for another couple of minutes and Dorsey cut it off.

"Gotta go, Serious. That working girl that got all this started, Star, called just before you. I think she knows something." He left the motel room he was now sharing with Felicia Bogdanovich, and with the Ukrainian police commissioner in tow, headed for Franklyn Street and the saloon called Bar, almost renovated from the recent shooting, but still stunk like an outhouse in July.

"Elmo said the feds screwed up and weren't able to catch the bad guys. They actually witnessed a hijack of the load. Damn, I wish we'd been there to see that."

"So, the Jacoby shipment was hijacked? If Dolinski is in

jail, Socrates is dead, who would this other party be?" Felicia's brow, knotted as snarled fishing line, danced around as she thought about this new problem. "We have many people involved here, Sol. And, it's been days since the name Mavis Brownell has surfaced. She has to be involved, but at what level? She was sure pissed off at Socrates." She reminded herself of her calls for help to Kiev.

Traffic was light and Dorsey was making good time, despite some wind that had kicked up, the initial offering of a big storm coming on shore highballing south from the Gulf of Alaska. It would be a cold and wet one with heavy surf when it arrived. It was storms like this one, coupled with massive amounts of fog that had helped to maintain the huge redwood forests along the coastal mountain ranges.

"I didn't find out very much from Kiev other than Dolinski was definitely setting up a narcotics operation, the Dziuba family was still working kidnaps and money laundering around the world, and many people seemed to be aware of Timothy Socrates. In other words, Sol they told me what we already know.

"Now you tell me somebody has tried to ace Jacoby and Sheik. We have four or five different narcotics operations going on all at the same time, and we are losing names left and right. Dolinski is out of it, Socrates is dead. We don't know much about Baranek and FCU, but at least we know where she is. That leaves Brownell and the Jacoby gang, and obviously a name or two that we don't know."

"We keep leaving FCU off the main plate, little darlin'. Baranek and Dolinski had to be a team, and while Dolinski seems known to some agencies, FCU and Baranek aren't.

What did Kiev say about them?"

"According to commissioner Babyak, FCU is not being investigated or even looked at, and the name Lori Baranek isn't known at all. She must be using another name, and the FCU is just an American thing. Kiev drew a zilch on that one." Dorsey had to snicker at another little Americanism.

"There's something wrong on that score, Felicia. Too much money, too well placed. A well-known international money launderer working with Brownell from the Dziuba family gang, working with Baranek who may have been working with Dolinski, and you tell me Kiev doesn't know any of this. Somebody's screwing with you, Felicia." His scowl would stop a Brahma bull in mid stride as he wheeled the monster Caddy onto Franklyn Street.

Dorsey parked right in front of the Bar, taking up half of a yellow loading zone and half of a red fire hydrant zone. "This'll kill his business for a while," he said, helping Bogdanovich from the car. "I'm more and more positive most of our answers are going to come from Lori Baranek. The FCU has to be in the business of financing these operations. I can't understand how else they could make the money they seem to have." He actually held the saloon door open for Felicia, rather than just crashing through it like an enraged rhino.

"Star should be inside. Last time she called is when I killed those three hoods that no one knew. I bet someone knows them now."

"Sol. Oh. Who is this?" Star doesn't like competition for Dorsey's attention, and there was a scowl on the young face as she looked Felicia over, top to bottom.

"Star, honey, this is Police Commissioner Felicia

Bogdanovich." He didn't say the word Ukrainian, and Star probably wouldn't have known what he was talking about anyway. "Whatcha got for me?" She gave Felicia a couple of mean glances, but started talking to Dorsey right away.

"I hate Santiago Navarro, you know that, Sol, so when he tried to sidle up to me last night, I wanted to run. He wouldn't let me. He said to tell you that some new group is trying to take over and they have some big guns with them."

"Is that all he said?"

"He said he thought the Sheik-Jacoby shipment was hijacked by this new group. That's all he said, Sol, honest."

"Thanks, baby, you did good to call me." He slipped a couple of C notes in her hand, called the bartender down and gave him a twenty. "Give this little pip-squeak a hit or two for me, Curley." Then he snarled, "And keep your hands off." He and Felicia headed back for the car.

"Looks like we were right. I wonder who this new group is? The only people left that we don't have our fingers on, are Brownell and FCU or Lori Baranek. That will be the connection, I think. Let's see if Serious will give us a few minutes alone with Baranek?"

"If Omar Sheik and Illiana Jacoby just lost millions of dollars of dope, there will be all-out war, Sol. He's a vicious killer, and from what I know of Illiana, she would shoot her own mother if it needed to be done. Those bodies you were talking about will be piling up pretty high and soon, I think." She was hoping they would get a break for lunch on the waterfront, but Dorsey drove right up to police headquarters.

"Here's something I didn't know about until this morning, Dorsey." Serious Elmo was wearing a wide smile, puffing on a horrible old black cigar.

"You're aware, I assume, that that's illegal," Dorsey said, gagging in the massive cloud of blue smoke. Elmo ignored him and continued.

"It seems there were three truckloads of Persian carpets that left the docks yesterday. That idiot Fleming only followed one. Omar Sheik may have pulled a fast one on everybody. Simpson's judgment isn't quite as sharp as Fleming believed it to be. He decided they should follow the truck with the lightest load because opium weighs less than carpet.

"He's probably right about that, but the DEA only thinks drugs. Sheik and Jacoby are also in the arms dealing business. Half a crate of automatic weapons and half a crate of opium will weigh quite a bit. Simpson belongs working with the feds." It was pretty obvious that Elmo was glad to get rid of "By the book." The crates were heavy, Illiana knew, because they were filled with automatic weapons. The Narcotics was coming on another vessel and wasn't due in for a day or two. "It looks like whatever they thought they found out from Socrates was wrong, and then compounded by piss poor thinking from By the Book."

Serious had a smug smile on his face, but changed back to his normal self immediately. "This might mean that we will have a visit from those fine folk at BATF soon, also. I wonder who I can pawn off on them," and he went back to chuckling and puffing.

Dorsey rocked back in the cane type office chair, in deep thought. "Serious, I just found out that Chago Navarro knew about the hijack before either one of us. He believes the hijack took place by a new gang operating here. Do you have any kind of description on the other trucks? It could be that Omar Sheik got his load and the new gang hijacked the wrong truck.

"Now would be a good time for Felicia and I to have a nice long talk with Lori Baranek. Somehow the FCU is tied up in this, and I'm still confused on what part Mavis Brownell might be playing. Have you had any contact with the DA's office? She should be worried about now. Socrates is dead and Dolinski is in custody. She may or may not know about Baranek. We know she has a direct connection to Socrates and Dolinski, but how about FCU? Remember, Brownell brought up FCU and me talking with Socrates the night we busted him. Baranek may have some answers for us. Remember, Baranek had a key to Socrates' condo and just walked right in. She's tight as hell here, in some way."

"I'll set it up, Sol, but only if you promise to be a good cop. Don't get handy in there. Remember, this is the cop shop, the interview will be recorded."

Sol Dorsey, with a wide smile and smart-ass attitude simply said, "You know me," as he and Felicia walked out the door.

"Be here at three, without the attitude."

Hand in hand, the two investigators headed down to the waterfront for some fresh cracked crab and cold beer. "I enjoy looking at the boats, knowing that I will never be able to catch as many fish in my lifetime as one boat can catch in a day. Maybe someday I'll buy one of those beauties and spend my golden years fishing."

"These are your golden years, big shot." He knew she was right. She was giving him a big, very positive smile that said many things past their lunch on the wharf. "Who is that guy, Sol?" She pointed at a man doing everything he could to get out of sight.

"I'll be damned. Hey! Santiago Navarro. Try to run from me and you'll regret it for a long time." Dorsey was at full speed in two seconds, leaving Felicia to try and keep up. He bounded down the rough planks of the pier, and leapt across about six feet of open water, landing on the deck of Navarro's boat. The drug dealer was trapped, cowering, sinking to the deck, waiting for Dorsey.

"I'm not doin' nothin' wrong, what you yellin' at me for?"

"You're always doing something wrong, Chago. Let's talk for a minute, shall we?" He pushed the little guy onto his feet, helped Felicia get on board, and sat down on a hold cover, facing Navarro. "You're on your way to prison, Navarro. You were involved in an attempted hijack and you're working to off a couple of people that were also involved, namely Illiana Jacoby and Omar Sheik. You're finished, shit head, so give me the details." He paused, not really expecting an answer.

"Hey, Felicia, we could just take this boat, and maybe cut this little prick up into bait, and catch all those fish I was talking about."

"Make him talk, first, Sol, then we'll cut him up. Do fish like grubby little drug dealers?" The two of them were laughing it up, and then Sol Dorsey slapped Navarro across the side of the head and got down to business. It was several hours later that the two investigators finally got their meal.

"Do you believe him? You Americans sometimes believe anything you're told. Do you really think some group from somewhere else is moving in? I think he was lying through his teeth."

"Yeah, me too, but he does seem to know a few things that we didn't. He never mentioned the Mexican connection and we know for sure they exist. I've known for years that the little shit head works for the Tijuana gangs. I'm glad you spotted him though. It will take a long time for the forensics boys and girls to pull that boat apart."

As they walked down the pier toward one of the sidewalk cafes, Dorsey was deep in his own thoughts. Out loud he said, "Somebody with a lot of money is trying to move into this territory and they aren't afraid of anyone who is already here, namely Jacoby and Company. You can't make these kinds of moves without someone knowing the names, and either we aren't asking the right questions or we're asking the wrong people."

~ ~ ~

"So, Serious, it looks like there are three distinct groups working the coast, Jacoby's is the largest, Navarro is small fish, and this new group, headed by someone called Bull or The Man, is moving in. We think his ties go back to the Ukraine the same as Jacoby's. This may be where Dolinski, Mavis Brownell, and Socrates fit in." The two large men bracketed Felicia Bogdanovich, and hogged most of the crab enchiladas as well.

It was late morning of the next day, and from the way Dorsey and Felicia looked, it had been a long night with very little sleep. "What the hell did you two do last night?" Elmo asked.

"Don't get personal," the big PI snarled, but his slight grin, shaded or half shut eyes told another story, and when Serious glanced at Felicia, he found just a hint of color in her cheeks. Actually, there had been some work involved, but for the most part, the late night hours were spent between the sheets. Dorsey would suggest something, they would try it, satisfactorily for the most part, then they would get serious and discuss the case. And, then another suggestion would be made.

"Sorry we didn't get back to talk to Lori Baranek, but Navarro had an awful lot to tell us, and he seemed quite willing, don't you think, Felicia?"

She nodded, but Serious answered. "Probably screwed up any chance at a clean conviction, too."

"Now, now, Serious. I didn't touch the little jerk. No, I mean it, I did not touch him. Well, maybe one little jab to keep him awake, but no marks. No marks, Captain, sir."

"Go to hell Dorsey." Even so, Serious Elmo had a slight grin on his mug. "I'm going to pass all of this on to By the Book, and then he will get extra stars on his report card from the DEA. That will keep him out of our hair.

"Your job, you two," he continued, "is to tie Brownell and Dolinski to the hijack attempt, and tie Jacoby and Omar Sheik to the delivery."

"Well, there just might be one more thing you've forgotten, Serious. There is the murder of the little dead girl, and the dead hit men. That's what started this whole mess."

"I've never eaten this much in my entire life," Felicia said as another platter was delivered. "I've never even seen this much food, more or less, eighty dozen crabs. Does anyone eat hamburgers around here? Or a steak once in a while?"

"I like steak," Dorsey piped up, "and it really tastes good

when crab season is over. Ice cold cracked crab is something I could eat every meal, unless I had a platter full of Maglio's crab enchiladas."

"Hey, don't forget crab cocktails, crab Louies, crab cakes. My mouth is watering just thinking about crab cakes. I love 'em," Elmo said, downing another pint of cold ale. The three of them ate enchiladas and drank cold ale for several more hours.

13

"Conner, get in here."

"Coming, Bull. You got some ideas on how they got the goods past us?"

"Damn right I have. You fool, they simply outwitted you, spun circles around your stupid head, and now have the entire load. You gotta start using your head if you're planning to keep working for me. Heroin and AK47s are pretty heavy, and you picked the lighter crates because you didn't think. You're like the drug cops, can't think past drugs.

"Now, I want to know who was in that big black SUV, and who was in that fish truck. The fish truck is most important because I would bet the SUV was filled with DEA and other feds. See? You thinkin' alike. Too many people knew about this shipment, and that means that somebody is talking. Find them and bring them to me."

Conner Figueroa didn't say a word, didn't dare, and headed out of Bull's office and made tracks for the Bar. "Hey, Shorty, you seen Chago around today?"

"Sol Dorsey got him a couple of hours ago. Beat the crap out of him. Francisco is leaving town, and it might not be a bad bet for you, too. Dorsey's in a rage, Conner, just so you know."

Figueroa walked to the back of the saloon, right next to

the door to the card room was the pay phone and a couple of booths that were a little private. He took a double shot of whiskey and a pint of beer with him, sat down and flipped open his cell phone and punched in some numbers. "We need to talk. Bull is going to tear this town apart, Chago is in jail, and Omar Sheik has his full shipment. I'm hanging out to dry, here."

"All right, Conner, take it easy. Meet me down near Pier 34. There's a bar there where we can talk. I'll be there in about half an hour. Be alone, Conner." He downed the last of his beer and started for the front door. Two men, dark skinned, probably middle-eastern by their looks, bulled their way in. Figueroa's eyes, wide with terror, tried to find a way out. There wasn't one, Shorty was already going for the floor, and the only other customer was too drunk to see the problem.

Figueroa was forced into the back of the Bar and into the empty card room. "End of the line, Figueroa."

"Who are you? What do you mean? What's this..." and the silenced revolver spit two big slugs into Bull's number two man. The hit men walked out the front door without saying a word to Shorty.

Once again, gunshots, sirens, cops busted up a nice day on Franklyn Street. The cop cars, ambulances, media types, and looky-looks arrived through sheets of torrential rain, the air pummeled by heavy claps of thunder, as from Thor's hammer, and many cowered from blazing flashes of lightning. The first major storm of the season arrived as expected.

~ ~ ~

"Yeah, I know him. Conner Figueroa. Sleazy little pimp

working to move into the narcotics world. Looks like they don't want him in their world, eh Serious?" The call came in before the gunshots were fired, and Dorsey immediately called Elmo and met him at the Bar. "I think I see a pattern, Serious. Santiago Navarro tries to hijack a shipment belonging to Jacoby and Omar, and so does some other group. I'd bet a lot of money that Figueroa was working for Navarro and the other group and somebody found out."

He was looking at Connor's body, thinking out loud in the Dorsey manner. "If they are killing themselves off, maybe we could just wait a week and this case will be solved. Connor Figueroa is a nobody, Serious, so why send two pros to wipe him out? Is he working for Navarro? For Brownell? For Baranek? Or, is there someone else that we don't know about?"

"This is a damn professional hit, Dorsey. Shorty said he never heard the shots. Two guys, silencers, revolvers so they don't have to police their brass. Damn professional.

"What have you heard from Brownell?"

"Felicia tailed her down to Pier 34, and she looked like she was meeting someone. She was angry when she left after just hanging around for fifteen minutes or so. Felicia followed her to Buchko's Grill, but didn't go inside. As far as I know, she's still there. I'm on my way there right now. I'll keep you posted." He left the bar, jumped into the 56 Caddy and spun tires leaving.

The Dorsey mind was clicking as he made his way through traffic and a thunderous storm to Buchko's Grill on Third. "Figueroa working for both sides and somebody finds out. And, the lovely Mavis Brownell waiting to meet someone at the same time Figueroa dies. I like the way this is adding up right now."

The storm was here, with heavy rain, dark skies split from time to time by flashes of lightning, thunder pealing through the canyons of tall buildings, and Sol Dorsey could feel the chill of danger in the air. It's the kind of chill that he would gladly call a thrill. "Danger is what keeps a man alive. It sharpens the senses, it makes one aware of everything going on around him. A man afraid to face danger isn't really alive, isn't really living the life he should be living. One doesn't go into combat without that fear, it's what drives a man, it's more than adrenaline, it may be the essence of testosterone. It's controlling that fear, using that danger to your benefit that allows a man to function during extreme danger."

A lovely spring evening altered by a spring time thunder boomer was how some people would look at the situation. For Dorsey, this just added to the drama, forced him to be as aware of what was going on around him, as it was possible. "People hide from this weather, from the danger of the elements. Not me. Damn, but I was looking forward to a few weeks of having that top down." The rain started slow, first a hint of mist, not fog, just mist, and built fast. As he cruised the city streets, sheets of water splashed across the windshield of that big Caddy, pounded the ragtop so hard it was like being in a tin roof building.

There was some light traffic, no pedestrians dared venture into the teeth of this tempest, and Dorsey had gunrunning, narcotics distribution, and murder raging through his mind, not some rain and wind.

"Jacoby and Omar are known killers, Dolinski and Brownell would have no qualms about killing anyone, and we have bodies piling up everywhere. Someone seems to know very much more than I do, and I don't much care for that." He tucked the big boat into the parking lot next to Buchko's Grill and made the quick dash through cold rain to the front door. Felicia Bogdanovich was waiting for him in the entrance alcove.

"Brownell came in and went straight back to the kitchen area. She has not come out, and I'm sure she hasn't seen me. Her official car is in the lot next door. I think you parked next to it."

"Good. Let's just go in as if we're on a date, take a table and order dinner. We'll play the waiting game. The headwaiter knows me as having cocktails with Mavis before. They speak Ukrainian most of the time, so you will understand what's being said.

"Does Mavis even know you're in the country, more or less working with me?" The thought changed the atmosphere as Dorsey became aware that so many people inside the restaurant seemed to be looking at them.

"No, and I'm sure she wouldn't know even who I am. I'll only speak English, Sol, but I'll do my best to let you know what I hear."

They took their seats and ordered cocktails from the old waiter that Sol remembered. "Nice to see you again, sir. We have more leg of lamb in the roaster this evening."

Dorsey chuckled a bit. "That was certainly the finest dinner I have had in a long time. That rain outside is cold tonight. Better bundle up going home."

"No problem with that, sir. I have an apartment upstairs."

Dorsey stiffened and gave Felicia a little nudge with his

foot under the table. As soon as the waiter left, Dorsey said, "Brownell has access to an apartment above the restaurant that her father once owned. And, remember, Felicia, these people have a tremendous amount of loyalty for her."

It was a couple of hours later, after a full meal, cocktails, after dinner drinks, and casual talk that the two left. And, there was no sign of Mavis Brownell. "Look, Sol, her official car is still parked next to yours. She's either upstairs in that apartment, or she slipped out the back without being seen. If I keep hanging out with you, I'm going to weigh three hundred pounds, just like you."

That got a warming smile from the big man, and he gave her a friendly pat on the butt. "My money is on upstairs. Give me the keys to your car, and you take the Caddy back to the motel." Simon Sol Dorsey was going to let someone drive his car? That was the truest sign of trust the man could give. "I'm going to do some lurking. If they are watching, they'll see the Caddy drive off and feel a little more comfortable." They traded keys, he gave her hugs and kisses, and slipped into rain soaked shadows. A closed business across the street offered shelter and a clear view of the restaurant's front door along with the parking lot.

"If she's not out of there within half an hour, I'm going to see if I can get into that apartment some way." He checked his guns, tightened his overcoat and pulled his hat down tight. The lightning continued with crackling thunder and heavy rain, and Dorsey stood in the dark entryway of Family Furniture and Appliances, glared at empty space between himself and Buchko's Grill on Third, and contemplated the case. The number of patrons thinned considerably as the evening wore on, and the rain, thunder, and lightning got more intense.

Dorsey had spent so many hours like this, followed wayward husbands and wives, business partners up to no good, criminals and other deviants, that it was second nature to just stand in the shadows, alone, cold, with a mind in high gear. "Sometimes I think I can see this case with clear eyes, and sometimes I'm wearing blinders. Brownell is up to her cute ass in this, so is Baranek, and there's at least a third party I don't know. Drugs and guns must be the catch of the day around these parts if the body count means anything."

~ ~ ~

Felicia parked the big Caddy and made the dash to her motel room. After these past few weeks she had discovered the pleasure of talking to herself. "That man has a way about him that I like. I like this idea of thinking out loud." The Ukrainian Assistant Police Commissioner took some files out of her brief case and spent more than half an hour on her computer. "I'll be damned. Sol was right," she said, pulled her cell phone, and made a call to Kiev.

"I'm positive you're holding out on me, Commissioner. You know who Lori Baranek is. You know about the FCU. You've been lying to me, Babyak, and you won't want to see me when I get back home." It was Dorsey who put the thoughts into her mind, and a few keystrokes on her computer proved him right.

"When you put that file together on the Dziuba gang, it had FCU investigations mentioned prominently. You lied to me when you said you never heard of FCU or Baranek." She listened for just a minute, then broke in, "Don't threaten me, Babyak, I just sent a brief to Kiev about our investigation at this end. Someone will be knocking on your door soon."

Half an hour later, with just a hint of a smile on her face, she took a shower and climbed into bed. "He'll be back soon, and I have some good news for him." She was warm, loved, and knew that she would never be able to spend the rest of her life with Simon Sol Dorsey.

I'm not prim and proper, but I'm also not a slob. I think I know why he won't take me to his apartment. Just look at this motel room, and he's only been here for a couple of weeks. I really like him but I could never live this way.

As Dorsey watched from the darkened doorway, the Assistant District Attorney appeared in the parking lot, had come around from behind the building. She got in her car and drove off in the blinding rain and wind. "So, not from the front, where anyone could see, but out the back." Dorsey left the relative safety of the doorway and loped across Third Street, through the parking lot, and ran into the barrel of a very large pistol.

"Do not move, Mr. Dorsey." The voice was heavily accented and Dorsey recognized it as belonging to one of the men that had been bodyguards for Dolinski.

So, he knows my name, which might mean that he is aware of my reputation. As a Dolinski man, why is he here in Dziuba country? These guys work on all sides, it seems.

The man used the big gun to motion Dorsey to walk up a flight of stairs to the second floor of Butchko's Grill. "I will kill you, Mr. Dorsey, so don't do anything stupid."

"Not me, pal," Dorsey said, as he started up the stairs. The wind was howling and rain was coming down in sheets, ice cold, the large drops driven and frenzied. A massive bolt of lightning cut through the sky, thunder blasted through the air at the same moment, and Dorsey went into action. "Like a stroke of luck from high above," Simon Sol Dorsey said, as he spun around and drove both feet into the face of his tormentor. The man's gun went off, the bullet slashing into the stairs. The two men tumbled onto wet pavement. Dorsey was kicking, hitting, and grabbing, all at the same time. It was his massive size and strength that won the day. He hit the man between the eyes, pulled his own large pistol, and shoved it into the man's mouth.

"Like I said, pal, I don't do stupid things." With his free hand, he had a death grip on the attacker's wrist, still holding the big gun. "Let go the pistol and you might live." The man let it go, Dorsey removed his own from the man's mouth, jerked him onto his feet, spun him around and blasted him on top of the head with his own gun. He was dazed but not unconscious and Dorsey wheeled him over to Felicia's car. "See, pal, you're the stupid one here. I'm putting a set of cuffs on you that I lifted from some cop a while back, and we're going for a nice little drive."

A tour of Dorsey's special place in the dunes north of the city was in his mind. "I need answers, and I need them soon, my friend, and you're going to provide them or not make the drive back. Even flinch on our little drive, and you will hurt for weeks to come."

He shoved the man in the car, got in, and started out of the parking lot. A second car immediately showed up on his tail, and Dorsey tromped on the accelerator, expecting the response he would have gotten from his Caddy's massive engine. Felicia's little rental didn't have it in it, and slowly moved out onto the street. "OK, screw head," and he slammed his prisoner across the face with his pistol. "One move, you die first, then your friends."

He drove fast down Third Street and into the center of town. "Three blocks more, and we're at the police station." The big black SUV was crowding, but Dorsey knew the streets better and kept him at bay, dodging, speeding, slowing, turning hard, but with the rain and wind, the little rental didn't have it. The SUV made a move to come around and run Dorsey up onto the sidewalk when red lights and sirens exploded around them. Dorsey slammed on the brakes and the SUV tried to make a run for it, but was blocked by two black and whites. Dorsey reached inside his jacket, found his ID and PI badge, and flashed it out the window.

"Sol Dorsey. What the hell have you got going now?"

"You've never had better timing in your life, Gregson. Nice to see you. Those goons are part of an investigation that I have going with Captain Elmo. Would you let the good captain know that we are coming to his office?"

"We had a call of shots fired, cars racing off, and were responding. You're right, Sol. Damn good timing. That big truck was about to demolish this little toy you're driving. Where's the Caddy?"

"Long story, Gregson, but believe me when I tell you these men are international killers." Dorsey found his cell phone, again in the third pocket he checked, and called Felicia. "Hi, pretty lady. I've got some big fish in chains. Meet me at Elmo's office. I think we'll need an interpreter also. Straight out of the old country."

~ ~ ~

The SUV was towed to the police lot and the three goons

inside were taken into custody, booked, then brought to an interrogation room. "Better idea, sergeant. Separate them, and keep anyone else from contact as well. They haven't had time to create a story, let's not give it to them." Elmo had the look of a winner after he met Dorsey and his entourage.

Dorsey's man was not booked, his pockets emptied and was brought to Elmo's personal interrogation room, adjacent to his office. His belongings were placed on the captain's desk. Elmo was wiping the sleep from his eyes, as was Felicia Bogdanovich, and Dorsey wiped gallons of rain from his face, his hat, his coat, and maybe even his shoes. "Nice of you to call us out in this weather, Sol. What the hell is going on?"

"Got your recorder on?" Elmo nodded yes. "Good, cuz this is pretty good." Dorsey spent the next fifteen minutes bringing Felicia and Serious Elmo up to date. "That big black SUV has been seen at so many of the places this investigation has led, and this jerk here is one of the men that worked for Dolinski. I'm sure that Brownell and Dolinski have partnered to take out Omar Sheik and Illiana Jacoby."

Before Elmo could say anything, Felicia jumped in. "You're almost right, Sol. I talked with my people in Kiev tonight and Dolinski's ties aren't with the Ukrainian gangs, they are with the Israeli's, and there's more. Don't interrupt now for a couple of minutes. The same as Omar Sheik, or more correct, Sheik Omar, Dolinski has something on Brownell and was trying to take her out of the picture. It gets even more complicated."

Serious Elmo had a broad smile on his face. "You are just like him," he laughed. "Get that big steam engine huffin' and puffin', and it can't be stopped."

Felicia took a breath, smiled at Sol, shrugged at Elmo, and continued. "My boss, Commissioner Babyak has been holding out on us. I got some files from my computer, and he has done an investigation of the Dziuba gang and connected the FCU and Lori Baranek to them. He lied to me when he said he had no idea who they were. I have filed a complaint against him, and this may cause a problem with me being able to stay here. It may be that I will be forced to leave."

"All right, let's stop right now." Serious Elmo was living up to his name. "Let's take this one thing at a time. I will do whatever it takes to keep you on this investigation, Felicia, if that's what you want. You have contributed immensely to what we have discovered so far, the investigation is leading right into your own department, and I have to say, I want you here."

"Yeah, I'm gonna go all in on that, too," Dorsey chimed in. "No way I'm giving you up. You may need to get a green card, though," and he was smiling when he said it, taking a little bit of the edge off the conversation. He knew it was much deeper than this investigation, it was something inside him that he had fought for all of his thirty plus years. Romance and the fun of it is one thing, that other thing, the one with four letters, completely different. He had fought it before and always won. Right now, he was thinking, *I don't want to win this fight, I want her.*

"What looks like something to you Sol, doesn't to Felicia," Elmo said, as he brought everyone back to the investigation itself. "And in turn, doesn't to me. Let's run through this. Sol, you go first, and don't be a smart ass. Too many people have died, and I'm sure more will join them. I'm simply not in the mood for more smart ass, right now."

"Me? Smart Ass? Oh, Serious, that isn't fair." He chuckled, Elmo scowled, Felicia sat quietly, wondered if all Americans were this crazy. Wondered if she was going to be able to remain. Wondered if her feelings for Sol Dorsey were real or just the thrill of the conquest.

She was thrilled with her thoughts but knew in her heart that it couldn't work. *I can't fall in love with this man. I am in love with this man. Now what the hell do I do?* Her thoughts were clouded by an investigator's judgment. *Damn it, I do love him.* Dorsey broke the reverie.

"OK, no smart ass. Here is what I think is going on."

14

"OK, I'm pretty much in agreement with Felicia on this." Sol Dorsey said again that he thought Brownell and Dolinski were partnering up with the idea of taking over the Omar Sheik-Illiana Jacoby narcotics operation. "It makes sense to me that Dolinski would put a knife in the back of anyone in order to get his way. Where does this leave Brownell? How does the FCU fit into all this? And we haven't even come close to solving the original murder of Melissa Jacoby." The word frustration was written across his big craggy face and a wise person would not want to provoke Sol Dorsey at this moment.

"And now we have the added problem of the commissioner of the Ukraine state police possibly involved with FCU, with Lori Baranek, maybe even with Dziuba influences. We know a lot of names, we seem to know what some of them might be doing, but we're miles from ending the investigation." Dorsey wanted a cold beer in the worst way, and wanted to wring Lori Baranek's neck.

Felicia apparently wasn't through telling her story. "Hold on, Sol, there's more. According to some of my people in Kiev, the Dziuba family is still active in the narcotics and money laundering business in The Ukraine and their influence extends to this country by way of Mavis Brownell. The commissioner will have a lot to explain when the investigators call him in.

"But, we're forgetting something very important. The person that is missing in our investigation so far is the one called Bull, and we may have been looking in the wrong place for him.

"I think we need to look at the Ukrainian translation of bull. It is bik, spelled B-I-K."

Serious Elmo didn't let her finish. "Frederick Bik, the international hit man, the man that takes care of the money and safety of some of the smaller criminal operations. Fred Bik, the Bull. You should have known that Sol, you've gone up against him before."

"That I have, Serious, that I have. Bik has never been a big time player, and this might be his move to a larger arena. Where is the connection between Omar Sheik, Dolinski, and Brownell? Something kicked this off, and led to the murder of Melissa Jacoby, the attempted hijack of Sheik's last shipment of guns and narcs, and the deaths of many people." Dorsey was pacing in Elmo's small office, Felicia was trying to find the same answer, and Elmo made a call to the detective he had interrogating the thugs that had made the move on Dorsey. But Dorsey wasn't through.

"Bull wouldn't have the money, he arranges the money. He is the moneyman, not Socrates. Socrates was the laundry-man, Bull is the money behind the narcotics gangs. Sheik and Jacoby had a huge shipment go by the boards not too long ago, remember. Bull lost a shipment, Bull gets even. Little Melissa Jacoby pays the price. Now, we have a hijacking attempt. Is this Bull? Is it what's left of Brownell's people? Is it a new gang entirely?" Both Felicia and Elmo seemed almost as confused as Dorsey.

"This is an international conspiracy, with too many players," Dorsey muttered. "I want a beer. No, I want to shoot somebody, beat the hell out of somebody, then, have a case of beer. The DEA is clueless, BATF hasn't made an appearance, and now, with the appearance of Mr. Bik, we have a whole 'nother ball game. Damn me," he said, watching Captain Elmo reach for the phone.

"Yeah, good," Serious said to one of his jailers. "Bring one of them up here. Wait. Get a uniform to get the one here in my interrogation room into my office. Give me ten minutes, then send in one of the others with an officer." He sat back in his chair with just a hint of a smile.

"Seems we have some answers close by," he said. A knock on the door and an officer brought the hit man in and slammed him down into a chair. "Thank you, Mason. Stick around and listen to this." Then to the goon that tried to kill Dorsey, he said, "Who do you work for?" The man wouldn't answer, and Elmo pressed a little harder. "Socrates is dead, Dolinski won't see freedom for another lifetime, Omar Sheik and Illiana Jacoby are going to be arrested soon, and the Bull doesn't have any juice around here. Right now, I can tie you to any of them, making you an accessory to several murders. Any one of them strike a bell with you?" Only silence.

Dorsey ripped the man from his chair and pushed his face into a wall. He had an arm twisted up behind the man's back and was ready to throw a punch to the man's kidneys. "You can't make a move on someone like me and take a chance on me finding out who you are. You are one stupid little pig, my friend. Now, let's see who you are," and he pushed the man back into his chair.

171

Dorsey reached across the desk and picked through the man's personal affects, opened his wallet. Elmo picked up the phone again.

"When you bring that man upstairs, bring whatever possessions he had with him when he was booked." He opened the wallet when Dorsey handed it to him. "Police procedures, Sol. Please. At least when we're in my office. Damn." The comment was given with a hint of a smile, and even Felicia Bogdanovich seemed taken aback by Dorsey's actions. The use of physical pressure during an interrogation is not unusual, anywhere in the world, and of course, has been widely known during the time of the USSR, and even today in the Ukraine.

"Yes, sir, Captain sir." He bowed slightly, and sat down. "Any identification in there?" Elmo emptied the wallet and was sifting through the papers.

"You're going to have to do the honors, Felicia. I can't read much of anything here. He does have an International driver's license, and it says his name is George Randall, but that's BS." He handed the papers to Felicia.

"This is mostly tourist stuff, Serious. I might have to do the interrogation. It is possible the man doesn't speak or understand English." She continued rifling through the stuff from the man's wallet. "There is a note that I think is contact information for Mavis Brownell.

"He speaks broken English, Felicia," Dorsey said. "He spoke to me when he shoved his gun in my ribs, and understood me when I kicked his ass."

"Will you look at this," she said, as she pulled a couple of pieces of paper from the bunch. "This man is part of the Dziuba criminal family in Kiev and was sent here to work with Brownell. I'll bet those other men are working for Bik and were going to make a hit on him. Sol, you just got in the way. They weren't after you, just this guy."

"So, we know that Mavis Brownell is up to here in this operation, but we can't prove anything." Sol Dorsey was contemplative for one of the few times, rocking back and forth in the office cane chair. "I still need to know why Bik is involved. Somebody put out a hit on Jacoby's daughter. That's the key to this whole thing. Was it Omar Sheik, her partner? Was it Mavis Brownell? Was Dolinski involved? Was it Bik? And, most importantly, why?"

Dorsey's mind was wandering, he needed to find that one elusive answer, the one that usually solved a crime. "Why?" he said again. "That answered and we have this all put together. It's always the 'why' of a case, not the who or the what. And why more often than not is money. Wanting money, more money, someone else's money, and this whole mess comes down to money. Someone fronted money and it got lost."

Sol Dorsey sat still for just a few seconds. "These moves aren't like ones I've known from the Bull in the past, Serious. Little Melissa was raped, her throat slit from ear to ear, and her body just dumped. The Bull I remember would have been a little more refined." This was one large man who got things done by way of physical mechanics most of the time, but who also had the capability of deep thought. "Do we have any contacts in the DA's office, at all?"

"Because of Brownell, it would be difficult," Serious answered. "Why?"

"We need to find that Sorenson fellow who was involved with the Jacoby girl's murder. He is the only name we know for certain, and who might still be alive. He might lead us to Bik or others in this mess. Can you go to Interpol or some other agency and put out a warrant, or can that only come from the DA or the feds?"

"That's good thinking, Sol. Damn good. I'll get that started right away. Of everyone we are looking at right now, Sorenson is the only one that has actually been personally involved. Everyone else is just suspect."

Dorsey doesn't do well just sitting, thinking, getting frustrated, and those around him at this moment could see that level of withdrawal ripping across his face. "Alright, that's just about enough. Serious, I need to talk to Baranek right now. Somehow, she, Brownell, Dolinski, Bik and God knows who else, lost a lot of money because of Omar Sheik and Illiana Jacoby and were using the daughter to recover losses. Always, Serious, always follow the money.

"Now, we find out that a shipment of guns and narcotics has arrived, probably for Jacoby, and a hijack was attempted, which failed. These people, whoever they are, have now lost even more money. Lori Baranek is up to her lovely neck in this, and I want to talk to her right now." He stood up as if to walk out the door, not even waiting for Elmo or Felicia to join him.

"Slow down, big shot. We'll get her up here, but you seem to have reached some kind of conclusion that I don't see yet." Serious Elmo was pretty fast but not as fast as Dorsey on this one.

"OK, Serious, here it is. I know this is true because I remember reading about it and putting it in my computer for future use. Several months ago a large shipment of narcotics and guns was intercepted on the docks, disguised as merchandise from several locations in the Middle East. Whoever was supposed to pick that shipment up didn't, and the trail went cold. The customs boys estimated a street value of several million, so it was one big loss. You remember that? It's at the heart of all this."

"I remember that." Felicia Bogdanovich jumped out of her chair. "There were direct ties to The Ukraine in that intercept, and we were furnished with lots of information that seemed to lead nowhere. It had all the earmarks of Omar Sheik and Jacoby, and had to be bungled at this end. Who fronts Omar Sheik's operation? There's our answer, Sol."

"More than that, Felicia, whoever fronts Sheik and Jacoby lost a bundle, and along with that is faced with at least two other groups trying to take over the operations." The big man sat back down and seemed to make strange noises as he mumbled to himself. One could see smoke coming from his ears, if one tried hard enough. "If Dolinski was working to out the Sheik-Jacoby operation, and if Brownell was working to do the same thing, that might lead me to believe that Bik is Sheik's front man." He rocked back and forth some more in the old cane chair. "Bik has never been that big a player, and that might be what caused the problems. He has always believed that he alone is smart enough to be at a high level in international crime. He isn't.

"I really do need to talk to Baranek, Serious. Just as soon as possible. And Felicia, we have these people, apparently all from the Ukraine, why don't you and Elmo concentrate on questioning them. Well, good, that's settled then," and again, he stood to leave. "Come on, Serious, make the call downstairs. I don't have all day, you know, I'm a busy man," and he chuckled as Serious Elmo frowned, but reached for the phone.

~ ~ ~

"We lost some good people on that hijack crap, Sheik. Good people. We didn't lose an ounce of stuff, though. According to my people, not only did another gang attempt the hijack, but the friggin' DEA was there as well. They got their car shot up real bad, but I doubt anyone died, or we would have heard about it."

The two were in Omar Sheik's Victorian home, green tea and toast points on a tray between them. Omar dressed in Dockers and a silk robe over a cardigan sweater looked like an elderly college poster boy from the 1950s while Illiana Jacoby was wearing a fleece sweater and wool skirt. Just a couple of business partners who were talking about a completed deal. The deal was measured in more than eight figures on their end, and they had people scattered throughout the west and Midwest waiting for their share. Money would flow through their fingers. "I'm so glad that idiot Hank wasn't involved in this. We would have lost another shipment, Sheik, and probably our lives."

"I paid the Man yesterday, my dear. He's still pissed over losing the last shipment, but with hands full of cash, he couldn't get too out of line with me. I'm afraid we would be targets of some big time killers if we lost this one too. As you said, thank God that fool Hank wasn't involved. You did a good job, Illiana. Very good."

It was doubtful that Illiana had smiled for months, but she gave a little nod toward her Egyptian partner. "We got lucky, Sheik. Very lucky. There were enough people working to rip us off, I figure they tripped over each other."

Omar Sheik offered a gentle chuckle back to her.

More green tea, more toast points, and more planning. "I think we have a leak somewhere that needs to be plugged, and soon. If another group is moving in on us, and the DEA knows about that and our shipments, somebody is talking about us."

Illiana agreed. She too was worried about a possible leak. "Are we OK on distribution? This would not be the time for a screw up."

"Everything's moving, no problems at all," Sheik nodded. "Our money is coming in fast, and I'm going to do the exchanges myself. No more little people like Socrates to take out a share or two."

"Good," she said. Unlike Omar Sheik, Jacoby was close to the operatives in her distribution network. She continued, obviously worried. "There are rumbles all up and down the coast that the Dziuba Family is going to try to force us out. Some of our distributors have been contacted, and it might have been them that tried the hijack. It was you that reminded me that Mavis Brownell is a Dziuba."

"I've heard some of the noises, too. I also heard that it was The Man that tried the hijack and may have been behind Melissa's kidnapping and murder. If that's the case, we might have to eliminate our own provider. I doubt it very much, the hijack part, that is. That would put a crimp in the operation. I've already started the line for our next shipment and may have to make some big adjustments."

"That can't be, Sheik. We've worked with Andrzej for years, and there's only been that one foul up, which we paid for."

"I don't know, old girl. The Dziuba Family will be fairly

easy to deal with. A nice round hole between the eyes of Mavis Brownell and that element will collapse, but if The Man is working to take us out, that will be a big fight. Big, Illiana, as in death."

She poured each of them another cup of tea, sat back for a moment, and then said something she had been afraid to say since arriving. "Have you ever had any dealings with Fredrick Bik? He could be behind some of the problems. That idiot husband of mine tried to set up a meeting between all of us, and I wonder if Hank didn't let too much out about us."

"I am so glad that fool is dead. I know the Bull personally and I would never work with him. At his best, the man is untrustworthy. One of the most self-centered, egotistical pricks I've ever known. You don't suppose Hank did something else just as stupid as losing millions of dollars, do you?" They shrugged, meaning, yes, I do believe Hank would do something that stupid. "We will have to follow up on the Bull. Right now, let's get rid of the Dziuba family."

Sheik Omar sat back in his large wing back chair, thinking out loud. "Two factions, Bik on one hand and Dziuba on the other. Dziuba is the stronger of the two, so they need to be eliminated first. The Bull, well as certain of himself as he is, he might just eliminate himself." They got a little chuckle out of that comment.

"We lost one of our better guns in the hijack, Sheik, but I have more ready to go to work. I think a well-planned hit on that bitch Brownell is the right move for us. We need to make it big, loud, and very public. Those are the hits I like. If The Man is working to out us, a strong move on the

Dziuba Family might just slow him down. And take them out of the picture. They don't have the contacts in the Middle East that we have, and I think we should consider dumping Andrzej as well. If it's Bull, he's gone, if it's The Man, he's gone.

"We're strong, Sheik, our contacts in Asia, South America, Mexico, and the Middle East are the best. We can go it alone and become even bigger than we are." She sat back and gave her partner a long look. "One of the things that has always worked for us is a lack of people. It's just us, Sheik, as you've said so many times. Now that Hank is out of the picture, the only people in the world that know what we're doing are us, you and I."

She was thinking of the large network of distributors they had throughout the western states, into Canada, and Asia. Sheik Omar and Illiana Jacoby had been building their network for more than twenty years, had a stable of hired guns, had major distributors that had always been loyal to them. It would be unlikely, she thought, that either Bull or The Man could take them out. And, only she and Sheik would know their plans.

"Yes, Bik, like in Bull," Sheik said. "He's always been on the outside, a protector and assassin, but I believe he's making a move into the international narcotics field, and possibly money laundering. He's very dangerous."

"Do you think he was behind the attempted hijacking?" She sat back for a moment and one could almost see a light come on. "Bik works for FCU, Sheik. I bet he is who FCU gets their money from. Damn, and we've helped him along." She tried to collect her thoughts.

"Bik has been transferring money to FCU for years, and

I've always thought that it was going for the protection and education of children. The FCU is working right along with the Dziuba gang to out us, and Bik is the man with all the contacts." She was angry and ready to kill someone, putting all her thoughts and those of Sheik together.

"You are absolutely right, Sheik. Bik has to be the one behind the attempted hijacking, and the FCU is probably our leak to the DEA. Son of a bitch, Sheik, they are ganging up on us.

"I'll put the hit out on Brownell, and I think it is time to consider more hits, on that Baranek woman, and on the Bull. We better consider only our own protection from now on, not let anyone get close to us, and clean up our back yard. Too many people are getting involved in our business, my friend. Too many."

Two lovely individuals, sipped tea in a soft and delightful Victorian atmosphere, planned assassination, and domination of their business. Sheik Omar walked quietly through antique and very expensive furnishings, his feet deep in luxurious Persian pile, his hands clasped behind his back. "Alright, old girl, here's the plan. You take out Brownell, and if you can find her, that woman from the FCU, and I'll see what I can find out about our friend Mr. Bik."

15

"Oh, Sol, I'm so glad to see you. Why am I being held in jail? What do these people want? I don't understand." Her eyes were wide and filled with tears, and Dorsey gave her a couple of points on performance.

"Can it, sweetheart. Googly eyes won't make it with me today. I'm not sure yet what the connection is, but it is plugged into you and the FCU, and many people have died because of it." He sat down across the table from her, slapped a large manila folder on the table, opened it, started drumming those strong fingers, and scowling right into her face. "Tell me about the Dziuba family, tell me about Bull, tell me about good old Charley Dolinski, so called cop from Kiev. I've got bodies piled up three stories high, and right now, I can pin some of their deaths on you." Those bright green eyes glared like laser beams deep into Baranek.

"Oh, and yeah, I almost forgot, good old Timmy Socrates, the international money laundering service rep? Man, so many dead ones, and all of them can be connected to you. You're gonna die, lady. Do you get it?"

The drumming continued, the glaring stare continued, and Baranek's whimpering continued. "It's all Mavis Brownell's fault, Sol. I was forced to cooperate or FCU would be implicated in drug dealing."

"Nice try, Lori. You and the FCU are implicated, and big

time. Dolinski is a dealer, an importer, and you were his American contact. You and Dolinski were working to take out Omar Sheik and Illiana Jacoby, and then the Dziuba family made their move, shoving you aside.

"Is that why you had little Melissa kidnapped? Is that why Tim Socrates is dead? Are you behind the hijacking attempt? Come on, lady, your time is short and I better hear some answers now," and he slammed his fist onto the table. Lori Baranek jumped out of her chair, shaking, and then the crying stopped, the sniveling stopped, and Lori Baranek's eyes narrowed. There was a new set to her mouth, to her entire being. Sol Dorsey was looking into the eyes of a lifelong criminal, a woman who had killed, who had had more than one adversary eliminated, a woman who was now going to work on Simon Sol Dorsey as he had never been worked on before.

"You're wrong, Sol, close, but wrong." Her voice was steady and strong, as Dorsey remembered from their earlier meetings. He still wanted to get to know her in a more animal situation, but he also wanted to reach across the table, grab that delightful throat, and thrash her all over the interrogation room. Instead, he indicated she should continue talking.

"Accessory to murder, implicated in drug dealing, implicated in criminal conspiracy, are crimes that will put you in federal prison for the rest of your life, Lori. I have enough evidence right now to charge you with several state and federal felonies, so start talking, and if you lie, I will take it out of your hide."

"Charlie heard that Bull lost millions of dollars on a Sheik/Jacoby screw up and thought he could put together a group to replace them, but he got greedy, Sol. That's when you got involved. Bull heard that Dolinski was going to grab this latest shipment of Omar's and decided to do it himself. That's how he lost the first shipment. He was going to hijack that one, but one of Sheik's front men screwed up the shipment and the DEA got it. Omar Sheik outsmarted both of them."

"The Fredrick Bik I know doesn't have the juice to be behind the Sheik/Jacoby operation, Lori. He's been known to be an assassin, he gets involved in certain money laundering deals, but he could not front an operation the size of Sheik's. So, if he can't front the operation, steal from it? OK, that makes sense, but where's your part in this, Lori?"

"That's not important, Sol. You need to protect Mavis Brownell, because Bull is sure that she and her family are behind the first screw up, and probably engineered getting the DEA involved and fouled up the hijacking he had planned. Bull is the money behind all of this, Sol." She was back to being a businesswoman, competent, not afraid, and willing to talk about everything she knows. "I can tell you more, but I want a deal. I am not involved other than knowing most of the people, but as you said, I could be implicated. Make me a deal, Sol, with Captain Elmo or the district attorney, and I'll tell you more."

"Big problem lady. How do you know anything about an attempted hijacking? How do you know about the DEA getting their noses in the door? You've been in isolation, Lori, no newspapers, no radio, no TV. You've got BS streaming through your veins, and if you don't start talking straight, you'll not see another minute of freedom in your life. Somebody is either feeding you this information, because it has all happened since you have been here, or, and suck on this baby, you are the brains and Dolinski, Bik, and others work for you." He pointed a long, tapered finger straight in her face, when he said 'you'.

"I can pin at least three deaths on you, probably more, and enough international conspiracy charges to keep you in prison forever. Start talking now. I want it straight, no bull shit, no cute little fluttering eyes, and I mean now," and that huge fist came down on the table one more time. The use of apparent anger is an intimidation factor often used in the interrogation process, and with Dorsey's size, burning eyes, and acting ability, it worked more often than not.

Dull green walls of the interrogation room, filthy walls, started closing in on her. The bright lights overhead, the long mirror, that is, two way glass, glared back at her, the heat had been turned up considerably and perspiration was evident. "I can give you names of the Dziuba family in Kiev and here in this country, and I can give you names of those that work for them in other countries. I don't know anything else." Tears were rolling down her cheeks, and the sniveling was about to start again.

"You're lying, Lori. You know one hell of a lot more than that. You know how the DEA got involved, you know how the hijack was going to take place, you know who killed whom. You and Dolinski? You and Bull? You and Brownell? I want answers and I want them right now." He stood up, towered over the woman, threatened her with his size, his strength, intimidated and, in her eyes, was willing to do harm.

Interrogators have as many tricks as those they

question, and Dorsey, a known professional, was working with a pro from the other side. "I think I have it. You are in with Bik. That would answer just about everything." *This lady is a chameleon. Now, she's crying again. She is really trying to play me. It's my turn to play. Maybe I'll be the nice guy.* To her, Sol Dorsey said, "That sounds more like it, Lori. You're involved up to your pretty little ears, but if you give us what we need to wrap this mess up, I might be able to ease some of the charges a bit. There are a lot of bodies floating around and I need all the answers." He was almost purring he was speaking so softly.

Behind the mirror, Serious Elmo and Felicia Bogdanovich along with the guy who ran the video recording unit, knew that Sol Dorsey was just about to crack this case. "He's very good, isn't he Captain," and she knew he was very good in many ways. "Brownell needs to be brought in for questioning, that twerp that tried to kidnap Sol needs to be grilled hard, and I need to let Kiev know what we just learned about Dolinski and Bik. We have to keep Dolinski here, Captain, or you may never see him again." Her own boss, the commissioner would see to that. Get him extradited to the Ukraine, and former Kiev cop Dolinski disappears. "You have to put enough pressure on to keep Dolinski in this country."

"Getting a warrant for an assistant DA isn't the easiest thing to do, Felicia, but I'm sure I can get it done. Make sure your people in Kiev know what we've found out, and I'll get the legal stuff going. Sol has to keep on top of this. He's the best investigator I've ever had the pleasure of knowing, and if you ever tell him that, you will be sent home in disgrace."

"Yes, sir, Captain, sir." She was spending too much time

with Simon Sol Dorsey. Serious Elmo gave her a big thumbs up. "Would it be OK if I learn the Dorsey procedure for interrogation? I've never really punched anyone. Shot them, yes, but never actually punched anyone." She was laughing hard and the video operator was choking, figured Captain Elmo would wring his neck if he broke out laughing.

"Damn, now I've got two of them," the Captain of Detectives said, as he walked back to his office. "Just talk to those bums we have locked up. Just talk," and he was gone.

~ ~ ~

"How about iced cracked crab, great chunks of fresh sourdough, and gallons of beer, pretty lady? Yesterday and last night wore me out." Dorsey and Felicia were in the motel room, covered in perspiration from a delightful workout, and about to climb in the shower together, which of course could lead to another workout. He had told her before, "A good investigator must always be in good physical condition."

On the drive back from police headquarters after a grueling interrogation session, Dorsey discussed how he thought things were coming together. "We don't have this little caper wrapped up yet, Felicia. We're damn close, but there are big loose ends dangling in the wind. The Sheik/Jacoby gang represents many millions of dollars with each of their ventures, drugs, guns, politics, and somebody lost millions of dollars because of a screw up that is blamed on one of their people. I don't think we know who that somebody is. What we do know is, somebody lost tons of money." He got quiet again, that meant his mind was in overdrive. "You need to talk to Kiev and find out what's going on there, get some background on this Baranek woman, how the hell is Bik connected, and who funds the Sheik/Jacoby operation. Too damn many questions, sweetheart."

"My contacts in Kiev are dropping away, Sol. Commissioner Babyak's compromised position is putting everyone in spotlights they don't want. I'm going to get the call soon, I can feel it coming, to return to Kiev and begin Babyak's investigation.

"I know we're on the right track, I just hope I have enough time left here to help you put the finishing touches to it. I guess by this time in our relationship it's OK to really say something personal." It was more question than statement and Sol Dorsey slowed the big Caddy.

IIe wanted to pull over, but of course there wasn't a parking spot in sight. He didn't give her time to discuss her personal feelings, instead, brought up some of his own. "I have some pretty strong feelings for you, Felicia, feelings I've fought all my life. How can a man like me, facing guns and terror every day, ask a woman to become part of my life? I chase down some of this country's worst criminals, get shot at, get beat up," he paused for just a second, and Bogdanovich slipped right into his conversation.

"You can because that woman feels the same way as you. I'm second in command of a nation's entire police force. Yes, Sol, they shoot at me pretty regularly too, and yes, I'm pretty damn sure I would like to spend the rest of my life with you." She smiled, and finished with, "But only if you learn to clean your filthy apartment."

The Caddy rocked with laughter, and back in the motel room, the conversation about the investigation continued.

187

"Fred Bik isn't capable of what we're seeing here. He is not the moneyman, but somehow he is involved in the attempted hijackings. There is a super power we don't know about, someone who fronts narcotics, guns, and god-knows-what around the world. He is the one who lost millions in the Sheik/Jacoby screw up, he's the one who kidnapped Melissa and he had her killed, but he's not the one behind the hijack attempt; he wouldn't be trying to hijack what he already provided. No, that has to be Bik.

"I would be willing to put lots of money on this, Felicia. The Bull is behind the hijack attempt, but I don't think we know who he's working with or for." Simon Sol Dorsey's mind was at full tilt until Felicia Bogdanovich took her clothes off, and then he became a puddle of jelly quivering like a little boy. "We'll talk about this later," is all he said.

~ ~ ~

She walked over to the shower in all her splendor, he stared and smiled like a teenager on his first fling at adult play land. "As you said, let's talk about this in just a little while, big guy. Wash your back, sailor?" And, the phone started ringing.

"I hate telephones," Dorsey bellowed, picking up his cell off the night table, roaring, "Dorsey."

"Don't take my head off, Sol. Listen close now. I just issued an arrest warrant for Mavis Brownell, and the DA is OK with that. I also contacted Interpol, and they have outstanding warrants for Sorenson already. It seems that man works under about a dozen aliases, has passports from all over the world, and we're not the only agency that wants to talk to him. I have men looking for Brownell right now."

"Thanks, Serious. Sorry for yelling, but ... uh ... never

mind." He clicked off and was in the hot shower in seconds.

~ ~ ~

Serious Elmo had two plainclothes detectives shadowing Mavis Brownell, and they sat in a sedan parked close to Butchko's Grill on Third. "Why does the Captain have us tailing the assistant DA?"

"Don't know, but he gave me the impression that he thought something might happen to her. Put in a call to the Captain, on your phone, not the radio. We may have to pick her up for protection or something. Damn, she is one good-looking lady. I'd follow her anywhere. Just look at those legs." The two laughed and agreed on the thought, and while one started to make the call, the other watched Brownell walk from the parking lot to the front door of the restaurant.

A large black SUV came down Third Street, slowed, and four or five rounds from a heavy gun, probably an AK47 rang out, Mavis Brownell was almost cut in two, and the large vehicle sped off. "Holy shit, let's go," detective Dave Johnson howled, trying to get the little sedan started. Patrons and help from the restaurant flooded the sidewalk, spilled into the street, and added to the uproar. Third Street soon had as many cops as Franklyn Street, the sounds of sirens echoed off tall buildings, radios blared, cops strung crime scene tape. One of the city's nicer neighborhoods ripped apart by drugs, crime, and big guns.

"I don't care what you're doing, Dorsey, get your ass down to Butchko's right now. Brownell was just murdered, and my men couldn't catch the bad guys. The hit came from a big black SUV. Sound familiar?"

"We're on our way." The two were just out of the shower

when Elmo called with the news. "Brownell is out of the picture, Felicia. Big time hit from a black SUV, probably the same one that has been following me. Serious wants us to come to that restaurant her father used to own. That's where she took it."

Frown marks across her forehead was all that changed when Dorsey spelled out the hit on the head of the Dziuba gang in the US. "Interesting that should happen not too long after you interrogated Lori Baranek. Dolinski is out, Socrates is out, Navarro is out, and Baranek is out. That leaves Sheik Omar and Illiana Jacoby, Frederick Bik, and whoever that other person might be, still in the equation. You know, Sol, I've worked quite a few international drug cases, but this one is really complicated. My people in Kiev say that Omar has been an international narcotics and arms dealer for decades, that Jacoby joined him more than twenty years ago.

"Sol, this makes them one of the largest gangs in the world. You're right, whoever backs their play has to be incredibly rich, and fearless. He has billions of dollars rolling in regularly. General Kalishnikoff's favorite weapon probably brings hundreds of millions alone."

"I still can't put Bik in the lead of all this," Dorsey said. "I'm sure he's involved, but I was certain he was working either with or for Mavis Brownell. We're missing someone, Felicia. Someone very big, powerful, and rich." Talking a mile a minute, the big man still hadn't gotten into his trousers. With a little boy's snicker, he looked her straight in the eyes. "Can't do two things at once, you know."

It was a short trip to Third Street, and Sol Dorsey was quiet on the drive. "Something you'd like to share, big guy?"

"Yeah, but I don't really know how to say these things. I have some pretty strong ways about me, you know, and I get all rangy and physical from time to time, and I think I am falling head over my ass for you.

"There. I actually said it."

"Well you did come close. Almost said it, and I know you will someday. Now, about that apartment of yours."

"Here's the deal," he said, not daring to look across the seat at her. "I'll hire somebody. OK?"

~ ~ ~

They drove into chaos entering Third Street. One of the city's better restaurants was the scene of a brutal gangland style murder of the assistant district attorney, and the cops had cordoned off blocks. Dorsey's big Caddy convertible was escorted to the restaurant where Captain Elmo was waiting. "Took you long enough. What the hell were you two doing?"

"Buzz off, Serious," but Dorsey couldn't keep the smile off his face, and when Elmo looked, neither could Felicia. "That looks like one hell of a lot of over-kill, Serious. Damn, they didn't hold back, did they?" He was knelt over the body and saw massive wounds to the middle part of her body. "This is a gangland hit, designed to send out messages. We are in the middle of a war."

He had been thinking that way for several days but hadn't put it into words. "There are some big moves being made here, and our little DA was in the middle, along with the FCU, and Sheik Omar, and Charlie Dolinski, and, well hell, I guess half the international drug dealers we know of.

"Have you got a line on Fred Bik? He's next, you know. This has to have originated from others working to take out the Sheik/Jacoby operation. Lori Baranek knew about the hijacking and DEA involvement before she was even arrested, I wonder if she knows about this." He couldn't let go of that little detail, that Baranek knew about action that took place while she was in solitary confinement.

"Nobody's seen Bull for about a month, Sol. Go back to your computer and put this together. Felicia, if you can put up with him for just a little bit longer, I think the two of you can finish this off before any more bodies come crashing down around us."

Dorsey had a pained look on his face, the computer was back in his apartment, and Bogdanovich seemed overly pleased at the thought, probably of getting to see how Dorsey lived on a daily basis.

"I think the only way we're going to get a handle on this is to either take Bik in or take down Sheik and Jacoby. Best to get both at the same time." One could see the gears churn, slam about in his large head. "I suppose the feds won't let us anywhere near Dolinski?" It was a question that sounded like a statement.

"You know," Felicia said. "There's one other big problem. We have ten-fold crimes, dead people, tons of narcotics and weapons, conspiracies by the gross, and we can't tie our suspects to any of it. There isn't a judge alive that would issue a search warrant for any of these people. It's all conjecture on our part."

Serious smiled at the thought. "You've done your homework on American law, Felicia. Unfortunately, you're right. You and Sol have to get all your stuff together in the same place and solve this damn mess."

Dorsey was getting impatient with how things were

developing. "I'm tired of all these people being one or two giant leaps ahead of us. That damn black SUV. Baranek knows things before they happen, the DEA can't think past drugs and foul up an attempted hijacking. It isn't a case of someone leaking this shit, Serious, it's a case of a well planned takeover of a well-organized gang, and we're following along after the fact."

He stomped around in the puddles from the storm, stared at the dead Brownell woman, saw bullet casings scattered around, poked at holes in the walls, half filled with spent bullets splattered in blood, needing some action. "I need to talk to that waiter inside," and slipped into the restaurant. Most of the staff sat at tables, a few were gathered near the bar, and officers were asking questions and kept everyone from discussing among themselves what they thought had happened. Dorsey walked up to the waiter that had been so friendly, had told him about the Dziuba connection, and just might know something about things he wasn't supposed to know anything about.

The waiter smiled, as Dorsey walked toward him. "Hello, again. What a terrible thing, little Mavis killed like that. Do you know why, Mr. Dorsey?" *So, the man knows my name, and I'm sure I never told him. Mavis Brownell must have told him something about me.*

"Yes, it is terrible how drug dealers get gunned down in front of family and friends." The old waiter took a step backward, eyes wide open over that statement, but didn't say a word. "What can you tell me about this family named Dziuba? They have deep roots in the Ukraine, and apparently are well healed in international narcotics and arms smuggling." Dorsey wasn't sure he should go this far out on that old limb he likes to hang from, but continued anyway.

"My associates and I were about to arrest Ms. Brownell on drug smuggling and conspiracy to commit other atrocities when someone intervened. Tell me what you know of all this?"

"My name is Michael Fillipovich, Mr. Dorsey, and Mavis is my niece. I know the old Dziuba family has been involved in criminal activity, back home in the old country, but Mavis has never been involved." His demeanor had changed dramatically from that of a waiter to that of a family member who had just been insulted. "I'm sure you're very wrong about the lady."

"No, I'm afraid I'm not, Mr. Fillipovich, I'm sure I'm not. Does the name Fredrick Bik ring a bell?"

"Mr. Bik eats here regularly when he's in town. Mr. Bik and Mavis have been friends for many years. He works out of Kiev and Paris, and has something to do with international finance, I believe."

"Thank you, Michael, you've been a big help. You have my condolences on the death of your niece, sir. I may have some more things that I will need to discuss with you, so don't go anywhere." He nodded to the old man, smiled and walked back outside.

"Listen up, you two. Bik is a regular customer here, is a longtime family friend of Brownell, and is due back in town shortly. He is who Brownell was partnering with to take out Sheik and Jacoby.

"I need another sit-down with Lori Baranek, Serious. She has the answers to this. Can you issue pick up and hold orders on Bik, Sheik, and Jacoby? If we get them aced, we might solve this damn riddle."

He looked at Felicia, smiled an almost evil little smile, and said something about needing food and companionship. She simply nodded, took his hand, and led him back to the Caddy. "Maglio's, driver," she said slipping in next to him.

16

"Somebody beat us to it, again, Sheik. The hit on Brownell was not ours, but I did get some information from my own man. Fredrick Bik was teaming up with Brownell when she screwed him over a hijack attempt that never quite took place, and that was the shipment that Hank fucked up. Bik blamed her for the screw up, not knowing it was our own." There was just a hint of an ironic smile on her face saying this, since it was her own late husband who was the screw up.

If she had given it any serious thought she could have understood why Melissa was killed. It was Hank's stupidity that brought that about, and if Hank had made the pickup, it would probably have been hijacked, which would have focused Andrzej's anger onto Bik and Brownell. Sheik Omar was starting to get the complete picture; his partner wasn't. Sheik Omar has the reputation of being the coldblooded killer while in reality it is Illiana that should. She has yet to actually mourn her daughter, and has celebrated Hank's demise.

"As near as I can figure it out, Bik jumped at the chance to work with Lori Baranek and the FCU and be the middle man. That fool Charles Dolinski almost fouled that up, got his ass in federal custody, and put Brownell in the sights of the local cops."

They were sitting at an outside table along the waterfront, watched the fishing boats, not really enjoying the antics of many tourists, had some tea and seafood cocktails; just another couple that seemed to be enjoying a sunny spring afternoon. The early morning fog had lifted some time ago, and the brilliance of a beautiful spring day was blinding as it reflected off a gentle bayside swell, the waves lifted each fishing boat in turn, as they made their way to the breakwater.

The newspaper spread out in front of Omar Sheik had headlines that screamed the death of an assistant district attorney, with hints of underworld connections. Spring in a big city wasn't always blossoms along an avenue or lovely ladies in pastel business suits. Sometimes it was death, money laundering, and narcotics dealers having a late afternoon business meeting along the seashore.

"Tell me just how much this Baranek woman knows about us. How is she connected, who is she working with or for, and why did you trust her in the first place? Illiana, this is very important to us. Too many people are getting involved in our business."

Illiana Jacoby was on the spot, Sheik was angry, and as he said, too many people had their noses in their lives. "I didn't know exactly how the FCU was funded, Sheik. It was just since Melissa's disappearance that I found out they were funded through arms and narcotics, and I only trusted her as far as helping find Melissa."

"I'm not as worried about her as I am about Bik and his family of mercenaries, and of what Andrzej might think of all this."

"Well, Andrzej got his money on the screwed up

shipment and on this last shipment. We are free of Socrates, and we have to plan on this next load of weapons coming on shore in two weeks. We need to eliminate Bik and Baranek, and as soon as possible. These guns coming in are going straight to Mexico, but it's easier to bring them in here first, then truck them down. That war between the cartels is making us very rich, dear lady.

"They have the U.S. border people all fired up about drugs coming into this country, about cartel wars, they don't even know that we are shipping weapons right under their noses into Mexico." Sheik Omar had a satisfied look on his face as he started to get up, thought for half a second, and sat back down. "What about that cop you heard about? Big son of a bitch who bangs people's heads."

"His name is Dorsey, Simon Sol Dorsey, and he's a private detective, not a real cop, but he is working with the cops. I put the word out on him, Bik, and Baranek this morning. Dorsey has a bad reputation, doesn't give a damn about rules and laws, and most of the dealers we use are terrified of the man. He's been nosing around Socrates and Brownell. He's pretty small fry, Sheik, I don't think we have to worry about him."

Sheik wasn't sure of that. "I've heard that he has some woman from Kiev working with him. Bogdanovich, or something like that. Is she the same Bogdanovich who is the assistant Ukrainian police commissioner?"

Illiana said she hadn't heard the name before, "But you have to remember that it's been years since I was in Kiev. I don't know anyone there."

Sheik Omar just grunted, and seemed to dismiss the subject. They finished up and headed in separate directions.

"I've offered good money to make sure the hits are taken care of, Sheik. I wish I knew who took out Brownell. We owe that person a debt of gratitude, but must also fear why it was done. If it was Bik, it means he's gone independent and might be after us as she was."

"According to some of my associates, Illiana, Bik was supposed to be working with or for Brownell. I don't think he would take out his own partner. The FCU is somehow the answer to this, the FCU and that Baranek woman. I'm not really worried, but we have to get this cleaned up. We have too much invested, dear girl, to get zapped by some little people that we can eliminate."

~ ~ ~

"I just got off the phone with Kiev, Sol," Felicia said as Dorsey came in the door of the motel room. He had managed to talk his way out of having to show her his apartment, had let her off at the motel, went back and picked up his computer and a hand full of file folders. "Listen to this. Lori Baranek put together the idea of the FCU when the Soviet Union came apart, and used it to create an international smuggling operation, which in turn funded the FCU. She set it up originally for smuggling people and money, and only recently got into the narcotics and weapons end of the conspiracy.

"At first it was just the smuggling, and that came about because of the old USSR systems, the spying, the KGB. People needed to be gotten out, others needed to be silenced, and some were just kidnapped and done away with.

"The concept was a really good front and she tied herself in with Bik while he was trying to get partnered with

Dziuba. She has a number of aliases, and may have worked her way into the Ukrainian police by way of Babyak." She paused for a minute, probably just to catch her breath, and Dorsey jumped into the conversation.

"And you call me a freight train." He patted her on the bottom end, snuck a quick kiss and continued. "Well, I was right, then. Lori is fully involved in this. She's a player, Felicia, a player. She changed her attitude at least three times when I talked with her."

"There's more, big guy. Bik has been working for some time to get himself set up with some of the leading candidates here, including FCU and Brownell. He and Brownell had a hijack set up to take a shipment from Omar Sheik and Jacoby when the shipment was seized by customs. Remember that?"

"Yeah, it all fits now." He was sitting on the edge of the bed, his laptop open, and was keying in some commands. "Here it is. Hundreds of millions of dollars' worth of heroin and cocaine, and just left on the docks for some reason. That's a huge loss for somebody. More than one gang involved, I'll bet.

"Let's invite Serious for some crab enchiladas and take this thing apart. We're very close right now to shutting down some big operations, but I wonder if we'll ever solve the murder of Melissa Jacoby."

"One thing I think I know," she said, giving Dorsey a little kiss on the ear, teasing the big man into distraction. "Dolinski is small fry at best. He thought he saw an opening into a big time drug operation, and all he did was manage to screw up other pipelines. We wouldn't have half the answers we have if he hadn't led us to them. Dolinski doesn't know as much as we were giving him credit for.

"My people in Kiev are screaming for me to get back there. This Babyak thing is boiling over, and I'm in line to be Commissioner."

"That's impressive. But you can't leave. I think we need to have a nice long ride up the coast, spend a night or two in a friendly coastal resort, and figure out where we are from a very personal standpoint. I don't want you to ever leave. There, I've said it." His palms were sweaty, and his heart was palpitating. As he said, he had been fighting this possibility all his life.

"You almost said it, big shot. Almost," and she giggled, looking for her sweater.

He closed the lid on the laptop, grabbed Felicia around the waist, and the two fell across the already messed up bed. "We can call Capitan Elmo in just a little while. I'm going to do some serious interrogating right now. Here's the first question. Why are you still dressed?" Two hours later, the phone in Serious Elmo's office rang.

"Where the hell have you two been? I've called half a dozen times. Look, Sol, quit being a smart ass, we need to talk."

"Yeah, Serious, sorry about that. The phone got accidentally turned off, and I guess the one here in the motel room isn't working either." He had a little boy's grin plastered across his broad face. He reached over and gave Felicia a pinch on the butt, and continued his conversation with Elmo. "We've been thinking about some iced cracked crab and sourdough French bread. You up to that, mein Capitan?"

"See you at Maglio's," was the quick answer, and the

phone went dead.

Felicia and Sol got there first and commandeered a large banquet, much to Maglio's torment. "Smile, Maglio. It makes for a much nicer evening. Hope you got a fresh boat load of crab, we're starved." With dollar signs in his eyes, the man from Palermo did manage a very slight smile, just about the time Captain Elmo came in. He wasn't alone.

"You brought By the Book with you? Are you out of your mind?" Dorsey was about to explode, but Elmo calmed him down.

"Tell Dorsey what you told me, Simpson."

"It's about Fredrick Bik. He's supposed to be picked up by DEA for some illegal narcotics he was attempting to transport into this country. They say he will be arriving in New Orleans sometime this week and that he might have connections to the hijacking attempt here, that you already know about." Simpson had the look of a strongly disciplined dog, eyes cast downward, no color to his cheeks, and he was nervously clasping and unclasping his hands. He was a beaten man, and this probably impressed Dorsey more than Elmo realized.

Dorsey looked at Elmo, then at Simpson, then at Felicia and back to Simpson. "Do you even know who Fred Bik is?"

"There's much more, Sol. Give the little prick time to answer."

Simpson never had a chance to answer. Two men with automatic weapons burst through the front doors of the restaurant and opened fire. Dorsey flung the table aside, had his nine-millimeter out and was firing when three slugs tore through By the Book. Elmo was hit once in the arm, but managed to get several shots off, and the two gangsters lay bleeding on the floor. One round from a large and horrible AK found its target in the middle of Felicia's forehead.

Black clouds of hate burned their way across Dorsey's face as he cradled Felicia's body. "This is now a very personal war, Serious. I want to talk to the Baranek woman first thing in the morning." He looked into her face, knew that he had just lost the only woman he ever loved. Emotions were a large part of the Dorsey character, and he would gladly kill everyone involved in this investigation. He knew he wanted to cry, to scream and rant, and knew that he would not do that.

The two dead gunmen were identified as guns for hire, probably from Chicago or maybe Jersey, and couldn't be tied to any local drug gangs. "This is Bik or Sheik Omar, Serious. They are the only ones left. Did those goons follow us? Well, hell, I've seen that black SUV around this neighborhood so many times." He was doing everything a man can do to keep his mind on his job. All he wanted to do was cradle Felicia Bogdanovich for the rest of his life.

Forensics people swarmed Maglio's for hours. "You need to have that arm taken care of Serious. I'm going to make a big scene down on Franklyn Street. I'll see you in the morning." His first stop was going to be his apartment, then the saloon simply called Bar.

~ ~ ~

The Bull was still angry, angry about the hijack screw up, angry about losing so much money, angry that people he trusted were betraying him left and right, and angry that his hired guns were either dead or in custody. It hadn't dawned on him yet that most of the screw ups could be traced right back to him. He has never liked New Orleans, probably because so many people involved in criminal activity in the Big Easy were so much smarter than he.

Bik watched the two DEA agents as they strolled down the street. He slipped into the little jazz club, and out the back. His driver was waiting, he got in the back of the large SUV, got hunched down onto the floor, below sight level, and the car moved out of the alley and into traffic. By the time the agents were aware of what happened, Bik was nearing a private airport on the outskirts of New Orleans. The Gulfstream 3 was already warmed up and ready.

"Glad you put this together Peter. Bastards are closing in on us and I need to be on the west coast as fast as this thing will fly."

"It's not good out there, Bull. We did take out Mavis before she got picked up, but no one seems to know where Baranek is. If Sheik Omar's people have her, they aren't saying, and there haven't been any bodies washing up."

"If I had known what a wimp Dolinski was, I would have shot the son of a bitch. Where is he?"

"He's in federal custody, and Kiev has a hold on him as well. When Brownell found out that you were going to fund Dolinski instead of the Dziuba Family, she put a hit on you both. The feds got him first, but you are still in some big sights. The whole damn Dziuba organization has guns out looking for you and Baranek." Peter took a short pause as the two climbed aboard the jet.

"And there's one more thing you need to know. Babyak has been removed as Ukraine police commissioner. Our tie to protection just went out the door, and you gotta believe Dolinski will give it up when they get him back there. Things aren't good right now, Bull."

Bik was settled into deep leather, watching nighttime lights from city after city as the fast little G3 screamed through thin air at forty thousand feet. His cocktail glass held a fair amount of Kentucky's finest cooled by two ice cubes, his cigar was lit, and he took on the appearance of a man in charge. Given half a chance, he would like to be seen as a rock star instead of a greasy drug peddler. He gave the impression that he didn't hear a word that Peter had said.

"Here's what I want, Peter," he said, as he sipped the good bourbon. "I want to know how my organization managed to screw up two hijackings. The Bull doesn't screw up, Peter. Don't ever forget that. The first one cost me more than one million dollars, and the second one, was to be even bigger." The anger boiled, he would gladly shoot the first person to look at him wrong. "First, my people find out that Omar just left his truck sitting on the docks for the DEA to find, then my own people hijack a shipment of fucking Persian rugs, get people killed, and go to work for Brownell." The anger was flowing from his pores, was bile in his throat. It was this uncontrolled anger that allowed Bik to make wrong decisions, stupid ones, regularly.

"Where are we going to land, Peter? I don't want to step off this airplane into big guns from feds or Omar or Dziuba."

"I've got a car waiting for us at Lake Tahoe and we'll drive down to the coast. Our flight plan is for Reno, but the pilot will land at Tahoe, then go on to Reno. He has no idea who you are, just a rich dude that wants to gamble without any publicity. You're safe, Bull."

~ ~ ~

Dorsey went to the motel and cleaned out his stuff, made sure that Felicia's stuff was bundled. He would have to go through it all, and what he didn't need for the investigation would have to be sent to Kiev. After several hours he headed back to his apartment. 'Those bastards were looking to take us all out, otherwise they would have hit us there at the motel." He sat at his kitchen table, still the home of many pieces of telephone, head in his hands.

"No," he muttered as he poured another cup of stale coffee. "No." He wanted to pound heads, shoot druggies, stretch necks. "No! No! No!" he screamed the words, slammed his hulking fists onto the table with each 'no', gnarled knuckles ready to destroy whatever they were aimed at, his shoulders could break through brick walls right now, and his emerald eyes were flame throwers of death. "I will avenge you, Felicia, I promise. And people will die because of it. I promise." He knew that several hours on Franklyn Street would put his head back on straight, or get him thrown in the can.

"It's Bik that set that up." He got his computer on again, and started putting together as much as he had on Sheik Omar and on Bik. "I know where Baranek is, and I'm going to nail her ass to everything that's happened. She knows things before they happen, and it has to come from Bik. Amazing," he was having a full bore conversation with himself by now, "that no one has a full picture on Jacoby and Sheik Omar. This is the largest international narcotics, weapons, and money laundering gang in the world right now. Amazing." The muttering continued for several more minutes and screen after screen flashed across the computer was welded into his mind.

"Sheik Omar is Egyptian or Saudi Arabian, or both, Illiana is Ukrainian, married to a bad cop, but running an international narcotics operation, and they have never bothered to use aliases, never even tried to work from outside the U.S. These people are damned sure of themselves, and except for Serious and me, I don't think anyone is even looking at them." He tried to remember if DEA agent Fleming had responded in any way when their names came up.

He finished his coffee, remembered to turn the stove off, shrugged into a brown leather bomber jacket and headed for Franklyn Street via a fine 56 Caddy ragtop. Fog was thick and cold, as wet and cold as Dorsey's mood, and he hoped that Curley would be working The Bar. With the Caddy safely parked, he checked his armament, slammed his way through the saloon door, and dared anyone to challenge him.

"Mr. Dorsey, you gonna break that door someday. Yes you are." Lefty Gonzalez was sitting at the first stool, gave the big guy a full on smile of welcome, filled with multitudes of white teeth.

"I hope so, Lefty. How's your nose. That was a good fight the other night. You'll be ranked one day soon, pal. You seen Star anywhere this evening?"

"Actually, she and the Princess Lolita just left. Said to hold their seats, they would be back in about half an hour. They had a John in tow, so they will be back soon."

Dorsey grabbed a stool and gave Lefty a fiver for his trouble. "Hey, Curley, you blind?" It looked like a long night; a bitter, foul, hateful night.

"Give me a double on the whiskey and a cold pint. Listen Lefty, do you remember a couple of years ago when I had a little deal going and was trying to find a guy named

Bull?"

"Yeah, Sol, yeah. He got away or something."

"That's right. I'm still pissed. I heard he might be coming back to town. You heard anything like that? He's a nasty bastard, and I owe him a big smack in the chops. The kind you gave out the other night."

Lefty chuckled. "Word is he wants to move on old Santiago Navarro or something like that. I remember Bull from my days in New Orleans, before I got my new manager. He had a hit squad for rent, Sol. Bad ass all the way, but not the brightest guy I ever talked with."

"That's him. It isn't Chago he wants, it's another gang, but he got in my face big time, and I'm taking him out. Try to keep me informed on whatever you hear. Deal?" A twenty flashed across the bar and Dorsey picked up his drinks and headed for the card room.

"Deal, Mr. Dorsey. Bull is looking for some hit people here in town is what I heard. He got some bad people on the street right now, and is looking for more. Some kind of big hit, but that's all I know."

Dorsey spun around. "When did you hear that, Lefty?"

"Yesterday, maybe late last night. Something wrong, Mr. Dorsey?"

"Yeah," is all the big man said.

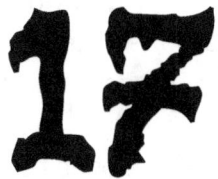

The cell phone brought him up from a deep alcohol drenched sleep. It took him three rings to recognize the sound, and another two to get untangled from Star. "Oh, Star baby, I'm sorry. I just needed some help last night, and you were there." He mumbled a couple more things in her direction before he finally answered the phone.

"Dorsey," he growled, propped up on an elbow.

"You better get down here fast, big shot. It's all coming down." Serious Elmo didn't even wait for an answer, just hung up.

"Wake up, Star. Gotta get moving, sweetheart. Come on, up, up, up," and he swatted her across the butt. He showered, thought about shaving and said to hell with it, and found tee shirt and jeans. "Get your ass out of bed, lady. I gotta get out of here." He bent over and gave her a kiss, patted her butt one more time. "You're a good friend, baby, and the one thing I needed more than anything else last night was a good friend. Thank you," and he tucked a couple of C notes into her pants pocket.

Dorsey headed downtown at a fast clip, and watched every car and truck that came anywhere near the Caddy. If one of them happened to be a big black SUV, it probably would have been shot to hell. He tried to boil Felicia out of his mind with hard liquor, and it didn't work. His anger boiled over twice during the night that he could remember. One erupted into a saloon-emptying brawl, the other his getting tossed out of a greasy spoon café when his eggs weren't proper.

He called Star Felicia a dozen or more times last night, had two bottles of cheap whiskey too many, broke down finally, as he sat in the Caddy. Star seemed to grasp at least part of the problem and managed to get the big guy home. "If he ever finds out that I drove his car, he'll kill me," she said to herself as she tried to park the monster. The fun part was getting him into the house.

"That was one well planned hit yesterday. Was it Bik, Omar Sheik, Baranek, or somebody we don't know behind it? Or retaliation from Dziuba people? Drugs and guns equal money, and there are tons of money flowing through this port right now, and we are kicking up enough dust that somebody is getting scared." It was a ten minute conversation, one sided of course, and he parked in an official car only spot in front of police headquarters.

As he got out, he realized he was forced to adjust the seat before leaving. "It's been days since Felicia drove this boat. Damn, I was really drunk. Who the hell drove my Caddy?" It was anger mixed with confusion mixed with hangover, and he had no answer.

The atmosphere in Captain Elmo's office was icy when Dorsey walked in. Drug Enforcement Agent Fleming was in one chair, Elmo was standing, and two uniformed officers were also standing. "'Mornin' Serious. Fleming. Got any coffee?" and he grabbed one of the chairs. "Bad night," was all he said.

Fleming's anger surfaced as soon as he recognized

Dorsey. "What's he doing here, Captain? We don't need any more amateurs working this case. I just lost a good man that probably didn't need to die."

Elmo, his fist, balled like hot steel, cocked with a hair trigger, started toward the agent, but Dorsey got there first. "Proper procedure, Captain. Always proper procedure," and Dorsey creamed Fleming, knocking him and the chair he was sitting in across the office. It looked like he was going to pull one of his large guns, but thought better of it as the two uniforms jumped in to stop anything else from happening.

"Get up, you little prick. Get up before I break every bone in your body." It was Elmo who grabbed Fleming and jerked him to his feet. "Thank you, Sol. I'm glad you saw agent Fleming start to get violent with me. You acted correctly in stopping him." He straightened up the chair and pushed Fleming down hard. "This will be reported to your superiors, Agent Fleming. Don't ever threaten me again." Dorsey couldn't hold it in and his laughter was probably heard downstairs, along with the clattering of furniture and bodies crashing about. The two uniforms did their best to control their humor, and not very well.

All the tension, all the hate, all the loss was behind that punch and Fleming will suffer that pain for many days to come. Dorsey tried to ease his pain with booze and trouble last night and it didn't work. Punching Fleming's lights out was like cutting a strand of cable that was cinched around his heart. "Thanks, Fleming, I needed that."

"Now, Dorsey, while I continue my conversation with the DEA, I want Officer Jackson here to escort you to interrogation room three. I believe you'll understand why when you get there."

"Thanks, Serious, and yes, I will follow correct police procedure. You bet I will." He pulled both his weapons out and laid them on the desk in front of the Captain, smiled, almost benignly, and he and Jackson headed out the door. "I was serious about that coffee, Jackson. Got any handy?"

"I'll bring you a cup right away, Sol."

"Bring a pot," he said, and walked into Interrogation Room Three. Interrogation rooms were not meant to be pretty or even slightly comfortable. In number three, the walls were a dull, dirty, avocado green, with splotches that may have been blood that had been cleaned up. There were body fluid stains, and graffiti offerings in more than one language. The conference table was steel, bolted to the floor, light fixtures were covered in metal cages, and that large mirror behind which a stenographer and camera operator were seated offered no friendly picture.

"Good morning, Lori."

"I'm so sorry for your loss Sol. Ms. Bogdanovich will be muchly missed in Kiev. I understand Commissioner Babyak has been exonerated by the investigation that was started by her."

It was impossible for Sol Dorsey to remain in that room. He walked out, intercepted Jackson, and sat on the other side of the mirror and finished the pot of coffee. He talked to himself, to Jackson, and the others, he muttered, talked, cajoled, and ranted, and no other voice could be heard. Among the things that were noted, were comments about "how the hell a woman in isolation would know that Felicia Bogdanovich had been gunned down. How the hell would a woman in isolation know that the Ukrainian police commissioner had been under investigation?" Half an hour later, Simon Sol Dorsey walked back into Interrogation Room Three.

"I understand Fred Bik is due in town today, Lori. Have you made plans to meet with him? According to my people, Sheik Omar will probably take him out before he can contact you. You," and he pointed one long finger in her face, "you filthy bitch, are now alone in this world." He crossed the room, pulled out a chair and sat opposite her.

"Did you really think Dolinski could take out Sheik Omar and the Dziuba gang? Damn, that would have been something. You should have stayed with your original plans of kidnapping and money laundering. Narcotics and weapons are for the big boys, not second or third raters." He looked her right in the eyes, growled from deep in his belly, balled up his fists, slowly opened them, and then slammed an open hand down on the table. Lori Baranek feared for her life.

"Actually, Lori, there is no one behind that two way glass right now. I told them I was sending you back to your isolation cell. That's right, it's just us, darling. It wasn't that long ago that I would have enjoyed being alone with you, but, damn me, it's all I can do to keep from strangling you right now," and he lunged forward, making sure he didn't actually touch her.

She whimpered, skulked, cried, and Dorsey laughed, threatened, and displayed an amazing amount of control. He never touched the woman. They spent another two hours together, two more full pots of cop-shop coffee, and Dorsey walked back up to Captain Elmo's office. Gerald Fleming was still there. "Learn anything?"

"Yup. Your boys do not know how to boil coffee. Oh, by the way, Bik is in town. Got here this morning. You have one big hole in your jail staff, Captain Elmo, sir. One big hole."

"You want to tell him, Gerry, or would you rather I did?" Serious Elmo rocked back in his chair, a monster cigar destroying the ecology of the police station and waited for DEA Agent Gerald Fleming to say something. The cigar smoke was supposed to be soothing to Elmo, was supposed, when blown in his face, to be more than irritating to Fleming, and it was Dorsey who was ready to keel over. Elmo wanted Fleming to spill whatever it was, and when he didn't, Serious Elmo did.

"Our stupid, now late, friend, Lt. By the Book Simpson, planted a DEA agent in the jail. It seems someone had slipped him the name of Lori Baranek, probably from something I gave him to give to Fleming, and Simpson decided to find out where she was."

"And you let him do that, Fleming?" was all Dorsey could say. "Is that what this meeting was all about in the first place, Serious?"

"That, and I wanted you to have a long conversation with Baranek so you would know just how much harm this fool caused."

"So, one of your jailers is a DEA plant? Why would a drug agent pass along all this information to Baranek? How much information did the agent get from her? Damn me, Fleming, I'm gonna punch your lights out again, just because I can. You fool," and he stepped forward but caught himself in time.

"We have an international case of narcotics, weapons, money laundering, at least two major criminal organizations in a fight with each other, and you play a little game like that. Small fucking minds playing small fucking games. You are one piece of worthless dog crap, Fleming." Dorsey was good at letting it all hang out, and Fleming was well aware that he could die at any moment.

"Where are my guns, Serious? I need them now."

"Ain't gonna happen old friend. Not quite yet. Get out of my office, Fleming, while you can." The DEA agent didn't need to be told twice. "Your boss will have my report within the hour, so prepare yourself, asshole."

~ ~ ~

"Those weren't the best, were they Illiana? Two so called professional hit men and they took out the wrong people before being killed themselves? A DEA agent and a representative of the Ukraine police? And Dorsey and Captain Elmo still alive? What the hell is going on, Illiana?" Omar was more than just upset, and had called Illiana as soon as he saw the paper in the morning.

"Once again, Omar, it wasn't our hit. I don't know where these hits are coming from. I put out a hit on Brownell and someone else made it first. I put out a hit on Dorsey, and again, someone else made the hit. Somebody knows what we're doing as soon as we make a decision.

"Those dead men are not our people." She was uncomfortable, being put down like this by Sheik Omar. "I know you're upset, but don't rag on my ass. I'm not Hank, and I don't screw up. We have a big leak somewhere, and we need to find it quick." The flash of anger took her partner by surprise.

"I'm sorry, Illiana. I'm very sorry, and you're right, I'm angry and worried. Who have you been dealing with?"

"Same as always, Omar. Petrus has been who I arrange most of our hits through. He has people all over the world. I've trusted Petrus from the day he arrived from the Ukraine. I don't think he would turn on us, but somebody sure has."

"All right, I'll get back to you. Don't call off the hits you already have in the works, but I'm going to find our leak and get us out of this mess. That ship load of weapons is due next week, and too many people know what we're doing." He didn't say goodbye, just hung up, leaving Illiana seething.

She slammed the phone back on its cradle, stormed into the kitchen of her apartment and poured a cup of tea. "He better be careful, talking to me that way," she mumbled.

~ ~ ~

"Tell me what has happened, Peter. I want to know everything." The Bull was sitting in the back of a large black SUV, enjoying the scenery of the drive through the Sierra Nevada from Lake Tahoe to the coast. With a fresh cigar, another taste or two of whiskey, he felt like he owned the world. "Does that fool Sheik Omar have another shipment coming in?"

"A boatload of weapons, Bull. They'll be hitting the California docks in the next week. Headed for the Mexican cartels through Texas."

"And, we have plans that will work this time?" The anger surfaced long enough to frighten Peter.

"I am doing the planning myself, Bull. No outsiders. Just you and me." He paused for a minute. "The hit on Sol Dorsey didn't go well. I brought two guys in from Chicago, they followed Dorsey and that Ukrainian woman to a restaurant, but other people got in the way."

"Tell me all of it, Peter. I'm damn sick and tired of things not working around here."

"They killed the Ukrainian and a DEA agent and wounded a police captain. Dorsey wasn't hit at all. Both hired guns were killed on the spot. I'm sure it will be traced back to Sheik Omar and Illiana Jacoby. She too had a hit on Dorsey. Dorsey is very dangerous, Bull."

"I've dealt with him before, Peter. I know, that's why I want him out. Did the Brownell hit go good?"

"Better than we could have expected. Again, all eyes are on Omar and Jacoby. The Dziuba Family is really pissed." Peter had a slightly suppressed smile on his mug as he said this, and that almost got Bull angry all over again.

"Don't get smug on me, Peter. I've lost hundreds of millions of dollars on the last two loads coming in. One more, and no one will work with me, ever. Screw this up, well, you know what I'll do."

"We'll be fine, Bull." He did indeed know what Bik would do. When he first got in contact with the Bik people, they had him tied up in a barn, and it was Bik himself who did the official employment interview. Peter lived through it only by making sure he only told the truth.

He continued, "Santiago Navarro got greedy. That's not how I operate. There is one problem I wanted to discuss, though. Who the hell is Lori Baranek?"

"If we're lucky, Peter, she will be our key to millions of dollars over and over again. She was working with a man named Dolinski to take out Brownell and the Dziuba gang and damned near pulled it off. Dolinski was just not bright enough and got himself all screwed up trying to take over.

"He's in federal custody and she's hiding under deep cover somewhere. I have to get in contact with her as soon as we get set up at the place in town. She has been running people and working some money programs and is ready for the big time with drugs and guns. She's the best contact we have."

He paused for a moment. "I want us to operate out of the condo in town, but I want our heavy armament at the coast house. I doubt that you've heard the name Andrzej, but he is our main target. If we get The Man, we own Omar and Jacoby. He is their source for money, and the only money left will be ours. They will be forced to work with us. See to it, Peter, that guns, people, and big strong cars are available at the coast house."

Bull hoped that if he was able to get close enough to The Man, that he would also probably be close enough to Omar and Jacoby to take them out as well. He didn't say this to Peter. *Peter's a kiss ass, that's what he is. Too willing to agree with me at all times. But, I need him right now.*

Peter knew about, The Man, but never heard his name. "I'll see to it Bull. As soon as we get to the condo, I'll get it set up." Bik handed Peter a large envelope. "These are the plans that I know of right now. Don't screw this up."

~ ~ ~

A large private corporate style jet was beginning its descent into LAX and the man that owned the plane was still livid with rage. "Yes, I understand I have my money returned, but money lost and with no interest, no profit, it is just money. Money, you must understand is something I have tons of. It is the profit that makes spending, maybe even losing some, the game.

"I have lost millions, and only my investment has been returned. Someone is going to die a very long, hard death." He hung up the on-board telephone, motioned for his traveling companion to come sit with him during the final minutes of the flight. "This is what I see, Sarah. Sheik Omar lost an entire shipment of narcotics, a shipment that I fronted. There was some stupidity on his part. Had the wrong man doing the job. Now, I find out that there was a hijacking scheduled for that load as well.

"Ironic, eh? I may have lost the load anyway." Andrzej never laughs, and didn't now, but there was a hint of humor in his manner. Sarah Palozzi, a tall blond Italian from high in the northern Italian Alps, known by many names in many international police agencies, was on board The Man's aircraft for one, maybe two, reasons. Her orders were to find Frederick "The Bull" Bik and kill him. Secondarily, she was to be Andrzej's bedroom companion when other duties weren't being taken care of.

"Now, I find out that the shipment that arrived a few days ago was to have been hijacked. I'm going to let Sheik Omar and his little killer companion, Illiana, off the hook for the time being. He paid me in full, but, here I go again, no fucking profit. But Bull? He dies the hardest way you can come up with. Understood?" And he put his arm around her, pinched one of her breasts with delicacy, and settled back for the landing.

It was a few hours later that another, much smaller, private jet landed at a private airfield on the northern coast of California. A large black SUV was seen parked near the fence along the roadway leading from the private airport, and it seemed to be following the cream colored Mercedes sedan that picked up the passengers on the jet. The sedan went to a large compound on the coast, just a few miles outside the city, and through heavy metal gates was seen to park near the main house.

"I don't know whose black SUV that was, sir. He followed us most of the way, even when I tried to lose him."

"I want you to take Sarah to my offices in town, and Sarah, if that car follows, have Sam here put you in a position where you can kill whoever is in the vehicle. Just kill everyone in that car."

"No Problem, Andrzej. I expected we would do that on the way in."

"Not with me in the car."

"I want to be seen, Sam, so I'll ride in front with you. You, with the rake," she hollered at somebody raking the garden, get in the back seat and keep your head down." Again, Andrzej almost cracked a smile.

Sarah Palozzi had a flare about her work, and there were many cops and investigators in Europe and Asia that can tell you stories. She once tied a man to a telephone pole, pulled his pants down, gave him an oral pleasure that few have ever had, then shot his penis and balls off and left him to die. She was known for being ruthless and was well paid for her abilities.

She had Sam open the trunk of the sedan, pulled out an Uzi, checked the clip, grabbed two more full clips, and got in the front seat of the car, cradling the gun for instant action. "Will we be having dinner tonight, Andrzej?" she asked as Sam fired up the sedan.

~ ~ ~

Sol Dorsey was an angry man as he stormed from the

police station. Captain Elmo was with him stride for stride, taking stairs two or three at a time, slamming doors open, scowling at anyone that dared to get close. "So your friend and mine, By the Book Simpson, bless his dead ass, put a DEA snitch in jail, who then was able to get information in and out. We know he didn't get close to Baranek, probably never heard her name, but he sure put the squeeze on us. It's not nice to say, but Simpson got his." They found the Caddy, and Dorsey was still talking.

"Lori Baranek gets information in and out, knows everything before it happens, and you can bet the DEA learned nothing. Now, the whole investigation is based on information she gave me from inside your own jail." They got in the Caddy and didn't move.

"It's ok, Sol. Go ahead and say it. I'm going to clean house as soon as we bet back, but I do want to know your feelings on this." Elmo's anger was different from Dorsey's. Dorsey broke things. Elmo considers the consequence before he breaks things.

"There's something else going on in that jail of yours, Serious. Not a DEA plant, but a longtime member of the police force who works for FCU or Bik or Omar Sheik. If Lori can get all this information, and brother she knows things we don't, does she also get information out?" He started the big Caddy and was driving toward Maglio's, only thinking of the case, and not getting any response from Serious Elmo.

"Well, damn it, say something."

"We can't go to Maglio's," Serious Elmo said at Dorsey's question. "Place will be closed for a long time, I'm afraid." Big balloon whites screamed in agony as Dorsey wheeled the boat down the street, pedestrians fled for their lives, off duty cops, and a homeless soul or two scampered out of the way. Elmo continued as if this happened every day. "There's always chili dogs and cold beer and Angelo's."

"You're buying. It's your cop-shop that's at fault here. Besides, I'm out of a job, remember? I was working for Felicia." The thoughts of Felicia brought a darker, uglier cloud across the big man's face. "I'm gonna kill every son of a bitch that even thinks drugs. Every damn one of them."

"Then I think we should start with Fred Bik," Serious said. "The Bull is behind just about every person that has died so far in this little caper of yours."

"Mine? You hooked me into this, Serious, and now I'm not getting paid." He was pushing the Caddy pretty hard and had to hit the brakes with gusto as he pulled into a parking place near Angelo's. "My little caper, my ass.

"Listen, Mein Capitan," Dorsey continued, "we have dead people stacked to floors deep, we know of massive amounts of narcotics, tons on automatic weapons, and international money people, and right now, this very instant, it's you and me doing all the investigating.

"Where the hell is BATF? DEA can only afford Gerry? We know of blood from how many different countries spilled all over these streets, and only one fed? Gerry?" He finally stopped talking and they got out of the car and headed for Angelo's. "Where do those guns go, Serious? We have a fair handle on the narcotics, and no idea where the big guns go.

"Well, damn it, say something."

"You talk too much," is all Serious Elmo said. They moved two tables together, ordered a pitcher of pale ale each, and told Angelo to bring chili dogs until they cried for help.

"Bik's in town, that we know," Dorsey said after pouring his first brew. "Lori knows it, but I doubt Bik knows she knows. I got the feeling that she was looking to ace the bastard. She's a real treat, Serious. I don't know if she can tell the difference between truth and lie. Bik has a property out along the coast, south of the bridge, and I would like to take a look at that place.

"I got one hell of a lot of information visiting Socrates' place, maybe I'll get lucky there too. Do we have enough information on the bastard to get a warrant, arrest or search?"

Serious Elmo had been pondering that problem. There was very little hard evidence of any kind. "As you said, Sol, we have tons of narcotics moving around, dead bodies everywhere, international gangsters driving around town shooting up the place, and no hard evidence.

"We're going to have to play this one the old way Sol, the way we used to. Make them make a move on us and take them out. This little caper of yours," and he had a grand smile saying it, "may never get to court. You and I both know that. Dolinski and Baranek might be ejected from the country, but we don't have anything to hold them on. Nada." He sat quiet for a minute. "The only thing we know for sure, Melissa was killed after being kidnapped, probably for something her father did. After that, it's empty streets and no brakes."

Dorsey drained his pitcher of ale while Serious was talking, motioned for another, and ploughed through a couple of chili dogs. "Damn good, Ang baby. Damn good.

Here we go again, Serious. Our Italian friend, Maglio, makes better enchiladas than any Mexican in town, and now, our Mexican friend, Angelo, makes the best chili, better than any Texan I know. What on earth is this country coming to?" He wiped a napkin across his broad mug, and sat back with a big smile.

Dorsey waited for just a moment before continuing, long enough for Serious to enjoy his commentary. "We're still missing someone, old friend. Sheik Omar and Illiana Jacoby run a major narcotics, weapons, and money laundering operation, and someone screws up a shipment of highly prized shit, loses millions of potential dollars, and for it, Illiana's daughter is kidnapped, raped, throat slashed, and dumped in the ocean.

"No, no, don't interrupt, I'm on a roll here. Someone fronts these shipments and was more than just pissed at losing it. Now, it appears that other international groups are trying to move in on Omar and friend, and are killing off all our suspects. That makes it a bit easier for us.

"Dolinski teamed up with FCU and Baranek, Socrates was with Brownell, Bik may have been trying to team up with Brownell, but switched sides when Dolinski went down, and mated with Baranek. Bik probably took out Brownell. Who took out Socrates? It could have been anyone of the group just named. Who put the hit on us? I'm picking either the Omar gang or Bik and Baranek. Baranek is smarter than Bik, and I bet she will be running his operation soon if we don't stop all this." He tried to take a breath, but his mind was just going too fast. Instead, he slurped half a pint of ale, took a deep breath anyway, and went right on.

"If there is someone fronting Omar and Jacoby, they have

to be aware that other forces are moving into the territory. Whoever that is, they almost lost another shipment with that attempted hijack. Their money, position, influence, is being threatened, and I would bet that Bik and Baranek are in someone's assassination sights right now."

"I've said it before, and will for a life time. When you get a head of steam up, that freight train called Sol Dorsey can't be slowed down." He took down a pint himself, and picked up his cell phone. "Thompson. Elmo. I want you to get with international people and get me the name of the biggest, baddest, meanest, and most wealthy person in international narcotics smuggling. And, call me as soon as your list reaches three. Don't take any other job until you finish this one." He hung up, smiled at Dorsey, and motioned for more beer and chili.

18

"Sam, you've been with The Man for a long time. Do you know where Bik's condo is in town?" Sarah was comfortable, her fully automatic weapon nestled in her lap, and she was ready for war. This was her specialty, taking out the people trying to wipe out The Man.

"Yes, ma'am. It's in one of the old industrial areas. Many of the old warehouse type buildings have been turned into condos. The Man has had me following all the vehicles that are known to be Bik's."

"That's how they made this car?"

"Probably."

"Does Bull have any other homes or locations?" she asked, fondling that wonderful killing machine on her lap.

"He has a large compound on the coast, just a bit south of the city. When he's in town he only uses that if he has visitors."

"Let's take a tour of that area first, then if that big SUV doesn't pick us up we'll head for the downtown condo. Keep a close eye, Sam. If that big black truck comes rumbling up behind us, you need to get in position for me to take everybody out."

"I'm with you all the way."

Another beautiful spring day along the coast of northern California, no fog, warm sun beating down, and with only a gentle breeze. This is a chamber of commerce day, and the drive along the coast proved it. Surfers daring the combers, sunbathers on the sun-warmed sand and in the water, volleyball nets every fifty feet or so for what seems like miles. The Mercedes was cruising at about the posted speed limit, letting those that always feel the need to be first pass, and Sam's eyes on the rear view mirrors as much as on the road ahead.

These kinds of operations could go wrong very fast, and Sarah had been in enough of them to be just a bit tense. If Sam couldn't get the sedan in position for her to shoot, if they were cut off by a non-involved driver, if they didn't see the hit car coming in time, all these problems had happened in the past, and Sarah wasn't fearful, but probably anxious.

She realized she was checking to make sure the safety was off every thirty seconds or so and forced herself to stop. Her window was down, the two back windows were down, and she was as ready as she would ever be. The gardener sat in the back, terrified, knew if something went wrong he would be dead, and had to take a piss in the worst way.

Sam slammed the sedan into the left lane, yelled, "Here they come. Very fast. I'll try to keep them on our right." The big black SUV climbed right up on Sam's rear bumper, two big AK47s appeared out the side windows and opened fire. The Mercedes rear window and trunk areas were fitted out with bulletproof glass and metal, the big slugs bounced off, ricochets may have endangered anyone within a quarter of a mile.

Sarah turned so she could shoot out of either back door window or her own front door window, and waited for Sam to give her a shot. It was a short wait, and it was the SUV driver that made the move. He whipped the big car to the right and hit the accelerator, which gave Sarah perfect shots. Her Uzi spit half a clip in what seemed like half a second, the SUV went wildly out of control, off the road into a ditch, rolled twice then went end for end once. The broken machine ended up on its top, wheels spinning, dirt still flying.

Sam slammed on the brakes and got off the road, Sarah was already half way out of the car and raced to the SUV. She slapped a fresh clip into the Uzi and emptied it into the bodies splayed about inside. She raced back to the sedan, and Sam made for the Andrzej compound, still trying to stay close to the speed limit. He learned a long time ago, the old maxim, "Don't give yourself away by doing something stupid like speeding or darting in and out of traffic." There were so many of these Mercedes sedans, and they all looked alike that Sam knew he could just flow with traffic.

~ ~ ~

"I can't just sit here and get shit-faced, Serious. I'm gonna take a drive out to Bik's coast joint and see if the guy is around. I can't just sit here another minute." The two of them had set a record for how many chili dogs and pitchers of beer they had put down, and neither one seemed to even know how much they had. "If the Bull is in town, and we know he is, we have to find him. We can't wait for him to make a move. He's here to take over from Brownell, Socrates, and Dolinski, and Lori Baranek already has plans to take him out. We have to stop all this."

Serious Elmo didn't question Dorsey's move. "Let me call the office, and I'll ride with you. It's a nice day for a drive along the coast in that boat of yours." In less than ten minutes the call was made, the bill was paid, and two very large men slipped into well-upholstered seats in a 56 Caddy convertible. It took less than half an hour to make the trip. They made two passes by the mansion and grounds and knew that Bik, or somebody was home.

"I see at least three black SUVs Serious. He must have at least half a dozen guns watching over things. We'll have to catch him outside this place, unless you want to set up a siege or something." He only slowed a bit on each pass and saw that there were cameras covering the grounds, and men in strategic places. There were heavy iron gates across the driveway, and a man stationed at a gatehouse. No open weapons sighted, but Dorsey knew they were close to hand.

"Let's go back and see if we can set up surveillance on his condo. We'll have better luck baiting him into a fight downtown than here."

The highway along this part of the coast was four lanes with a large center divider filled with vegetation, small trees and bushes, lots of flowers, which made it impossible to use as a U-turn point. There were breaks in the vegetation for turns, spaced about a half mile apart. Dorsey had trouble getting the Caddy to make a full U-turn on both of his passes by Bik's mansion. "Yeah, we need to check out that condo."

All he got back from Elmo was a grunt and a nod, and he moved back up to traffic speed. He hadn't gone half a mile when one of the SUVs came screaming down the highway, passed the Caddy like it was going backward, and seemed to not pay any attention to Dorsey and Elmo. "Let's tag along, shall we?" Dorsey said, and got another grunt and nod from Elmo.

The big truck sped down the highway for about three

miles, then did a power one-eighty through the median, kicking up everything that grew there, almost hit a car, and sped back toward the Bik mansion, wheels so hot blue smoke drifted in the salt air.

Dorsey did his best to get the Caddy turned around, but a 56 Caddy doesn't behave like modern vehicles, and he was at least a mile, maybe more behind the SUV when Sarah Palozzi made her move. She was back in the Mercedes and gone before Dorsey and Elmo arrived on the scene.

"Now there was a hit gone bad," Dorsey said as Elmo called in the event to police headquarters. Within minutes there were a dozen police vehicles, many more cops, and radios crackling with a description of a Mercedes sedan that wouldn't be seen again. There were four bodies in the SUV, none of them Fred "The Bull" Bik.

"I wonder who the hell was in that sedan? Whoever it was, they knew they were going to be targets, and took out the hit men. Damn fine job, Serious. Damn fine job." Dorsey gave each of the bodies a good look-see.

"I've seen two of these guys. I thought they were Dolinski apes, but I guess they either work for Bull or Baranek. We shut Baranek's connection with the outside off just a few hours ago, so these must be Bull's people. Was Omar Sheik or Illiana Jacoby in that sedan? Or is there still someone we don't know pulling our chain?" The Dorsey frustration level was very high and he simply didn't have any answers. He slammed doors, pounded one fist into an open palm, kicked dirt, and stomped around the area. He also knew full well the answers weren't there.

"I thought we had this narrowed down to three options, Serious." He named them off, "One, the Sheik/Jacoby gang, two, the FCU Baranek trust, or, three, the Bull. All of this started because of a lost shipment that was for Sheik Omar and company. Jacoby's daughter slaughtered, hit men dead, and now, all-out war between heavily armed and wealthy narcotics gangs. So, it's that top man, the man that funded that lost shipment that is behind all of this. Who the hell are we looking for, Serious?"

"Ease off, Sol. You have the answer, just not the name. If these are Bull's people, and I have to believe they are, then that sedan either carried Sheik Omar people, or it carried the big man, the money man." Two or three eyewitnesses had given their statements, and all they could remember was the Mercedes sedan, and there are thousands of them matching that description in northern California.

Serious directed a bunch of cops to do the follow up, made sure they knew this was his murder/narcotics investigation, not traffic or something dumb like that, and grabbed Dorsey before he exploded.

"Let's go back to the office and see what names those guys have come up with." The trip back was very quiet, both men concentrated on filling in the blank spaces.

"I'm going to put in that independent front suspension, with power steering and power disc brakes, Serious. It took a long time to get this beast turned around back there. They just whipped that SUV, set up a slide, put the power to it, and did a beautiful one-eighty. I had to back up twice."

Elmo chuckled and knew that Dorsey's mind was back on full charge, frustration level back to high rage, not worse, and answers would be coming soon. "You know, Sol, I think I'll pass on dinner tonight." Both men were laughing, driving in bright sunlight on a beautiful spring day, headed back to town.

~ ~ ~

Illiana Jacoby was nervous as she sat at a small table along the waterfront, didn't see the crowds of tourists, didn't hear the sound of salt water lapping at pilings or boat hulls, only worried about why Sheik had been so demanding that they meet ASAP. She barely knew there was a cup of tea in front of her, and was startled when Omar suddenly appeared.

"What's wrong, Sheik? Why the meeting? Has something happened to the shipment that is coming in? I have already started putting together the plans for moving everything. That last shipment moved very well, despite the hijack attempt." All the questions just flooded across the space between the two.

"No, dear lady, everything is fine for this next shipment. The Bull is in town, arrived yesterday, and is making enough noise to bring every federal agent on the west coast to town. He is spreading the word that we are finished, that if anyone wants what we supply they need to go through him."

"He's always been a fool, Omar. Always."

"There's more. The Man is in town as well and Bull pulled a hugely stupid stunt yesterday. He tried a hit on The Man. He wasn't actually in on the hit and all four of his people are dead, but The Man is in a rage." The two had vivid pictures in their mind on what that rage might be like. "Do you remember the name Sarah Palozzi?"

"How could I forget," Illiana said. She felt a ballet of cold fingers dancing down her spine at mention of Palozzi's name. "That is one evil woman, Sheik."

"The Man brought her along on the trip to take out Bull. Fred Bik is a dead man and doesn't know it. She wiped out the hit squad. But Andrzej is sure that he has someone close to him that is feeding information to The Bull.

"Anyway, The Man wants me to have dinner with him tonight. He doesn't think it's a good idea for all three of us to be together in the same place at the same time. I want you and at least two good men with big guns nearby. As close as you can get without being seen. The Man is sure something is going to happen."

"I'm glad it's you having dinner with him. I don't think I could handle that. I'll pull the two men I have tailing Dorsey and have them with me. Where's dinner, Butchko's on Third Street?" She said it with a straight face, but the crinkle in her eyes gave her away, and Sheik Omar laughed out loud.

"That would be something, eh? No, Andrzej has a large office complex downtown, and we'll have a catered affair on a roof top garden. I think one man with a rifle on a nearby building, and another near the entrance. You can be where ever you feel is best. Here's the address, so get started now and get this set up."

Illiana went straight to her apartment and made some calls, then took a cab to a location about two blocks from The Man's office building. Dinner was scheduled for nine and it was already four, and she knew she didn't have enough time to do this perfectly. *It's a good night for a hit, too. No moon, no clouds, no wind. I hope Bik just continues to be stupid, and we'll get him. That will make me very happy, seeing that man die.*

~ ~ ~

Dorsey let Elmo off at the police station and headed for his apartment. "Who the hell are you?" he bellowed when he opened the front door and found a large woman standing in his hallway.

"I'm Mabel, your cleaning lady. You owe me a lot of money, Mr. Dorsey. Have you ever had this place cleaned before?" She held a mop in one hand and was wiping perspiration from her face with the other. "You don't need a cleaning woman, you need a skip loader and three lumber jacks."

"Oh, yeah," Dorsey mumbled, "I forgot. What's that?" he said, pointing at a room off to his right.

"That's your living room. You telling me you've never seen it before?"

"Don't remember, I guess. So, how much do I owe you?" He was reaching into a pocket to find some cash. "I remember Felicia saying she was going to hire a cleaning woman, I just forgot, I guess."

"She told me a hundred bucks to get the place straightened out, then fifty bucks a week to keep it that way. We're stretching things with that first hundred." She was a stout woman with a southern European background, and Dorsey was intimidated and embarrassed.

"Humph," he grumbled, handed her two C notes, gave her a big Simon Sol Dorsey smile, emerald greens shining brightly, and said, quietly, "Thanks."

"I'll be in every Wednesday, Mr. Dorsey." She put the mop away in another room that Dorsey didn't know existed, and left. He glanced into the living room, shook his head and headed for the kitchen, just as the phone started ringing.

"Wow," he said, seeing his kitchen, almost as if for the first time. He turned the coffee on, answered the phone, and sat down at the now clean table. "Wow," he said again, instead of hello. "OK, OK, it's just ... never mind, I'd rather not tell you right now. What's up?" Serious Elmo spent about two minutes talking before Dorsey could get a word in.

"So what you're telling me is, this man we might be looking for only has one name, Andrzej, has never been arrested for anything, at least under that name, and flits about the world in large private jets? Damn me, Serious, there must be more than that." Sol Dorsey sat at his bright newly cleaned kitchen table, and was staring into a computer screen after calling up the name 'Andrzej'. He had a full mug of hot coffee at his side.

"Interpol has a line on the guy, he appears to be connected to international arms smuggling, narcotics, and political kidnapping and assassination. They think he's in this country right now, but the guy is pretty elusive. He has holdings all over the world, including California. That's it, pal. That's all I got."

"You know, Serious, he might not have a criminal record because he's the front man, the money man. Somebody has to make huge sums of money available for each of these cargo ship drops. He breaks the law, but not in such a manner that most investigators would even know about.

"I have all of Felicia's files from Kiev, so between hers and mine, let's see what I can come up with. Thanks Serious. Anything more on that shoot-'em-up on the coast?"

"The dead guys are from the Ukraine, probably brought

here originally by Dolinski or Brownell, but working for Bik now. Partnered up with the guys that tried to get you a few nights ago.

"By the way, my people thought they had the Jacoby woman, but she has moved from their old home. They are looking, and we can't get a handle on Sheik Omar either. They are a slippery pair. We'll keep looking. Anything from your end?"

Dorsey looked around his spotless apartment, decided it wasn't worth it to open that can, and simply said, "No, nothing yet. "I'll call you later."

19

Illiana Jacoby was a thorough woman when it came to setting up a kill or doing protection work, and had her crew assembled, each man with a high powered rifle, in pieces, inside a suitcase, and Petrus had brought one for her as well. Illiana had the men gathered and she gave the orders of the day. "We want to be fairly close in order to protect Sheik and The Man. We don't want to be seen, either, so here's where each of you need to be," and she laid out some maps of buildings.

On one map of the main office complex, the doors in and out were well marked, surrounding buildings where her people would have good sight lines were highlighted, and escape routes were well defined. "I want these cars ready to go. No foul up on this. If there's any kind of problem, I don't want us in the middle of a bunch of damn cops.

"The man has his own people at the entrance and exit points of his building, so all we have to do is watch the surrounding areas. Make sense? A hit would not come from inside, it would come from one of these surrounding buildings. That's where we have to be. Don't take any chances. Shoot to kill, and shoot first."

She decided on four of her best guns for this operation, so, there were five people moving into locations surrounding the Andrzej office complex. Illiana was on the roof of a building directly connected to that complex, and was looking across at the rooftop garden where dinner would take place. It seemed strange to her, but it looked like two or three of these large old warehouses, now ultra-high rent condos, shared common walls.

She was in plain sight from the garden area, but was out of sight from surrounding buildings. Petrus was in the building to Jacoby's right, and the other three gunmen were moving into place.

Jacoby saw one flaw in her plan. While she could see the roof garden, would be able to see Andrzej and Sheik, she would have to make herself visible in order to see the other roof tops surrounding her. There would be no other way, she decided, but it bothered her.

Petrus, in position with his rifle assembled, pulled his cell phone out and dialed a number. "Bull," he said.

"Yes, Peter, are things going as planned?"

"Just like you said, Bull. I can see Illiana, I will have both Omar Sheik and The Man in my sights after I kill Jacoby. I'll call you as soon as I'm through here. The other men she brought along are going to come after me, but I've hidden a car they don't know about, so I should be able to get out."

"Good, Peter. Call me when you can."

It would be light for another hour at most, but the fog was sure to roll in, and with it an evening chill. Sheik Omar and Andrzej would enjoy gas fired fire pits spread around the roof top garden, with the city and large bay sparkling in the evening glow. Large men with large weapons would also be in attendance for the buffet soon to be offered.

~ ~ ~

Dorsey tried three times to call Serious Elmo, but the Captain of Detectives was either not answering his phone, or he couldn't. "Damn it. Well, I can't wait," he said, and checking his armament, headed out the door. As he slipped behind the wheel of the big Caddy, his cell rang. "Dorsey," he bawled.

"Take my head off, Sol. I've been in interrogation. What's up?"

"This guy Andrzej has offices here in town, and from chit-chat on Franklyn Street, something is about to happen there. Known guns for hire are being deployed around the building, and the tension on the street is pretty high. I've had two calls in the last hour, and they are from people I trust."

"Give me the address, I'll meet you there."

"If you bring people, don't bring black and whites or uniforms. I think either Sheik Omar or Bik have plans to hit this Andrzej guy. According to Lefty Gonzalez, Bik has been rambling around Franklyn Street for several days, trying to buy hit men, and I guess he's been successful."

The two met up about a block from the office complex where five guns were awaiting Bik's hit, and Bik had at least three other men on the scene as well. It was Bik's plan to take out the Jacoby/Omar people first, then Andrzej. That would make him the man, and with help from FCU, he would be able to fund most of the narcotics and weapons deals on the west coast and central U.S.

"Let's go up there, Serious," Dorsey pointed to a building that overlooked the Andrzej building. "Might even be guns up there already." They had officers, some in suits, some in more casual attire, not uniforms, spread out around the area, sent men to each of the areas where they could watch entrances to buildings, and headed to their chosen spot. "I'm glad you decided to bring an army. From what I gathered on Franklyn Street, every hired gun in town has been given a high paying position.

"This is more like it, Serious. I hate just having to sit around and think. Running, fighting, shooting, and thinking, that's OK, but just thinking? That's crap." They found the door to the roof of the building slightly ajar.

"Somebody's already here, Sol." He tried to look out onto the roof without moving the door. "One guy, near the ledge, with a scoped rifle," he whispered. "I don't see anyone else. Ideas?"

"Yeah, shoot the bastard. No, let's see, how about one of us just walking out the door. No, damn, Serious, can he see the door directly?" Dorsey was having a little bit of fun at Elmo's expense, but the last question was legit.

"He's pretty intent on watching the main building off to our left. He's got his back to us right now. Come on, very quiet, now." They slowly opened the door, thankfully no squeaks, moved behind one of the ventilators that seem to be in profusion on top of most buildings. The two snuck from ventilator shaft to ventilator shaft. Peter was standing near the edge of the building, probably twenty-five feet or so from the two burly men.

From where they were, they could see a woman on the other building, and she too had a scoped rifle. "That, Mr. Dorsey, Sir, is Illiana Jacoby," Elmo whispered. "Is this guy going to shoot her, or are they planning to shoot Andrzej?"

"I think I know this guy," Dorsey whispered. "Do you remember Navarro talking about a guy named Peter? That's him. He's a Bik man." Dorsey was on his knees behind the ventilator, and had a big smile creeping across his mug. "Jacoby is here to hit Andrzej, Bik is here to hit Jacoby. Hell, Serious, we can just sit and watch."

"Just can the damn smart ass, Sol. Damn." He knew what Dorsey said was pretty funny, just the wrong time for someone named Serious. "Can we take this guy out without waking up the neighborhood, in particular Jacoby and company?"

"You got a stun gun with you?" Dorsey said this in complete smart-ass mode and Serious seemed to say, without saying it, oh hell, yes. I always carry one.

"Oh, yeah, now you're cooking." Serious Elmo slipped his nine-millimeter automatic back in its holster and pulled a little stun gun from a waist pockct. Vcry small, it was a weapon that would stop a man cold, but not necessarily do permanent harm "This thing is supposed to have either millions or thousands or something of volts when it hits. Knock a guy flat on his ass, I know that."

Some police agencies used the large type stun gun, carried in squad cars, but Elmo had carried the little pocket type for several years. "I've practiced with it, but never actually used it on someone. Hope it works like the ads say it does."

He got down on his belly, and slowly inch-wormed his way to another ventilator shaft. Looking back, he saw Dorsey go the other way, for back up just in case the man didn't go down from the heavy shock.

It was late spring, just about sunset on California's northern coast, and that usually meant it was time for the fog to roll in. Slow tendrils of moist air, then a bit heavier, and finally, visibility was down to mere yards. The romance of gossamer lace might look good in someone's poetry, but when you're in it, it wasn't necessarily pretty, and Dorsey said to himself, "It sure as hell isn't romantic."

Dorsey watched as Illiana Jacoby looked over to see if this man, Peter, was there. *That's strange*, he said to himself. *Peter works for Bik, and Jacoby knows he's here.* That goof-ball light that would come on in comic strips flashed across Dorsey's face. *This son of a bitch is playing both ends, just as he did with Navarro. I'll be damned.* Dorsey picked up a flicker of movement, and watched Peter roll on his side, and twitch like a dog having nightmares. His rifle was on the deck, and the man could not control what was happening to him, couldn't grab the rifle, and couldn't even scream or holler a warning to Jacoby.

Serious Elmo gave a thumb's up, moved closer to stay under the casement, out of sight, and threw a set of cuffs on him. Dorsey crawled over to the area. "This guy works for Bik and Jacoby, Serious. This is a Bik hit on Jacoby and a Jacoby hit on Andrzej. Damn me, we have hit gold. Get one of your men up here to take care of this fool, and let's watch Jacoby for a while. Maybe we can get one of your men up to that roof where she is in case we need to take her out."

Serious used his cell phone, not the radio, and called two of his men up, making sure they understood they had to stay out of sight while on the roof. "Look at this, Serious." Dorsey had the man's wallet out. "His name is Petrus. Must be Ukrainian for Peter, I guess. Driver's licenses from three states, and in three different names. This is a good bust, my friend, damn good." He thought for just a minute, couldn't control himself, and continued. "And I used perfect police procedure. I let you hurt the man, not me." He got a flaming glare back from Elmo.

It was a slow process moving Peter off the roof, he came to for a moment, but a slam to the head with the butt of a pistol, offered by Sol Dorsey put him back to sleep. "It's OK, Serious. I'm not a cop. He has no rights when he's with me." If they weren't in such a precarious situation, Serious Elmo would be all over the big man, but all he could do was give him the evil eye. Dorsey just continued with his shit-eating grin.

They were behind one of the ventilators, and Dorsey pointed out what appeared to be a party getting underway on the roof of the Andrzej building. "Watch Jacoby now, Serious. If she's here to take out this Andrzej guy, this is the time." Several people were milling about in the rooftop garden area while what looked like waiters and table servers began bringing out plates, utensils, and food. "He's having a dinner party, buffet style, I guess." There was a rattle of automatic weapons fire from down on the street, and Elmo's cell phone vibrated at that moment.

"Elmo," he said, listened for a minute, and slipped the phone back in his pocket. "Three armed people tried to get into the Andrzej building, and were killed by fire from inside. Glad I have some men down there. They went in immediately and have two goons in custody. The guys trying to get in are dead."

"Look at Illiana, Serious." Dorsey pointed toward the party, and then at Jacoby. "See the guy in the brocade jacket? She just gave him a wave and he returned it. Is that Sheik Omar? And the guy standing just inside the doors, there. Almost trying to hide. See him? Is that Andrzej? All

247

our suspects lined up like ducks at a carnival. Can I shoot someone, Serious, can I?"

"Will you ever can the smart ass stuff, Dorsey? Damn." Elmo had his cell phone out again. "I want at least a dozen black and whites to come in to this area, using all the streets. No vehicles leave the area, no pedestrians leave the area. I want a complete shutdown of this four-block area. And, I want to hear sirens. Lots of sirens. I want these people to know they are going down."

He sat back against the ventilator shaft and studied Jacoby, then the roof garden, then the surrounding buildings. "There have to be people on these other roof tops, Sol. I wonder who tried to get people inside the office complex? Was it Bik? If Omar is already with this guy Andrzej, and Jacoby seems fine with that, who was trying to break in?"

"I'd make book on Bik. He simply isn't the intelligent person he believes he is. His man Peter was supposed to take out Jacoby and Omar, and I'll bet a bunch that those were Bik men trying to get in." Dorsey's attitude was back on the case at hand, and he had one more problem.

"If Andrzej had people in the lobby of the building, I would think there would be a lot more guns in various other places inside that building. Your men might be walking into a trap." He was intent on the roof garden, saw that waiters and food had disappeared, and the only people visible were hired guns. "It looks like Omar and the other dude are now inside ready to play hide and seek."

~ ~ ~

"Gunfire down below. Clear this rooftop now. Sheik, are your people in place?" Andrzej was in full command, his personal cadre of body guards moved to rehearsed positions, big guns locked and loaded.

"Illiana just gave me the thumbs up, Andrzej. I would not be surprised that the guns from below are your men, and that Fred Bik is behind the problem. Illiana has men stationed on roofs around this building, so if anything goes down, she can handle it."

The Man had a cell phone out as he moved down a hallway leading off from the garden area. "Sarah, bring the car to that underground garage as quickly as you can. Yes, of course, bring at least one other person with you besides our driver. Be careful, there have been gunshots, so there will be cops everywhere soon." He came to a set of steel doors at the end of the hallway, went through and closed the doors that locked automatically. Sheik Omar was left in the hallway.

Down two flights of stairs, Andrzej slipped through another set of doors and into the building next door. From there, he raced up one flight of stairs and through another set of doors that led into a third building. He was now at the far end of the block, one block from his own building. *That's why I bought this building. I can move a full block from my own offices, and no one knows it.* He found the service elevator and took it to the basement garage to await Sarah Palozzi.

Sheik Omar was left deserted, and the anger boiled. He slipped back out toward the rooftop garden to try to make contact with Illiana. When he came out onto the garden, gunfire from where Illiana should have been rattled and echoed through the air. Omar was trapped, knew his best bet was to get out of this building as fast as possible. He couldn't find any of Andrzej's men and ran toward the elevators.

He knew Illiana had made plans for how she and the men could get away if something went wrong, but he had no such plan. He felt he would be safe with Andrzej, didn't feel he needed an escape plan.

"That bastard is throwing me to the wolves. You won't get away with this. We will take you out Andrzej. Illiana and I will kill you, and filet you, and hang your guts out to dry," he screamed, filled with panic as he raced toward the elevators. Sheik Omar was the one that screwed people, he wasn't the one to be screwed, has killed for far less.

~ ~ ~

The squad cars that Elmo ordered were coming into the area, sirens screaming, and Illiana Jacoby tensed up, brought the rifle to the ready. "Look at her, Serious. She's about to take flight. Get some people on her, or she'll be gone."

"Already done, Sol. Watch now," and he pointed at the roof top doorway. Three uniformed officers and two men in suits, all with guns drawn, exploded onto the roof. Jacoby turned, and without taking aim, started pulling the trigger on the scoped rifle. One officer went down, and Illiana Jacoby died instantly from a hail of bullets.

Gunshots echoed through the high rise office buildings as officers and hired guns blasted away at each other. The three remaining Jacoby men were taken, one dead, two wounded, and as officers moved toward the front entrance of the Andrzej building, they were forced back by heavy assault type weaponry. "You were right, Sol. There are more guns inside that building. We have to get either Sheik Omar or this guy Andrzej alive. Ideas?"

~ ~ ~

"Captain, you need to come down here right away." It was one of Elmo's lead men calling. "This man we have in custody has a cell phone, and we have a direct number to the man Bik. I think we can trace that to a location."

"On my way. Come on Sol, this is right down your alley." They left three officers on the roof to keep watch over the roof garden next door, and headed down to the street. "Peter has a cell phone with Bik's number. He called a time or two tonight. I think we can get Bik."

"I want him, Serious. It was his hit that took Felicia. I know it was, and Bik is mine."

"Don't kill him, Sol. We need his ass alive."

"I'll do what I can not to, but I won't guarantee anything."

They spent about fifteen minutes with forensics people as they worked over the cell phone, followed electronic pathways that aren't supposed to be followed without court approval, -- who has time for that, -- and came up with a location for Bik. "It seems that our good friend Mr. Fred (the Bull) Bik has a condo right here in the city. He's about three blocks from here, and that means he has heard every siren that came into the area. Probably all the gunfire as well," Serious Elmo said as he walked toward his car. Sol Dorsey was one step ahead of him.

"I bet he is already half way to his ocean front mansion, Serious. And, that's where at least one of us has to be. The other has to stay here to make sure that Sheik Omar and Andrzej are taken down. Want to flip for it?" and he dug into his trousers to find a quarter.

"Always the smart ass. OK, Sol, you go get Bik, I'll get Omar Sheik."

~ ~ ~

"Sirens, boss, and lots of them." One of Bik's protectors came into the study where Bik was having some more of his good bourbon, waiting for the call from Peter that everything went well.

"Get the truck, Dom. We got to get out of here now. Hurry." He grabbed a jacket, made sure he had his nine-millimeter under his arm, and followed the bodyguard out to where a large black SUV was parked. They drove down five levels through the parking garage and hit the street, Bik in the back seat, weapon in hand. One other big black truck moved in behind, and they raced through town toward the beachfront property. The fog rolled in fast, wet, and cold, making the streets slippery and dangerous.

"If you don't do it yourself, it doesn't get done. Peter screwed this up somehow, and every son of a bitch in town will be gunning for my ass. Move it, Dom, we need to get out to the coast now."

Bik didn't understand that he had spent most of the previous two nights going up and down Franklyn Street trying to hire guns. Oh, no, that wasn't the problem, it was Peter that screwed up. "That bastard Sol Dorsey is behind this. I'll bet Peter turned on me. He's a dead man and doesn't know it."

Bik had his cell in hand, calling the mansion. "I want that helicopter waiting for us when we get there." He paused a minute, then, "What?" The voice on the other end told him they would not be able to fly out because of the fog.

"I don't give a damn about fog. Get that chopper ready

now." He didn't wait for an answer, just closed the phone and put it away.

The two black SUVs blew off traffic lights, passed cars on either side, and broke every possible traffic law, as they whipped through the city streets and onto the highway leading to the coast. They were almost to the compound when Dom lost control of the heavy SUV. The fog put down a covering of water almost as slick as ice, and Dom took the SUV into a slide, over corrected, slid out of control the other way, and slammed into a passenger car trying its best to get out of the way. Dom was almost knocked unconscious when the air bag deployed. The SUV stalled and Dom couldn't get it restarted, again because of the air bag deployment.

"Get in the other car, Mr. Bik. Hurry." Bik jumped out, found the other SUV alongside with the door already open and jumped in. Dom sat behind the wheel of the first truck, his mind as fogged as the coast, unable to start the engine. He shook off the wreck and quickly jumped out of the car.

Two men in the passenger car, while not injured seriously, were busy dialing cell phones for help. Dom walked over and shot both men through the head, went back to the SUV, opened the hood, ripped fuel lines off the injectors, and set the fuel that was spilling out on fire. He ran from the highway, and headed for the coast, to make the last mile to the mansion along the shoreline.

Dom stumbled and fell several times, as he fought through fog so thick he tried to find the water line by listening for the sound of the surf. Slippery rocks, deep tidal pools, and incoming surf slowed him considerably. He could hear sirens coming up the coast road as he flailed his way to the mansion.

253

~ ~ ~

Simon Sol Dorsey knew where Bik was headed, as he wheeled the 56 Caddy onto one of the boulevards, putting his foot deep into the accelerator. He followed the carnage left behind from intersection to intersection, as he followed Bik out to the coast. Heavy fog and many crashed and disabled vehicles later, Dorsey reached the coast road, cruising as fast as he dared through the wet shroud of fog. He saw the burning black SUV, stopped for just a moment to make sure no one was inside, found the two dead men in the sedan, jumped back in the Caddy, and drove, faster now, toward the Bik compound.

He stopped alongside the highway, about three hundred yards from the mansion and moved cautiously toward the compound. He could see fog shrouded lights and hear activity as he got closer. "Looks like they're setting up for a major get away." He pulled his cell phone out and called Elmo.

"He's here, and has lots of protection. No way can I get in from the front. I'm going down toward the water and see if I can get in that way. There was a wreck involving one of Bik's vehicles, and I can hear emergency vehicles coming. Can you have some of them take up positions near Bik's front gate?"

"Good idea, Sol. Keep me informed. Things aren't very good here, right now. I'll tell you about it when I can," and broke off the connection.

"Damn good," Dorsey said, putting the phone away. He threaded his way between walls, trees, bushes, and rocks toward the sound of crashing surf. *Sure as hell can't get there by eyesight*. He stumbled through a rock field, almost fell into a tidal pool, and finally could see the surf. He followed the tide line, which led him to the compound and found that walls extended down to the high-tide line.

Just as he started to move toward the wall, he heard someone stumble behind him. With his big forty-five in hand, he got down as low as he could, and tried to see who might be coming toward him. He had a hard time seeing the surf through the fog, it was so thick.

In one breath, he was cursing the fog, and in the next, praising it. He knew whoever was coming would have seen him if the fog hadn't been there, but still cursed it because he couldn't see. Out of the mist, he spotted a man, stumbling over the slippery rocks, and let him get as close as he dared, then stood up and slammed him across the head with his automatic.

The guy took the hit, but didn't go down right away, and Dorsey had to hit him twice more before he went limp in the wet sand. *Tough old bastard, eh? Well, let's see who you might be,* and frisked him, finding two automatic pistols, and a wallet with several forms of identification in several names. Dorsey rolled the guy onto his stomach, pulled his right arm behind his back and put a cuff on, then pulled his left leg up and put the other end on his ankle. "Stay," he said with that shit-eating grin, and started toward the compound wall, worked around it, filling both shoes with water, and found himself on a little beach area. To himself he muttered, *Yeah, Serious, I know, can the smart ass.*

Dorsey was crouched in some bushes, as low to the ground as he could get, and watched as several men emerged from the veil of fog and moved across the open lawn between the big house and the sea wall. Bright lights were reflected in the fog and made visibility all but impossible. Dorsey thought it was like driving in the fog with your lights on high beam. The brilliance is bounced right back in your eyes.

The men were involved in a loud argument as they came across the lawn. Dorsey couldn't pick up very many words or phrases, and then the fog lifted just a bit and he saw a small black helicopter sitting in an open area off to the side.

"I'll be damned," he said. "That fool Bik wants to fly out of here in this fog? Ten feet in the air and they'll be lost, surrounded by high wires, trees, high fences. Even Bik isn't that stupid." Dorsey checked himself, thinking, not saying it out loud for one of the few times in his life. *Of course, he's that stupid. He spent hours going up and down Franklyn Street trying to buy gunmen and wonders how I know about it? How did his hit go so bad?* He also could remember that it was Bik that got away from him one time, and he renewed that vow to take him out tonight. *"Yeah, yeah, Serious, but I'll try not to kill the fool,* he said to himself.

As he watched, the argument grew louder, men threw up their hands in disgust, and then he saw it was Bik doing most of the yelling. "Get that chopper fired up and I mean right now. Do it, or I will shoot your balls off where you stand." He had his automatic out and was pointing it at a man wearing a flight suit.

"I can't fly in this fog. We'll die within two minutes if we lift off into this crap. It can't be done, Mr. Bik. It can't."

Bik fired once at the man's feet, and then put the gun to the pilot's head. "Get in that airplane and fire it up now." In the pilot's mind, he could die with a bullet to the brain or die in a helicopter as it floundered through a springtime pea-soup fog. He got in the chopper, Bik got in on the other side, and Dorsey listened as the jet engine slowly wound itself up. The turbines screamed, seemed almost a prelude to what Dorsey knew would be screaming from the two men inside when the bird came down in flames or pieces.

Fred Bik, the Bull. Bullheaded fool. That thing is probably fully fueled and if I wait until they are almost out of sight in this fog, and shoot the pilot, the explosion when they crash could keep those other goons busy enough for me to get clear of here. Can't take them on. There's just too many. Dorsey wanted to call Serious Elmo, let him know what was going on. "What did he mean a few minutes ago? He said things weren't going well at his end. He should be watching this scene play out." The mumbling continued as the turbines on the helicopter reached the right pitch for takeoff.

Dorsey had the forty-five in his hand, contemplating the best shot. "This will be a good thirty yards, and piss poor visibility," he mumbled as he inched through sand, grass, and brush, trying to get closer. "What I need is an RPG," he snickered "PIs don't carry rocket propelled grenades," he almost laughed. "I have that long barrel forty-five, and it's because of situations like this that I carry it." He was crouched, giving himself a good firing platform when he heard sirens closing in on the mansion and compound.

"The army is here, but not in time. I still have to do this." The turbine was wound up tight and he saw the chopper begin to lift off, do its little gyroscopic dance, leveling off. "Come on baby, nice and slow, up a little more, just a little more now," and he pulled the trigger, sighted again, pulled the trigger again.

The little black helicopter went out of control, rolled over on its side, put its nose down, and dove into the gathered group below. When it hit, fuel lines and tanks burst, and the explosion that followed knocked Dorsey back about ten feet. He found himself flat on his butt in a tidal pool.

When he got to his feet, he could hear more sirens, then volleys of gunfire from the front of the compound. "The Bull is out of business," is all he said to himself. He floundered out of the tidal pool, cussing up a storm, then stopped as he watched the helicopter burn, and saw the dead bodies of Bik's guards.

"Sergeant Rafferty, it's Sol Dorsey. Glad you guys could make the party. There's a guy all trussed up in handcuffs down the beach a few yards. Probably responsible for that wreck up the highway and the two bodies. I've got to get back downtown."

"We've got it covered, Dorsey. Did you do all this? Amazing."

~ ~ ~

"I had a hard time getting through the police line, Andrzej. This whole block is closed down. I'm not sure we can get back out." She held the back door of a light green Mercedes open for The Man. "There was heavy gunfire as I pulled in. Do you know where the hit is coming from?"

"Bik. We need to get back to Paris as soon as possible. I have a jet standing by, a nice Gulfstream, down the peninsula. You remember that little airport down there? We've used it to come in. Can you get us there quickly?"

"I remember. You need to get under that back shelf there, Andrzej, so I can get us back through all the cops. Don't move once we start." She helped get The Man tucked in, took her seat back in the front, made sure the extra man was secure, no guns visible anywhere, and motioned for Sam to head back out of the parking garage. They were stopped by two cops at the entrance to the garage.

"Hi. Thanks for letting me go to make sure my father was OK. I wanted to bring him out with me, but he said he felt safer in the condo, knowing you men were out here protecting him." Her smile was devastating, there were long legs showing, and cleavage enough for sixteen cops, and the cops ate it up.

"OK, Miss. We'll see to it your dad is safe. Turn right, go up about two blocks before you make any other turns. There are some bad things happening, so follow the directions any other officers give you."

"I will. Thank you again. You men are so brave. Bless you," and she smiled what most men would consider an invitation to bliss, had the driver turn right, and headed south to a private airport several miles down the peninsula from the city.

"That's one damn fine looking piece of action right there," the taller of the two cops said to his partner. "I think I'd follow her just about anywhere."

An hour later, a private corporate type jet lifted off through the fog and set a course across the North Pole to eventually land in Paris as Andrzej and Sarah enjoyed each other's company in the manner the two cops were thinking about after she drove off.

"I'm afraid I will have to get my ass back to work as soon as we land, dear heart. I want you to make sure that Bik does not live another week." The Man got contemplative after saying that. "I've probably lost Sheik Omar, but I had no choice if I was going to get out of that trap."

He sat back in the luxury of the Gulfstream, trying to put all the pieces together. "Nobody but my own people, Omar, and Jacoby knew about our plans. How did Bik find out? Either someone working for me, or someone working for them could have told Bik.

"One thing for sure, Sarah. I have to find another source to fund. I'm not going to lose the kind of money I've been making just because I have lost Sheik and Illiana. The Dziuba family is torn apart now, that fool Babyak in Kiev screwed himself. I'm actually going to miss working with Illiana and Omar. Keep your ears open, and spread the word. Only big time, no little pukes like Bik or Navarro."

~ ~ ~

"Captain, we've found a man you need to talk to. He may have been part of the garden party buffet you mentioned earlier. Should I bring him down?" Serious Elmo had headquarters set up just inside the Andrzej building after securing the lobby area, and sent officers on a search and destroy effort throughout the building. Many of the condos had not been rented or sold, on Andrzej's orders, and many held hired guns that had to be flushed out.

Reports coming back to Elmo were usually preceded by heavy gunfire, and so far, no one had been taken alive. This was good news coming down the radio link. "Yes. Bring him down here immediately. Be very careful, these are dangerous people. Clear him of any possible weapon, cuff him, and don't take any crap off him."

"On our way, cappy."

Elmo wasn't the least bit happy over his end of the mission so far. In his mind, everyone has either been killed or managed to get away somehow. He blasted the hell out of two officers that had been told that no one comes or goes from the immediate area. "I sealed off one full square block of this city and you let a car with a woman and two men in it, first to come into the area and then to leave?"

His temper was raging, and he worked hard to calm himself as best he could. He told the men to report to his office the next morning. "Get your butts out of this area while you can. One word from either of you, and you're both fired. Get the hell out of here." *I should have pulled a Dorsey and just shot the bastards,* and he had to chuckle at the thought.

The elevators opened and three officers escorted a man in a brocade dinner jacket out. "Claims he doesn't speak English, Captain. I don't believe him." The lead officer pushed Sheik Omar toward Serious Elmo. Omar, always dignified, always the European gentleman, now being treated as a common criminal. Omar glared at the officer, glared at Captain Elmo, and found himself shoved into a chair, and with his hands cuffed behind him, almost falling out of the chair.

"I have bad news for you, Sheik. Illiana Jacoby is dead, most of your men are dead, and Andrzej has apparently flown the coop, leaving you to face the death penalty." He looked over to the officers. "Did you read him his rights?" With an affirmative nod, Elmo walked Sheik over to a desk.

Sheik Omar seemed to be unresponsive, giving the impression he didn't understand what was being said, right up to the words, 'death penalty'. "That's what I thought. 'No speaky, no speaky' my ass. Sit down," and he pushed Sheik down, a wry smile across his Egyptian face. "Think that's funny, eh? Well, here's the situation, just in case you aren't fully aware." He pulled some papers out of his brief case when his cell started buzzing.

"Elmo," he snarled. "Yeah, slow down, Dorsey. Start over and nice and slow and deliberate, OK? Damn, you are a freight train sometimes." He listened for a full minute, said thank you, and turned his attention back to Sheik Omar.

"Seems as though The Bull doesn't want you around anymore, Sheik. That was my partner, Simon Sol Dorsey, I think you've heard of him. Well, you don't have to worry about Bik the Bull. He's a bit crispy right now. So are the men who were supposed to protect him. Kind of like yours, eh?"

There was another interruption as an officer came into the lobby at a fast pace with a file of papers. "These came across the fax about half an hour ago, Captain. Looks damn important to me, so I brought them down."

"Alright, let's see." He started reading, looked up at Sheik, went back to reading, and about every ten seconds or so, stopped to look at Sheik Omar. "Well, well, well," he said. "The Ukrainian Police Commissioner is dead, and one of Felicia's people has forwarded all this information on one Lori Baranek. So, Babyak did know who she was. Hmmm," and he glanced at Omar, pulled his cell phone out, and punched in some numbers.

"Listen to this, Sol. I said listen, so shut up. It seems that Babyak has committed suicide and one of Bogdanovich's people has sent me a big old file on Lori Baranek. Babyak knew more than a little about the lady. They were partners.

"I have Sheik Omar in custody and am about to transfer him to the jail. I think we lost Andrzej because of a couple of my people. Meet me in my office in an hour. I think we can just about wrap this thing."

"I'm on my way. That fool Bik was trying to have a helicopter fly out of his compound in this fog. Almost everyone at the place is dead. I did capture without killing him, one of Bik's bodyguards. I think the attorneys in town are going to be busy for a long time on this." Elmo could hear his laughter even after he clicked off.

It was a long slow ride back into the city and Dorsey had some time to put things together. "First free time I've had to try and figure this out," he mumbled, not trying for a world speed record. "If the Ukrainian police commissioner was working with Baranek, why did she get me involved? She didn't," he remembered. "She got stuck with me when Jacoby's daughter was kidnapped. That simple little snatch cascaded into the biggest case I've ever been on."

It was obvious that Sol Dorsey wasn't finished with the case, either. "There's still something missing and I don't know what it is. Everyone is out of the picture now, but the picture is still out of focus." He found a parking spot at the cop shop, Compacts Only of course, tucked the Caddy in and headed up to Elmo's office.

The place was overflowing with cops, federal agents, Ukrainian agents, and now, a PI. "Howdy all. Listen, I've called you all together," he started with his Dorsey flourish when Elmo cut him off.

"Can it, Sol," Serious Elmo scowled. "Everyone out. Get out of my office. Not you Dorsey, and not you Fleming. Everyone else, out, out." He made a uniformed cop scatter when he glared at him, found his chair and sat down. "You, Jackson. Coffee by the gallon." He racked back in his chair, found one of those ugly big cigars of his and destroyed the atmosphere.

"That was a stupid move on your part Fleming, to try to put some kind of snitch into my jail. I have written a report on it and it has been delivered to your supervisor. I don't know if you did it or if Simpson did it, but you could have destroyed this case." Fleming started to say something and Elmo shushed him with a wave of his hand. "Now, you, Dorsey," he began as Jackson arrived with the first pot of coffee.

"Thank you, Officer Jackson. Listen, let's not do this in here. Jackson, take the coffee and stuff down to interrogation, uh, room number three. Put a couple of extra chairs in there, and after you do that, bring Lori Baranek in to visit with us." The smile spread clear across his broad face, he blew a stream of blue smoke toward the ceiling, and looked straight into the emerald Sol Dorsey eyes.

"Didn't know we had her, did you Fleming. You and Simpson didn't even know who she is. Come on Sol, let's see if we can figure this crap out. You see, Simpson or Fleming, or both, put this undercover DEA agent into my jail, and didn't even know why they did it. He didn't get the information to and from Baranek, that was one of my own people who is now under arrest." He blew some more smoke in Fleming's direction along with a smart-ass grin.

"I really hate those cigars of yours, Serious, but in this case, what the hell, go for it." The chuckle was there along with the sarcastic look, and Elmo continued talking as if he hadn't heard a word.

"I know I'm missing something and I think Baranek might have those answers. When we get down there, Fleming, you keep your trap shut and you might learn something."

21

Jackson motioned Fleming to follow him, and Dorsey held back just a bit. "So, mine Capitan, tell me how you have managed to keep Fleming from having federal agents come here and take you down. You beat the crap out of him just a few days ago."

"We came to a wonderful, and mutual agreement. I told his boss what he and Simpson did, and he knows he is going to catch hell very soon. I'm sure the idea was Simpson's, and I don't like knocking dead people, but it was as stupid as I can remember him doing.

"The only thing he accomplished was to get three of our jailers fired for not telling me or any other division chief what had happened. But, remember, because of it I found that we had a bad jailer, so there are good points to this. Simpson got away with it because he was still Lt. Simpson in their eyes." Elmo was still angry over that episode and he hadn't even had a chance to talk to the two cops that let Sarah Palozzi through his dragnet around the Andrzej office complex.

"Because of this case, there is gonna be a big shake-up around here," he said. "My department, mine, Dorsey, my name all over it, screwed up big-time, and heads are gonna roll."

"I just hope yours isn't one of them," Dorsey said. "We

just brought down an international drug, guns, money conspiracy. Are you ok?"

"Yeah, I'll be fine, Sol, but the big-shots upstairs will be watching. I found the problems and they're being corrected, but, it is my department. I'll be on the radar scope for a few months."

The two men walked into the interrogation room, joining Officer Jackson and Agent Fleming. "OK Jackson, keep that coffee coming after you bring Baranek in," Elmo said, "and don't forget the extra chairs. Get up, Fleming, that's my seat." He wasn't going to give that federal agent a single hair's edge.

Dorsey was pacing around the small room, stopping at the large mirror/one way glass for just a moment. "You have extra people in on this, don't you Serious. Who besides your people are in there?" Dorsey could almost feel extra eyes looking through the glass at him. "Think they would mind if I brushed my hair just a bit?" He ran his hands through his brush cut, picked at his nose, just a bit, then waved hello before turning to take the seat Lori Baranek would be sitting in.

"You never give it up, do you? Well, you're right. Because of the complexity of this investigation, I have invited several agencies to sit in on our interrogation of the Baranek woman. A major player got away, most of the others are dead, and even the two suspects we have, Baranek and Sheik Omar, are not U.S. citizens, which means that federal agencies will take the case from this point."

"Why wasn't I told this, Captain?" Fleming fumed.

"Because your actions almost contributed to us not

being able to solve the damn case. To put it bluntly, you aren't even a fair investigator, Fleming. And, I believe you're a fool, besides.

"Behind that mirror is a high level FBI agent, an ATF agent, and a DEA agent. My own people are there as well, and we have had a camera rolling since we walked in. Want to pick your nose again, Sol?" He got a good chuckle over that, and said, "OK, Jackson, bring Baranek in." Dorsey was giving him the best evil eye he could conjure when Jackson popped in with a couple of chairs.

"You gentlemen on the other side of the glass have already been briefed on what Sol Dorsey and I have discovered so far. There are large gaps in this investigation, and I think many of those will be closed after we have a chat with the Baranek woman." He finished when a knock on the door announced Jackson and Lori Baranek.

"Hello, Lori." Dorsey was the perfect gentleman, gave the lady a big smile, and almost reached out to pinch her butt. He caught himself just in time, took a quick look at Serious Elmo and knew he had been caught in the act.

"Sit down, please. You remember Captain Elmo, I think, and this is DEA agent Gerald Fleming. We need to bring you up to date on a few things. I guess you already know that your pipeline to the outside was shut off a few days ago, so you don't know some the things that have transpired."

She was more subdued than Dorsey had ever seen her, and his first thoughts were that she was feigning, putting moves in his head, but as he watched, her eyes moved slowly from his to Fleming's, then to Elmo's. The usual smile to Dorsey wasn't there, and she was more than just haggard. *She is beaten and she knows it,* he said to himself.

"Officer Jackson, will you do the honors, then leave the room please." Elmo had Baranek stand and Jackson read her rights. "Thank you. You see, Lori, you have been held as a material witness to some damn serious crimes, including murder, conspiracy to commit murder, and who knows how many narcotics, weapons, and financial laws you have broken."

Before Elmo could go any further, Sol Dorsey chimed in. "Along with international treaties, and laws in other countries, including the Ukraine. Speaking of the Ukraine, did you know your old pal, Ukraine Police Commissioner Babyak was dead?" Her head whipped around, her eyes blazed with anger, her fists balled up, and she gave herself away.

"I thought so," Dorsey smiled. "Here's what I see, Lori. Don't try to stop me because the freight train is leaving the depot." He gave Serious Elmo a fine smile and continued. "I was having a hard time trying to understand why so many criminal organizations were moving in to our area. Jacoby and Omar Sheik have had this territory pretty much sewed up for years, but of course that curse called money makes people do strange things.

"Everything started in Kiev with first the Dziuba family wanting to oust Jacoby/Omar. Mavis Brownell was sent to this country to set it up over a long time period. She was a child when she got here. First, getting her law degree, then marrying someone with no Ukrainian connections, then going to work for the District Attorney, that way having access to any investigations that might be taking place.

"Sound familiar, Captain Elmo?"

Elmo's eyes were pinpoints of anger. "Very familiar. Almost like Baranek's story, eh Sol?"

"Yep, one and the same. You, Lori were sent here by police commissioner Babyak to do exactly what Brownell did. You set up the FCU as a front, made it seem completely legal and you did business in the open. FCU business, that is. You made several mistakes, the worst of which was bringing that ape Dolinski into the gang. He opened the door for us, gave you up, gave Socrates up, gave Brownell up, all because of his stupidity and his desire for money."

Dorsey sat back and watched the emotions flash through Lori's face. He could almost read her mind, he thought. "Look at her face, Serious. There's hatred, that's expected, but now she knows that we have most of the names, and she knows how implicated she really is." He gave her a full-blown Sol Dorsey smile, the one that was designed originally to put her in his bed. He sat back in his chair and took a long slow drink of coffee.

"There were three things that destroyed your little game, Lori," Elmo said, picking up from Dorsey. Felicia Bogdanovich, the assistant police commissioner in the Ukraine, came to me for some information on a narcotics investigation she had going in Kiev. Her investigation dovetailed with what Dorsey had going following the death of Illiana's daughter, Melissa. You brought Dorsey into the investigation because of that death. Damn me, lady, but that was dumb.

"You had no fear of a private investigator looking into a teenager's disappearance. Even if it was Illiana's daughter. Very dumb, lady."

Dorsey let out a good laugh on that, glared at Fleming

just for the hell of it, and got back in Baranek's face. "You and Babyak on one hand, Brownell and the Dziuba family on another, little guys like Navarro getting in the way, and then, along comes Fred, the Bull, Bik to really screw things up. And all because you were trying to run Jacoby and Sheik Omar out of business. Only you and Omar are alive right now," and as he said that, he slammed his open hand onto the table. Baranek jumped back in her chair.

"That's right, Lori, darling, everybody is dead, and you and Omar are left to face all the charges that have been piling up. Bik tried to do a one-upsmanship on you guys, tried to take out the moneyman himself. Yes, Andrzej seems to have gotten away to wherever vermin like him live. Just you and Omar.

"Got anything to say about all this?"

"I want a lawyer."

"Figured that would be about it. One big problem, though. You aren't a U.S. citizen, so you are here in this country illegally, but even so, our constitution does give you the right to an attorney. And, the laws you have broken, for the most part are federal, so we're going to turn you over to the federal agencies, and one by one, by one they will take you apart, limb from limb. First, the FBI, then ATF, then DEA, and oh, yes, let's not forget Homeland Security, and with a little luck, maybe the Postal Service.

"Goodbye Lori, hope I never see you again."

~ ~ ~

The big Caddy wheeled down Franklyn Street, cold fog swirling, clinging, creating little dances among neon signs, fouling the windshield wipers, and Sol Dorsey didn't really care. "Come on, Star, smile. This is our night to celebrate."

The little prosti sat cuddled up to the huge man, his hand on her thigh, and she liked that part of it, but she wasn't smiling. "I just found out that the police lady that was with you for the last several weeks was your lover and she was killed. That's so sad, Sol. So sad." Sol Dorsey belonged to Star, she knew that, but she also knew she could never have him in that way. "Did you love her, Sol?"

He pulled the Caddy over into a loading zone and turned in the seat to face her. "Yes, Star, I think I did. I don't think I'll ever let that happen again. You're my girl, Star, now let's go party up this filthy street."

~ ~ ~

He traced the incessant ringing to his cell phone, on the kitchen table, a sure and easy target, but his hangover was so bad he simply answered the phone. "Dorsey," he bawled, then listened. "As soon as I find my pants, Serious. Damn, it isn't even sunrise." Serious informed him it was three in the afternoon, and he had a quick smile on his face as he woke Star up. "Up and at 'em, old girl. Time to go to work."

The trip to police headquarters was quick, no fog, little traffic, and a roiling, boiling hangover. "Have Jackson bring coffee, cold beer, and a pitcher of bloody Mary's, and not in that order," he said, trying to sit down without disturbing his head. "I'd like to say never again, but I won't."

Serious Elmo was enjoying watching Dorsey's theatrics. "I need you to help me put the cap on this thing. How about enchiladas and cold beer at Miguel's?" It took just a minute for the two of them to bolt the building, push the Caddy to legal limits, and park in front of the best Mexican restaurant in the city.

"Hi, Mike, nice to see you. Bring beer until we say no,

and platters of enchiladas, green chili burritos, and maybe a shot or two of your famous tequila. This is a business meeting, so just keep that stuff coming." Sol Dorsey needed this.

Serious got right down to business. "I understand the what, I understand the who, but I don't know the why yet. Any ideas?"

"I think I hit on it when I was with Star last night. Of course, everything traces back to money, we both know that. Money drives the world, politics, marriage, narcotics, war, you name it, it all traces back to money. But, I think there is a bit more to it in this caper. Babyak and Baranek, Brownell and her family, wanted to take Jacoby and Sheik Omar out and take over their operation. Bik wanted something a little larger, he wanted Andrzej's part in all this.

"You see, Serious, even the largest businesses, multinational corporations for instance, need seed money, major loans if you will, to continue. That was what Andrzej provided. When Omar wanted to bring in a load of narcotics or a boat full of AK47s, he got his funding from Andrzej, and when it went out to the distributors, he paid it back with hefty interest.

"Bik held himself in pretty high esteem, and the brain power simply wasn't there. He gave himself up by being stupid, and in the process, brought everybody else down. We need to say thank you to Dolinski and Bik. They are responsible for us cracking this case, My Strong Willed Capitan.

"My big regret on this little caper is losing Andrzej. On the other hand, all the international police agencies now know who he is and how he operates. He'll go down one day, they all do."

He stood, and with the flourish of a Marine General, gave an outstanding salute to Elmo, to the delight of Miguel and the other customers.

"Put it in a can, Dorsey."

Thank you for reading.
Please review this book. Reviews help others find New Pulp Press and inspire us to keep providing these marvelous tales.

If you would like to be put on our email list to receive updates on new releases, contests, and promotions, please go to NewPulpPress.com and sign up.

ABOUT THE AUTHOR

Johnny Gunn the pseudonym of a retired journalist. He says, "I ditched college after the first year by being hired by a radio station as a full time reporter, and the merry-go-round never stopped. I can't say I miss the day-to-day newsroom chaos, but I love allowing my characters to do their thing, not have to report someone else's thing."

During his fifty-year career, he published and edited *The Nevada Observer.com,* an internet news magazine; *The Virginia City Legend*, a weekly newspaper; and *The Rhythm of Reno,* a monthly entertainment magazine. Also he was senior editor at *AdNews*, serving the advertising gurus, marketing mavens, and other creative souls in Nevada.

Several years ago, he started transitioning from hard news to fiction (There are many that say these two are the same), writing short stories and having them published in some fine literary journals and magazines.

He and his wife live on a small hobby farm about twenty miles north of Reno, Nevada, and share space with a couple of horses, a flock of egg-laying chickens, some meat rabbits, and one goofy goat.

www.NewPulpPress.com

www.ingramcontent.com/pod-product-compliance
Lightning Source LLC
Chambersburg PA
CBHW060526260626
47161CB00003B/775